# SKY
# DADDY

# SKY DADDY

A NOVEL

## KATE FOLK

 RANDOM HOUSE · NEW YORK

Published in the United States by Random House, an imprint and division of Penguin Random House LLC, 1745 Broadway, New York, NY 10019.

RANDOM HOUSE and the HOUSE colophon are registered trademarks of Penguin Random House LLC.

LIBRARY OF CONGRESS CATALOGING-IN-PUBLICATION DATA
Names: Folk, Kate, author.
Title: Sky daddy : a novel / Kate Folk.
Description: New York, NY : Random House, 2025
Identifiers: LCCN 2024015301 (print) | LCCN 2024015302 (ebook) |
ISBN 9780593231494 (hardcover ; acid-free paper) |
ISBN 9780593231500 (ebook) |
ISBN 9780593978672 (international edition)
Subjects: LCGFT: Novels.
Classification: LCC PS3606.O446 S59 2025 (print) | LCC PS3606.O446 (ebook) |
DDC 813/.6—dc23/eng/20240415
LC record available at https://lccn.loc.gov/2024015301
LC ebook record available at https://lccn.loc.gov/2024015302

Printed in the United States of America on acid-free paper

randomhousebooks.com
penguinrandomhouse.com

1st Printing

First Edition

*Book design by Debbie Glasserman*

The authorized representative in the EU for product safety and compliance is Penguin Random House Ireland, Morrison Chambers, 32 Nassau Street, Dublin D02 YH68, Ireland, https://eu-contact.penguin.ie.

TO MY FRIENDS,

NEW AND OLD,

THE ONES I HAVEN'T TALKED TO IN A WHILE,

AND THOSE I HAVEN'T YET MET

*All men live enveloped in whale-lines.*

—HERMAN MELVILLE, *Moby-Dick*

*Planes are the whales of the sky.*

—LINDA

# PART I

Call me Linda. My tale begins in January, when I was invited to a Vision Board Brunch hosted by my co-worker Karina Carvalho. According to Karina, the vision boards, crafted from common drugstore materials, could be used to manifest anything a person wanted in life. I was receptive to the idea, as I'd always subscribed to the notion of an intelligent universe, a web of predestination in which we all were tangled. Only such a cosmic force could bring about my dream of marriage to a plane—what others vulgarly refer to as a "plane crash." I believed this was my destiny: for a plane to recognize me as his soulmate mid-flight and, overcome with passion, relinquish his grip on the sky, hurtling us to earth in a carnage that would meld our souls for eternity. I couldn't alter my fate, but perhaps, with the vision board's help, I could hasten its arrival.

Karina had told me about previous VBBs, which her friend group convened at the start of each quarter, but this was the first one she'd invited me to, and I took it as a sign she wanted to deepen our friendship. I was so excited to see the evite in my inbox, I RSVP'd "yes" before considering the risk of revealing my dream to a gathering of normal women. I suspected Karina's friends would balk at a vision board comprising only photos of planes, or worse, crashed planes strewn in postcoital debris. The imagery might offend Karina most of all, as she was fearful of flying and had vowed never to set foot on a plane again. It was this quality that first drew me to her when I came to Acuity, where we both worked as content moderators for a video-sharing platform. I'd found her trembling in the break room, and learned that she'd just witnessed gruesome footage of plane wreckage in her queue of flagged videos. I comforted her, resisting the urge to inquire about the specifics of the wreckage and whether it could be viewed elsewhere on the internet. I'd always considered aerophobes my spiritual comrades, their fear and my desire flip sides of the same coin, and from that day forward, I knew Karina and I shared a special bond.

As the VBB approached, I'd reached an impasse. I couldn't truthfully present my vision, nor did it seem wise to craft a fraudulent board. I didn't want to give the universe the wrong idea, which might cause it to mix up my destiny with another person's, as when a traveler picks up the wrong suitcase at baggage claim. I began to think it was safer not to attend, though I knew Karina would be disappointed.

On Thursday, Karina and I went to our usual happy hour at the sushi place on the ground floor of our office building. The VBB cycled venues, with a different member hosting each quarter, and this Sunday, it was Karina's turn.

"I'm making three types of mimosa," she said, her brown eyes gleaming beneath fluffy mink lashes. "Celia will be at work, so we'll have the whole house to ourselves." Karina lived with her fiancé, Anthony, at his mom's house in Daly

City. Like me, they lived in a room off the garage, though unlike mine, their room had a window. I'd never been, but I'd seen pictures of the space, and it looked cozy: tile floor, tulip wall sconces, *Scarface* poster, Anthony's immaculate sneaker collection lined against a wall.

"Will Anthony be there?" I asked.

"Probably, but he'll stay downstairs." Karina frowned, setting down her sake cup. "Don't you like Anthony?"

I recalled previous happy hours during which Karina had expressed dissatisfaction with Anthony, always for good reason. There were the flirtatious Instagram messages she'd discovered between Anthony and his coworker at the fast-casual pizza restaurant. There was his novelty T-shirt business, into which Karina had sunk large sums of her earnings, with little promise of her investment ever paying off. There was his habit of forgetting important dates, such as Karina's birthday and their anniversary. I'd learned to be cautious when speaking of Anthony, to discover exactly where Karina stood on the subject of the man on that day before voicing any sentiment.

"I've only met him a few times," I told her now. "I like whoever you like, Karina." I was impressed by my own diplomacy. Perhaps I'd overheard someone saying this on the bus.

"Well, he likes you," Karina said. "He's always asking, 'What's Lindy up to?'"

"That's nice of him." I was surprised to hear that Anthony held any opinion of me. I took a sip of sake. "I'm not sure I can make it on Sunday," I said carefully.

Karina's eyes narrowed. "Why not? I thought you were coming."

"My landlords are having a garage sale," I lied. "They want me to help out."

"You really don't want to miss it," she said, gnawing an edamame shell. "The Q1 VBB is always the most powerful. It sets the tone for the whole year."

I told Karina I'd try my best, though I'd already decided against going. While it pained me to squander an opportunity to nudge the universe on behalf of my destiny, the risk of exposure was too great. I could not do anything that might compromise my position in society—my job and my housing—which in turn would threaten my prospects of marriage to a plane.

From happy hour, I took BART to SFO, hoping the AirTrain would boost my spirits. I planned to ride the Red Line's loop for an hour or two, my typical routine when I hungered for connection with my loves but couldn't afford to take a flight. The train rounded a bend, approaching Terminal 3. Through the window, I glimpsed many fine planes resting at their gates. Jet bridges nuzzled their temples, their rear ends pointed provocatively toward me. A beefy Boeing 777 pulled back from F4, pivoting on his slender ankles with surprising grace for such a big fellow. Parked at F12, I spotted an old friend who went by the tail number N78823, an Embraer 175 bound presently for Phoenix, according to my flight-tracking app. I'd accompanied N78823 to Salt Lake City a few months ago, and found him to be a playful lover, teasing me with a round of turbulence as we descended into SLC.

At the Terminal 3 stop, the doors opened and a pilot boarded my car. I was shy in his presence, as I always am around pilots, granting them the level of respect others extend to doctors and members of the clergy. This pilot was stout and snub-nosed, his face resembling that of an Airbus A350. He was around fifty, with silver hair protruding from his pilot hat. He wore his uniform of black trousers and a jacket with four stripes on each cuff, indicating he was a captain, a pilot in command. He settled onto the seat across from me. As the doors closed, our eyes met and he smiled in the polite but distant manner of a celebrity. I wouldn't dare to disturb him, though I wished I could ask him many things, such as which model of plane was his favorite, and whether he felt an emotional attachment to the planes, as a farmer loves the horse that assists his labors.

The train rumbled on. As we approached Terminal 2, I was struck with an idea for how I could attend the VBB after all. I could place a pilot on my vision board as a stand-in for my goal of marriage to a plane, claiming I wished to marry a pilot instead. If the universe took my request at face value, and supplied me a pilot husband, I'd make the best of it. I would have access to discounted flights, and a companion to talk about planes with. Though I'd take no pleasure from sex with this pilot, or any person, I would submit to the act to please him, and remain in good standing as his wife. I'd be caressed—infrequently, I hoped—by fingers that had recently touched the most intimate parts of a plane, and been anointed.

Of course, I'd prefer to skip the middleman, launching myself directly into the aluminum embrace of my soulmate: whichever plane would finally recognize my worth and claim me as his bride in orgasmic catastrophe. But I'd recently turned thirty, and perhaps it was time for compromises.

I leaped from my seat and stood impatiently by the doors until they opened to the BART station. Normally, I'd have remained on the AirTrain for another five or six revolutions, but tonight, I couldn't afford to linger. I had a vision board to craft!

SINCE I'D MOVED TO SAN FRANCISCO A YEAR AND A HALF AGO, MY life had attained a pleasant stability, in contrast with the waywardness of my twenties. I worked in the Hate & Harassment vertical at Acuity, scrubbing comment threads of hate speech and death threats in accordance with the parent company's terms and conditions. It was the first job I'd ever been good at, and I was proud of my status as H&H's top-performing mod. I was paid twenty dollars an hour, a large chunk of which went toward nine hundred dollars' monthly rent on a windowless in-law apartment in the Outer Sunset that I rented from the Chen family, who dwelled in the house and did their best to ignore my moldering presence in the room built inside their garage. Karina was my only friend, though I knew she had many friends besides me. I was grateful for the drippings of companionship she offered, in the form of our weekly happy hours and occasional mall excursions.

Though I enjoyed spending time with Karina, I'd been careful not to reveal too much of myself to her. As a rule, I avoided forming deep connections with other people. I knew my fate could manifest upon any flight, and I didn't want to burden additional loved ones with grief. I kept in touch, sporadically, with my family in Southern California. My mom remained in my childhood home in Irvine, from which she sold patterned leggings through a multilevel marketing scheme. My brother, Al, worked in fracking in Bakersfield. We texted sometimes, our relationship having improved since the two years I'd lived with him and his then-girlfriend, now-wife, Denise, along with another couple, Brenda and Roxy. My dad had died four years ago—colon cancer—which was unfortunate, as he'd been my favorite family member, the only one who'd indulged my interest in planes, though I'd never revealed to him its full extent.

I believe I was born loving planes. As a child, on the rare occasions my family flew, I felt a thrill unmatched by anything else I'd experienced. No roller coaster, video game, or bouncy castle could compare to the exhilaration of takeoff. I begged my parents to fly more, and my dad, always up for adventure, compromised by taking me plane-spotting. We'd park on an access road behind John Wayne Airport and spectate through the chain-link fence. I sat on my dad's shoulders, peering at the planes' handsome faces through binoculars. Together, we made up stories about where they were headed, and which important people were on board. As

I aged into adolescence, my love for planes took on a sexual dimension, and I felt I had no choice but to reject my dad when he tried to bond with me over what had long been our shared interest. My desire for planes, alongside an awareness of the fate for which I was bound, crystallized on board a flight to Chicago when I was thirteen—but more on that later.

When he died, my dad left me his beloved boat, a 1989 Sea Ray Sundancer named *Wendy*. I sold *Wendy* for nine thousand dollars, far less than she was worth, and spent the money on a monthlong flight binge. In my grief, I was desperate to unite with my soulmate plane, whoever he turned out to be, but I learned the planes couldn't be pressured into choosing me before they were ready. My binge left me penniless and demoralized, and I'd turned to Al for help, which was how I'd wound up living with him in Bakersfield for a regrettably long interval. I had vowed to never again put myself in such a position, establishing rules to forestall another binge: I adhered to a strict budget; I allowed myself to fly only to a single destination and back; I lived in a windowless room, from which I could not view the sky's traffic. Hearing the cry of planes above me as I lay in bed, while not being able to see them, added to the romance of our separation.

On the last Friday of each month, I flew wherever was cheapest, usually a regional hub, such as Salt Lake City, Denver, or Phoenix. I preferred to fly near a mountain range, whose choppy airstreams, I hoped, would embolden a plane to yield to his lust for me, as alcohol primes a human lover for intercourse. The city surrounding the airport was irrelevant, as I never left the secure sector. It was all about the flight itself, a date I'd purchased with a plane—preferably a variant of the 737, though like most deviants, I couldn't afford to be picky. Like dating, death by plane crash was a numbers game. Such an event was vanishingly rare, with odds of one in eleven million. Still, those were far better odds than winning the Powerball, a chance of one in three hundred million. The people I saw buying lottery tickets at 7-Eleven would surely think my dream was insane, but theirs was thirty times less likely, so who was the madwoman, really?

Of course, I believed my connection to planes transcended raw statistics. With the vision board, I hoped to persuade the universe to deliver my fate sooner rather than later, while I was still young enough to enjoy it.

From my pilot sighting on the AirTrain, I returned to my cube in the Chens' garage. I sat on my bed, my flight map looming on the wall behind me, routes I'd traveled sketched in crisscrossing red string. I consulted the grimy screen of my laptop, a hand-me-down from Al, seeking photos I could print out and glue to my board. Images of planes climbing to cruising altitude, in clear skies or against sherbet-hued sunsets. Lewd shots from below, that long stretch of belly, fish-smooth and flanked by testicular engines. I amassed dozens of juicy plane pics in a special VBB folder on my desktop.

Next, I searched the term "pilot" and found an image of a white man with a crew cut and aviator sunglasses, tan arms crossed over his chest as he stood in midday sun near the nose of a 747-400. I wondered if this man was really a pilot or merely a stock model, the bottom of the food chain of professionally attractive people. I imagined his hardscrabble life in Los Angeles, waiting tables at night and auditioning for reality shows and pharma ads during the day, struggling to distinguish himself in a field of blandly handsome men. But even if he wasn't a pilot in real life, he sufficed as a symbol for my board. I found another image, of a pilot similar to the first one, but this time, an action shot. The pilot peered into a jet engine, one hand placed suggestively along the inlet lip.

In addition to the pilots, I secured an image of Guillaume Faury, the CEO of the Airbus corporation and one of my personal idols. Faury posed in a gray suit on a runway, next to a lovely A220-300. The plane's windscreen betrayed no hint of nervousness. He seemed not to mind the presence of his boss—indeed, the biggest boss of all—a man who could, with an email, condemn the plane to a repair facility in El Salvador or a boneyard in New Mexico, from which he might never emerge. I admired that plucky A220 and resolved to mimic his confidence in my own work dealings.

I closed my laptop with a sense of accomplishment. I would save the images to a thumb drive and print them the next day at a copy shop I'd seen from the bus. I was excited for what my vision board would set into motion—though I didn't know then how powerful it would be.

2 The next morning, I waited at the corner of Nineteenth and Taraval for the bus that would convey
me to Acuity's office in Daly City. It was a clear day,
and I took stock of the sky, as I'd been in the habit of doing
all my life. As a child, I was shy, prone to daydreaming, and
my fantasies always involved the sky and a realm above it, a
secular heaven populated by rabbits and horses with wings.
My dad taught me the names of different clouds, enabling
me to distinguish between the high, wispy cirrus, the patchy
altocumulus, and the low-hanging stratocumulus. As my interests matured, I progressed from clouds to the harder stuff
of contrails, which I learned to read like tea leaves, by a system of my own devising. An abundance of contrails was a
sign my day would go well.

Presently, I fixated on the boldest line in the sky, a con-
trail still in the process of creation. By squinting I could
make out the plane that expelled the vapor, a shining silver
dot at the head of the trail. I consulted my flight-tracking
app, which identified the plane as a 737-900 named N8770Q,
en route from Seattle to San Jose. The sight of the distant 737
filled me with longing. It had been three weeks since I'd
flown, and at times like these, I feared my connection to my

loves was waning. I was eager to renew our bond after work with a visit to the Elephant Bar in Burlingame, my usual Friday night routine when I didn't have a flight booked. I'd order a side of fries, the cheapest item on the menu, and spend a few hours watching planes land at SFO through the bay-facing windows before the host dislodged me, an amiable battle we waged each week.

I boarded the bus and stood in the front section, my body pressed against those of students bound for San Francisco State University, a cluster of brutalist buildings just past Stonestown Galleria, where Karina and I sometimes ventured after happy hour to browse tipsily at Forever 21 and Sephora. I rode to the end of the line, the Daly City BART station, where many commuters climbed the platform to board trains that would carry them north, to offices off the downtown San Francisco stops, or south, to the Millbrae station, where they could transfer to Caltrain, which would ferry them farther south to the tech campuses of Silicon Valley, including our parent company's headquarters in Menlo Park. I wished I could take BART to SFO again, perhaps daring to enter the airport itself. I'd gaze longingly at the security checkpoint, beyond which lay my personal nirvana. Sadly, I could not permit such an indulgence. I had to earn money that would fund future flights, as well as rent and food. I waited dutifully at the stoplight to cross John Daly Boulevard.

Acuity occupied the third floor of a building lined with narrow tinted windows. I was a few minutes early, as a life devoted to air travel had molded me into neurotic punctuality. I stowed my phone in a locker at the edge of the moderation floor, in accordance with company policy; they didn't want us taking photos of the content that crossed our queues. Our terminals were arranged on long tables, cardboard dividers set between the monitors to prevent what Christa, the stocky blonde who oversaw human relations at our site, termed "cross contamination." As usual, I headed to the exterior row, nearest the windows.

The night-shift workers had departed at 6:00 A.M., and I was nervous to discover the condition in which they'd left the terminals. The custodial crew made their rounds between night and day shifts, and again between day and night, but their work was often slapdash, and sure enough, today I found a clump of tissues tucked between my monitor and the cardboard divider. I scanned Karina's terminal to ensure she wouldn't find any similar remnants. One morning, I'd found a small heap of fingernail clippings tucked between her keyboard and monitor. I quietly removed the pile of keratin before Karina saw it, knowing she'd make a big deal of it. Karina was a germophobe, and she would view the nail shards as a provocation. And perhaps they were, as debris seemed likelier to wash up at Karina's terminal than mine, though maybe the night-shift worker who used her terminal was simply filthier than my own nocturnal double.

I settled into my swivel chair, donned my headphones, and logged in with my credentials. On my portal, a backlog of posts had accumulated, awaiting my review. These were posts the moderation software had flagged, requiring a human intellect to weigh in. The software's artificial intelligence was refined by each decision we input, though our own decisions were cross-checked with the software and our efficiency ratings climbed the more frequently we concurred. I was happy to be paid twenty dollars an hour to flatter a machine that would soon replace me.

First up were a few dozen comments on a CNN video of interviews with survivors of yesterday's mass shooting at a church outside Dallas. *OBVIOUS CIA PSY-OP*, read one; *classic false flag*, read another. *Wake up, sheeple!* read a third comment, a common refrain, along with a few comments linking the event to billionaire George Soros. These were all fine, according to the terms of service. I clicked the green button for each post, which would allow the comments to remain visible. But the next comment—*crisis actors should be executed!* along with the names and addresses of several victims' family members—was not allowed under the ToS. I clicked the red button, which flagged the post for removal and placed a temporary lock on the offending account.

Next, the queue fed me a string of flagged comments on a video of a teenage girl's morning routine, calling her such names as *slut, bitch, cum dumpster, ugly whore;* but thanks to my expertise, I understood these comments were in good fun, playful ribbing among friends. One comment read, *OMG I hate your perfect skin you cunt,* which the video poster had "liked" and replied to with a kissing-face emoji. I was intimidated by the girl's popularity. When I was her age, I'd been exempt from such camaraderie, but I couldn't permit envy to impede my judgment. I applied the green button to the comments, allowing the girls to continue enjoying their youth.

Karina arrived, ten minutes late, on a cloud of gardenia perfume. She smiled at me sheepishly and went about sanitizing her space with disinfectant wipes. Today she wore a turquoise silk dress with a ruffled neckline, a white blazer, and red pumps. "Dress for the job you want" was one of her favorite sayings, though I wasn't sure what profession corresponded to her outfits. Perhaps a cruise director or a local news anchor. Karina was three years younger than me, prettier than I'd been at any age, and better maintained, with smooth skin and a well-formed skeleton. She carried a Louis Vuitton tote, which Anthony had given her last year to compensate for forgetting her birthday. Her engagement ring sparkled as she wiped down her terminal.

Karina then draped an antimicrobial blanket over her chair, lowered its seat—her night-shift double must have been lanky—and sank into the chair with a sigh that conveyed her dread toward the eight hours that lay before us. The Violence vertical seemed ill-suited to Karina's sensitive disposition. I was confused why she stayed, month after month, without at least requesting a transfer to H&H, Porn, or Spam. Karina's credentials surely qualified her for better jobs. She held a bachelor's degree, spoke Spanish and Portuguese, and was friendly and likable, unlike the rest of us. Why remain in this role, subjecting herself to videos of torture and gore? I'd asked Karina this in my first week at Acuity, and she'd replied simply that it was what she deserved. I was curious why she'd think she deserved punishment, but I refrained from further questioning. Karina would reveal her secrets to me in her own time, if she wished to.

I hoped to be the most efficient moderator in my vertical for the third consecutive month. At the end of each month, the top mod in each vertical received a one-hundred-dollar bonus. Our scores were written on a whiteboard by the door, updated daily by Christa, with our employee numbers standing in for our names. I glanced at the whiteboard now and was pleased to see that my number, 83944D, remained at the top of the H&H column. Karina, who'd told me her number was 28839C, had sunk to the very bottom of the Violence vertical. I was sorry to see her low ranking. I wished I could help my friend, but I reminded myself she was on her own path, guided by the universe's all-knowing hand.

AT 11:00 a.m. I RETRIEVED MY PHONE FROM THE LOCKER AND ADjourned to the wellness room for my mandatory nine-minute break. The room was a converted office, painted lavender. On one wall hung a painting I was fond of, which depicted the sun setting over the ocean. A narrow window provided a view of Interstate 280, though the blinds were drawn over it as usual. Pushed into a corner were felt boxes of toys and craft materials. The seating options were an overstuffed armchair and a yoga ball that needed inflating. On a side table sat a pyramid-shaped meditation timer set to nine minutes.

I activated the timer, sat on the ball, and fished in my

jeans pocket for my shard of plane. I'd purchased it on eBay for forty dollars and carried it everywhere, as a talisman and a tool of sexual gratification. The piece was white and roughly rectangular, the size of a domino. According to the listing description, it was part of the hull of a decommissioned 737-800. I tucked the shard into my mouth while I perused photos of planes on my phone. First there was the A320, who possessed, in my opinion, the handsomest face of any commercial airliner. I proceeded to the 787 Dreamliner, whose beauty was augmented by his lovely name. Next up, a vintage magazine ad of the retired McDonnell Douglas DC-9, a plane that flaunted a certain "bad boy" appeal, having been involved in 276 aviation occurrences with a combined 3,697 fatalities in his forty-nine years of service, among the worst safety records in the industry.

Having enjoyed these appetizers, I moved on to the entrée: the 737. The 737 was my ideal plane, the sky's narrow-bodied workhorse. His modest size made him more approachable than the wide-bodied fellows, such as the pompous 747 and the aloof A380. I scrolled through the dozens of 737 photos I'd saved, my eyes growing teary with affection.

As I admired these fine specimens, my thoughts drifted, as they often did, to my first love, a 737-800 named N92823, whom I met when I was thirteen. It was on board N92823 that I had my first taste of the destiny that awaited me. My family was flying to Chicago, where my dad had been invited to an actuarial convention. A rumbling commenced during the second beverage service. Then, the plane dropped. Around fifty feet, according to a report issued by the National Transportation Safety Board a year after the incident, though it felt like free fall. My body lifted, constrained only by the belt across my lap. All was calm for a moment, and then the plane pitched again, his nose dipping and rising erratically, so that it felt like we were in a boat on choppy seas.

The cabin filled with screams and prayers. All the while, a cord of energy crept up my spine. I was filled with a warm liquid sensation, a feeling of inevitability, along with wave upon wave of pleasure, what I would later understand had been my first orgasm. My mom gripped my forearm, but I hardly registered her touch. I was alone with N92823, who I believed had recognized me as his soulmate. I wanted the turbulence to go on and on, to build to a climax, the plane diving nose-first into the earth. A perfect death! I saw that my life had always been defined by this sublime end. It would have been ideal to die with both parents beside me, Al in the row ahead, our family preserved as we were in that moment— never to grow old and develop diseases, to shrivel and suffer, and to succumb to unremarkable deaths. For the first time, I understood my place in the world, and when N92823 leveled, I sobbed. My dad reached over to pat my thigh, mistaking my disappointment for relief. It was no big deal, he assured me, just a little turbulence. But he was wrong. It was a big deal indeed.

The NTSB report concluded that we'd encountered a patch of clear-air turbulence—though I had my own theories. N92823 had been in operation only two years at that point. We were both adolescents, and I hoped our flight had been as formative for him as it was for me. I became N92823's biggest fan, following his moves on a flight-tracking website. I stalked the perimeter of John Wayne Airport when he was scheduled to fly through, taking distant, grainy photos of his handsome form with a digital camera. As he was often bound for Chicago, I asked my parents if we could fly there again, claiming to have become enamored of the stalwart Midwestern city. "Chicago? You kidding me?" my mom said. "You spent the whole trip in the bathroom. You had your chance at Chicago."

When I turned eighteen, I got a job at the Subway in Terminal C at John Wayne, hoping to save my wages toward another date with N92823. But before I could reach this goal, my love was placed in storage after a mechanical issue on a flight from Newark to San Juan. I wondered if he'd grown impatient, awaiting our reunion. Perhaps his malfunction was an act of protest against the unjust world that kept us apart. As far as I knew, he remained imprisoned in a boneyard somewhere, his veins pumped with preservative oil, his windows covered with reflective shields to protect his interior from the sun's rays. His body had likely been scavenged for parts on behalf of operational aircraft. I had forced myself to move on to available planes, but I'd always be grateful to N92823 for providing a standard against which I'd judge all subsequent lovers.

The timer's chime snapped me back to reality. I tucked my shard of plane in my pocket and returned to the moderation floor.

. . .

IN THE BREAK ROOM, KARINA ASSEMBLED HER LUNCH ON THE coffee-stained table: a Tupperware of raw kale and shredded chicken left over from last night's dinner, and a Dannon Light + Fit vanilla yogurt, which she bought by the case. As usual, I'd brought nothing, preferring to feed upon the break room's snack reserves to save money. Christa had made a Costco run last week, and I'd been extracting most of my daily calories from the replenished stash. I appreciated our employer's largesse. They were not legally required to feed us, and yet they did, four times a year—boxes of frozen food and snack packs of trail mix, Nutri-Grain bars and fruit gummies, a pallet of Rockstar lemonade—all of which we ran through within a month, to await the next windfall.

"We could take a walk," I said, as I scrounged the cabinets.

"What's the point?" Karina said. "Leave the building so we can be impaled by a piece of sheet metal that fell off a truck? No thanks." As this seemed like a random concern, I assumed she was referencing a scene she'd witnessed this morning in the Violence queue.

I heated two vegetarian egg rolls in the microwave. We were careful about what we said in the break room, as we all believed, without evidence, that the microwave was bugged with a listening device, so that Christa, or Scott, the regional manager, or perhaps even Scott's supervisor at the parent company, could monitor for signs of discontent among their contracted employees.

"You need to eat better, Linda," Karina said, glaring at my

egg rolls, whose grease had burned a patch of translucence into the paper plate on which they rested.

"It's free," I said with a shrug.

One of the interior row dwellers—Adrian? Aiden?—entered the break room, cast a look of perfunctory lust at Karina, cracked a Rockstar lemonade, and left.

"What are you up to tonight?" Karina asked. I always dreaded this question. I couldn't reveal my usual Friday plan of going to a bar to ogle planes, nor could I say I was doing nothing, which would draw attention to the barrenness of my social calendar. I feared Karina would realize she was my only friend, in which case she might wish to withdraw her friendship, sanitizing her life of me as she sanitized her terminal each morning.

Today, however, I had an excuse I knew would please her. "I need to work on my vision board," I said coyly.

Karina's eyes lit up. "So you're coming?"

I nodded. "The garage sale was postponed."

"Great!" she said. "I can't wait to see what you put on your board."

"What do the other women put on theirs?" I asked. I never missed a chance to learn what other people did.

"Everyone's different," Karina said, licking yogurt from her spoon. "Esme tends to focus on her career. Morgan's more focused on family stuff."

"What about romantic goals?"

"Those are fair game, too. The vision board is how I got Anthony to propose, after all." Last October, Karina had showed me a photo of her Q4 vision board, which featured a diamond ring hovering above a couple kissing on a beach. Anthony had proposed over Christmas. I was glad Karina had gotten what she wanted, though I'd initially hoped she would manifest some other guy.

"You really think the board made him do it?" I'd been skeptical on this point, as it seemed to me that Karina's devotion to Anthony was irrational and that he'd be wise to trap her in a marriage contract before she came to her senses.

"Totally. He needed a nudge." She put down her spoon and eyed me. "Do you want to meet someone, Linda?"

"I'd like to find my soulmate," I said, thinking of N92823. Whenever I flew, I imagined a repurposed piece of him was embedded within the plane I occupied, even if it was only a lowly bolt or screw.

"The vision board would be a great way to set an intention around dating," Karina said.

I bit into an egg roll, scalding my tongue on the cabbage within. "I'm a little nervous to meet your friends," I said quickly, before she could probe my dating history.

"Don't stress," Karina said. "They'll love you."

AT LAST, I ARRIVED AT THE ELEPHANT BAR IN BURLINGAME, AN excursion I'd looked forward to all week. The restaurant was housed in a friendly building with zebra stripes painted on its sides. At the host stand, I greeted my adversary, Jose. He was thin and stylish, with a fade haircut and a single dangling cross earring. As usual, I claimed that while I appeared to be a party of one, I was in fact half of a party of two. This was a lie, but a necessary one, as a single patron had no hope of securing a booth with a view of SFO's runways.

"I can seat you at the bar while you wait for your friend," Jose said, which caught me off guard. This was the most resistance he'd offered yet. The bar was useless to me, as it was far from the windows and offered a view only of TV monitors playing sporting events.

"She'll be here any minute," I said. "Can I wait in a booth?"

The restaurant was mostly empty, as it was only five-thirty, and my request was reasonable on its face. Jose must have decided the fight wasn't worth it, and he led me to a table along the window. I'd gotten away with it again, though I feared my days in the booth were numbered.

Through the window, I watched planes land on a runway jutting into the bay. It was dark, the winter sun having already set, and I tracked planes by their signal lights as they streamed in from the east, a steady procession guided by air traffic controllers stationed within the torch-shaped tower. A server arrived at my table, and I ordered a Diet Coke without breaking my gaze from the runway. A plane emblazoned with the Emirates logo touched down, his landing gear bouncing on the tarmac, and I flinched, my pulse quickening.

I was eager to discover what my vision board would set into motion. Perhaps it would result in my marriage to a pilot, which would in turn enable my marriage to a plane. I imagined my pilot, already fully assembled and going about his affairs in the days before our paths converged. He could be flying one of the planes I presently watched, his form tucked inside the plane's noble head. It would be nice to have him here with me. He would add commentary to the scenes we saw through the window, making observations about physics or mechanics or something as the aircraft touched down. My dad had attempted a similar narration on our plane-spotting excursions, but his knowledge of aviation was limited, and I suspected he made things up sometimes. A pilot was better equipped to reveal the plane's secrets. I knew that a pilot's skills were put to the test during takeoff and landing, the most dangerous segments of any flight. While takeoff was uniquely orgasmic, and landing had its own erotic appeal, I preferred the intervening period of cruising, when the plane's intelligence dominated, in the form of his autopilot software, along with, I believed, a spark of something akin to a soul.

The server returned for a third time and asked, with a note of impatience, whether I wanted anything else. I placed my usual order of fries, the cheapest item on the menu. I ate them slowly, stretching them until I'd had my fill.

3 On Sunday, I took the bus to Daly City and walked west, toward the address listed on the evite. The sky above me was cloudless and scarred, gloriously, by six contrails of varying thicknesses, corresponding to how recently the planes that excreted them had passed overhead and how low to the ground they'd been flying. I was so distracted, I crossed against the light and was met with a chorus of honking.

I'd dressed carefully for the VBB, in light-wash jeans, a purple sweater Karina had persuaded me to buy on one of our post-happy-hour trips to Forever 21, and a denim jacket, also from Forever 21, which I'd purchased because I'd seen young people on the bus wearing them. They were SF State students like Kevin Chen, son of my landlords, who presumably had some stake in the world, being enrolled at an accredited institution. I carried my rolled-up vision board under my arm. I'd spent forty dollars at the copy shop; printing wasn't enabled at our office, but even if it were, I wouldn't have dared to print such scandalous images at my place of employ. It pained me to part with this sum, which represented a quarter of the airfare for a roundtrip from SFO to

SLC. However, if the boards worked as well as Karina claimed, this initial investment would pay dividends.

I made my way through curving blocks of boxy, pastel-colored houses. My anxiety mounted as I approached Anthony's mom's house, which was painted light blue. I was proud of my board, but I feared the response it would receive from the VBB's other attendees. I didn't want to embarrass Karina. I wondered if she was unaware of my weirdness, or if she recognized it and didn't mind. Perhaps she only tolerated me because she needed a friend at work.

I heard the haunting cry of engines and looked up to find a plane passing directly overhead, heading northeast at around six thousand feet, low enough that I could discern the details of his sexy undercarriage. I opened the flight-tracking app on my phone and discovered this gentleman was a 777-22ER named N792UA. He'd taken off from SFO three minutes ago and was headed to Zurich, where he'd arrive in ten hours and seventeen minutes. I nodded to N792UA. If I'd had a hat, I would have tipped it. His appearance was a good omen, filling me with courage in my endeavor.

A silver BMW pulled to the curb, and two women emerged. The driver was a tall, regal woman with light-brown skin, wearing gold hoop earrings and a floral-print wrap dress; the passenger was a short woman of Asian descent, wearing a fleece half-zip pullover, jeans, and checkered Vans slip-ons. I was grateful to see the second woman dressed casually, as I'd worried I was underdressed. The tall woman popped the trunk of the BMW, and from it they retrieved two rolled posterboards.

The woman in Vans noticed me standing across the street, and I waved, hoping she'd recognize me as a fellow passenger bound for the VBB ship. She waved back with a confused look. The two women proceeded up the stairs to the front door. Karina stepped out of the house to greet them, and while she was hugging the tall woman, she looked over her friend's shoulder and spotted me.

"Linda!" she said. "What are you doing over there?"

I crossed the street and climbed the stairs. When I reached the top, Karina threw her arms around me. "I'm so glad you came!" she said. She touched the edge of my rolled posterboard. "There it is, huh? I can't wait to see what you came up with."

I followed Karina inside. She wore a dress I'd never seen, in a red paisley print, which plunged at her chest and cinched at her waist. As she led me to the kitchen, I noticed Karina held her body differently here than she did at work. She seemed relaxed as she stood behind the butcher block arrayed with mimosa components: bottles of champagne and orange juice, and three small bowls of fruit garnishes.

"Which would you like, Linda?" she said, gesturing to the spread. "I have raspberry, pomegranate, and classic orange."

I pointed to the pomegranate, though it made no difference to me. Karina clapped her hands.

"Excellent choice."

There was a rustling at the door behind Karina, and a moment later, Anthony emerged from their downstairs lair. He was a handsome fellow, with sparkling blue eyes and a wide, affable face reminiscent of the A310. As usual, his facial hair had been barbered in a sharp line from chin to side-burns, drawing attention to the square diamonds in his earlobes. He wore an oversized teal T-shirt, presumably of his own design, on which a goblin-like creature smoked a cannabis cigar.

"Hey, Lindy," he said, drawing me in for a hug. "You're on board with the boards, huh?"

"It's my first time," I said. Anthony smirked. My cheeks flushed as I realized I'd accidentally said something sexually provocative. A virgin I wasn't, unfortunately. I'd had sex maybe ten times in my life, with two different men. Afterward, I always felt disgust, along with a bloated emptiness, as when I'd eaten a large quantity of popcorn for dinner.

I surrendered to Anthony's charm, which was comforting on this fraught social occasion. He was a familiar object in a sea of unknowns, a life vest I could strap on.

"Did you make a vision board?" I asked.

"Nah," Anthony said. He opened the fridge and withdrew a bottle of Glacier Freeze Gatorade. "No guys allowed at the VBB."

"That's not true," Karina said. Anthony kissed her cheek lustily, and she swatted him away. "Go back to your cave, you creep," she told him with affection.

"Karina never shows me her boards. They're a state secret around here."

"You never asked," Karina said, though surely Anthony was right that the boards were a secret from him. Karina couldn't show him her engagement-themed board from last quarter, revealing that she'd wielded the universe's infinite

power to coerce him into proposing. Other people didn't like
to feel their free will had been tampered with; they under-
estimated the appeal of surrender. As I watched Karina and
Anthony flirt, I found myself rooting for their relationship.
Karina loved this man the way I loved planes. Knowing this,
how could I begrudge their happiness?

Anthony winked at me and disappeared down the stairs.
At last, there was no escaping the other women. I moved to
the living room with Karina.

"Everyone, this is my coworker and dear friend Linda,"
she said.

"Oh, you're Linda!" the woman in Vans said. "We've
heard so much about you."

The women in the living room—the two I'd seen outside,
plus two others—stood to introduce themselves, shaking my
hand in a firm manner that would have pleased Guillaume
Faury, whose spirit I'd endeavored to trap inside my board.
The tall woman was Esme, while the woman wearing Vans
was Stacy. There was also Morgan, a freckled woman with
red hair and large teeth, and Judy, whose neck seemed overly
long. We settled into the living room furniture—Esme,
Stacy, and Morgan on the couch, Judy on an armchair. I
claimed the second armchair, though I worried Karina would
have nowhere to sit.

"I was happy to be invited," I said. "I've never made a vision board before."

"Of course," Esme said in a chilly tone. "All are welcome."

I found this hard to believe. Surely they wouldn't let in
anyone off the street.

"It's a silly thing we've been doing since college," Judy said. I didn't like how the women were minimizing the ceremony. I'd hoped they took the art of manifestation as seriously as I did.

"Where'd you go to college?" I asked.

"Stanford," Stacy said with an ironic eye roll.

"Except for Karina," Morgan clarified. "She went to SF State."

"My housemate goes there," I said, though I wasn't sure this term accurately conveyed my relationship to Kevin Chen. Kevin was a member of the family and lived in the house, while I maintained a spectral presence in the garage.

"It's a good school," Judy said. The other women murmured in agreement, a bit too strenuously.

"Where did you go, Linda?" Esme asked.

"Nowhere," I admitted. "I took an English class at a community college once, but I never turned in my final essay." An awkward silence ensued.

"College isn't right for everyone," Esme said.

Judy agreed, adding, "My cousin makes six figures as a plumber."

"That's a great job," Stacy chimed in. "Totally recession-proof."

"Has anyone heard from Nikki?" Morgan asked. I was grateful she'd changed the subject. I sank further into the armchair, hoping to make myself invisible. I sipped my mimosa, admiring how long and lean my fingers looked against the glass, like the string cheeses I stocked my mini-fridge with. From their conversation I gathered that Nikki was about to give birth. I assumed this was why she was unavailable today, though it seemed a risky moment to shirk the universe's influence.

I scanned the room, admiring the decorating choices of Anthony's mom, Celia. She was a nurse and a devout Catholic. According to Karina, Celia had also pressured Anthony to propose, so he and Karina wouldn't be living in sin in her garage. A portrait of Celia with Anthony's dad, who I understood was no longer around, either dead or simply gone, hung on the far wall, above a credenza topped with a lace runner and an assortment of glass figurines in the shapes of animals. Sunlight flooded through the front windows, bathing the left side of my body in a nauseating heat. I turned to see a two-foot wooden crucifix with an agonized Jesus hanging on the wall behind me. I flinched and was grateful I'd already drained my glass, as otherwise I'd have spilled my mimosa.

Judy laughed, not unkindly. "He's something, isn't he?"

"Let me get you a refill," Karina said, having materialized beside my chair. She took the glass from my hand and returned to the kitchen.

"So you and Karina work together?" Morgan asked, and I was horrified to find the other attendees' focus retrained upon me, as though my reaction to the crucifix had reminded them of my presence.

"We do," I said.

"What's that like?" Morgan pressed. "I've read articles about those places."

"I love it," I said. "It's the best job I've ever had."

"Linda's the top mod in her vertical," Karina said, placing the topped-off mimosa glass in my hand.

"It seems like pretty intense work," Esme said.

"Why don't we get started?" Karina said with an abruptness that suggested she wanted to avoid discussing Acuity. While I'd been focused on the décor, Karina had ferried in trays of croissants and glass cups of yogurt parfait, which stood on the coffee table like offerings on an altar, untouched by all. She brought a straight-backed chair in from the dining room and perched at its edge.

Stacy tore the nose from a croissant, which seemed to signal the start of things, as though the knob of pastry were the pin of a grenade. Esme volunteered to go first. She stood in front of the window and unfurled her board. The other women leaned forward to inspect it, and I mimicked them. Esme's board was divided into four sections, with each quadrant comprising a cheerful collage of images. The top left quadrant was devoted to fitness. Esme pointed to a photo of a woman doing an advanced yoga pose, her elbows on the floor and her legs raised to the sides, in an enviably winglike configuration.

"I want to work out five days a week, with three days of HIIT and two of hot yoga," Esme said.

"God, I wish I had your energy," Morgan said. "Enjoy it now, because once you have kids, exercise is a luxury."

Esme smiled stiffly at Morgan, seeming annoyed by her interjection. "That brings me to the next section—personal relationships and family," Esme continued, pointing to the lower left quadrant, which featured images of a man and woman drinking coffee and laughing, a pregnant torso, and a teddy bear. "I had my IUD removed. Ian and I have started trying." The other women congratulated her. Esme, blushing, moved quickly to the third quadrant, which displayed two human hands clasped in a handshake, a woman in a power suit walking down a city street, and a roomy corner office with a view of downtown San Francisco.

"I'm planning to ask for a promotion to lead portfolio manager," Esme said.

"Hell yeah," Stacy said. "You deserve it, babe."

"Finally, and most importantly," Esme said, pointing to the fourth quadrant, which contained a photo of a woman sitting in lotus position, "I want to work on developing a spiritual practice this quarter. I might even go on a meditation retreat at Green Gulch."

We clapped. Esme curtsied and allowed her board to re-spool around itself. I felt daunted and wished Karina had given me more guidance in crafting my board. I hadn't known I was supposed to divide my goals into quadrants.

Stacy's board contained text, in addition to images of dogs, mountain trails, and leafy greens. *She has fire in her soul and grace in her heart,* read one snippet, scarily. *SELF-CARE,* commanded another. Morgan's board focused primarily on her children, two red-haired boys under the age of five, along with images of Costa Rica, where her family was planning a summer trip. Judy hoped to go on a backpacking excursion in Joshua Tree with her wife, and commit herself to mentoring younger female employees at the education startup where she worked. Each time an attendee finished displaying her board and was feted with applause, my anxiety ratcheted up another notch. Still, I was determined to go through with the embarrassing spectacle, as Karina had said showing the board to others was a crucial step in transmitting one's intentions to the universe.

It was Karina's turn. Her board consisted of wedding-themed photos, generic shots of a bride and groom at an altar, along with pictures of babies, stock models like the pilots I'd found for my board.

"I'm hoping we can set a date for the wedding this quarter," she said, her voice hushed in case Anthony was listening from the basement, I presumed. "I'm not in a rush, but I'd like to start looking at venues."

"You haven't set a date?" Morgan said.

"Not yet," Karina said. "Anthony's been busy with work and his side hustles. He's hoping to hit big with his T-shirts this year. He's looking into partnering with a streetwear brand."

Esme leaned forward, uncrossing her legs. "Isn't the novelty T-shirt sector fairly saturated at this point?"

Karina seemed thrown off by Esme's question. "Anthony's got his own niche," she said, with less confidence than before. "He sold out of a few designs over the holidays. I'm so proud of him."

From their tepid responses, I gathered the women had the same reservations about Anthony I'd held in the era prior to an hour ago, when we'd had that nice exchange in the kitchen.

"I'm sure you'll set a date," I said. "Anthony's a great guy."

"Thanks, Linda," Karina said, smiling at me.

Morgan peered at Karina's board over her mimosa. "What about your professional life?" she asked. "No goals in that department?"

"Not at the moment," Karina said. "I'm happy at Acuity."

"Are you, though?" Judy said gently. "I worry the work is traumatizing you."

"It's not so bad," I said. "We get free snacks and a nine-minute wellness break every day."

"When you're ready for a change, I know plenty of companies are looking for people," Esme said, ignoring my comment.

"My sister says they're hiring at Airbnb," Judy said. "I bet she could get you an interview."

"Maybe you should all mind your own business," Karina said. Everyone—we humans, the glass animals on the credenza, Jesus on the wall behind me—remained still, as if the air had gelled. Karina rolled up her board and lowered herself with great dignity into her chair.

"Linda, you're up," she said.

Conditions were more awkward than I could have imagined. Yet somehow, the way the mood had tilted into conflict, fraught with relational context of which I was ignorant, felt freeing. I would throw myself on the chopping block for Karina's sake. I stood before the window and unrolled my board.

The women's eyes scanned the images. I couldn't bear to look at my board, though I'd memorized its layout. The best photos I'd procured of planes shot from various angles, their wings and faces and one naughty landing-gear shot. The pilots. Guillaume Faury.

Stacy was the first to speak. "Wow, look at all those planes!" she said.

"I always thought pilots were kind of sexy," Judy said.

Esme stood, glass in hand, and scrutinized my board at closer range. "Are you thinking of a career change, Linda?" she asked.

"No, I want to marry a pilot," I said. "Now that I'm in my thirties, I figure it's time to get married."

The women crouched one by one to examine my board. They seemed delighted, as though it were the morbid artwork of a child. Stacy curled up on the floor at my feet.

"Your board is fucking amazing, Linda," she said. She seemed a little drunk.

"Pilots are gone a lot of the time," Morgan said, as she settled back onto the couch.

"That's true," Esme said. "I've heard they have high divorce rates."

"I don't think it has to be a pilot," Karina said. "That's just an example. A guy with a good job. Right, Linda?"

I nodded, grateful she'd translated my board into acceptable terms.

"Who's that?" Stacy asked, reaching up to tap Guillaume Faury's stoic face.

"That's Guillaume Faury, the CEO of Airbus," I said, feeling insulted on Faury's behalf that these women didn't recognize him, and that Stacy had poked him.

"So you want to marry a CEO?" Morgan said. I sensed she was mocking me, but I pretended not to notice.

"Oh, I don't want to marry him," I said. "He's pretty old, and I think he lives in Europe, anyway."

"Why does she have to date a CEO?" Esme said to Morgan. "She could be one herself."

I nodded again, or perhaps I'd never stopped nodding. "I'd like to be the boss," I said, hoping this would please them.

"Fuck yeah," Stacy said.

"And what do the planes signify?" Karina asked. I'd dreaded this question, especially from Karina, as I worried the plane imagery would trigger her phobia.

"Travel," I said. "I'd like to travel more."

Karina nodded, and I knew I'd passed an important test.

"Next time, you might want to add some images from particular destinations," Esme said. "The more precisely you can express your vision, the better."

Next time! I couldn't believe it. They seemed to like me in spite of my board, which was so different from theirs. I'd shown them a sliver of my true self, and they'd accepted at least this partial measure of me. I felt an overwhelming affection for these women, recalling those teen girls from my moderation queue who'd harassed their friend, calling her a cum dumpster. Perhaps I'd finally been inducted into a similar sorority.

I decided to wrap things up before they asked me a question I didn't know how to answer. I rolled up my board, and they applauded. Karina crossed the room and hugged me. I breathed in the familiar smell of her perfume, along with the waxy scent of her scalp.

"One more thing," she said. "That was a great first effort, and I really like the unified theme, but for your next board you might try not leaning so heavily on one type of image. You don't want the universe to think you're obsessed with planes."

Everyone laughed, and I laughed along with them, while inwardly, I prayed the universe was canny enough to decipher my board's coded meaning. We stood and joined hands for the final stage of the ceremony. Esme led us through a manifestation mantra she'd learned at a corporate retreat: "Universe, empower me to become the best version of myself, in accordance with your infinite wisdom."

4 I journeyed home from the VBB feeling high. At last, I'd found a way to assert my desire to the universe, rather than waiting passively for my moment to arrive, as I'd done most of my life, with the exception of the flight binge following my dad's death. That experience taught me that simply flying nonstop wasn't sufficient to budge the statistical probability in my favor. The universe would not be cudgeled into delivering my fate prematurely, and I sensed it did not appreciate my petulant demands. I hoped my vision board had conveyed that I'd humbly accept my fate, whenever the universe saw fit to bestow it. Best of all, I'd transmitted my intentions while fitting in reasonably well with Karina's friends. Karina herself seemed to like me more than she had before the VBB. She'd kissed both my cheeks at the door, perhaps in a nod to Guillaume Faury, whose inclusion on my board was assumed to hint at latent Francophile tendencies I did not in fact harbor. "See you tomorrow, *ma chérie*" were her last words to me.

As I walked to the bus stop, I called my mom, to whom I hadn't spoken since my yearly visit at Christmas. We'd always had a strained relationship. I knew I wasn't the daughter she'd hoped for, whereas Al was the perfect son—confident, athletic, in possession of conventional ambitions and romantic desires. Growing up, the battle lines in our household were clearly drawn: my dad and me versus my mother and Al. But now that my dad was gone, I'd have to settle for the company of my surviving parent. I was excited, and I wanted to share my good news with someone.

She answered on the second ring. "Hello? Linda?"

"Hey, Mom," I said. "How are the pants?"

On my last visit, I'd found the house infested with leggings—stacked on the dining room table, draped over the couch, loose pairs tangled together as though engaged in an orgy. "The last shipment was bad," she admitted. "More holes than usual."

"I'll take some, if you can't sell them," I said.

"Okay, hon. I'll send a few pairs."

"Is Ron there?"

"He's coming over soon, with the boys." Her boyfriend Ron's sons, Teddy and Ron Jr., were large, pale men in their early twenties. During Christmas dinner, they'd sat next to each other and remained uncannily quiet, like beautiful white cows.

"I have some news," I said.

"Is everything okay?" My mom was always apprehensive about my well-being, and I didn't blame her, but her concern irritated me now that my life had taken such a fortuitous turn.

"More than okay," I said. "I've decided I want to marry a pilot."

"Oh, that's nice, sweetie. Did you meet someone?"

"Not yet. But I've laid the groundwork." I told her about the vision boards, and she said she'd heard about them from her friend Trish, whom I distrusted, as she was also involved with the pants scheme.

A clamor erupted on her end. "They're here with Chipotle," she said.

We said, "I love you," sealing the call, so that if one of us perished in the night, we'd have less regret than otherwise. On the 28 bus, I headed north on 280, to Junipero Serra, where we veered left onto Nineteenth Avenue. The bus's northbound route carved through the Sunset District, Golden Gate Park, the Richmond District, and the Presidio; made a loop at the Golden Gate Bridge; and continued east along Lombard Street with its strip of cut-rate hotels, terminating at the heart of Fisherman's Wharf. I rarely rode it beyond Taraval, however. I got off there and walked west, to the Chens' house.

The Chen family lived in a burnt-orange house on Thirty-eighth Avenue. I entered through a side door to the garage, half of which was occupied by my in-law apartment, a pre-fabricated, enclosed structure with dimensions of twelve by twelve feet. The rest of the garage was used for storage and laundry, though I was not permitted to use the washer and dryer. Sometimes, on those occasions when I'd failed to monitor for activity in the outer garage before leaving my cube, I encountered Mrs. Chen using them and was forced to make small talk with her.

My room featured an en suite bathroom with a sink, a

toilet, and a shower. I'd never had a private bathroom before, and this luxury motivated me to be a perfect tenant. When I'd come to see the space, Mr. Chen told me I would be their first renter. He seemed uneasy about the arrangement, as the room was surely not up to code. The ad had said they were looking for a single person, someone quiet, preferably a student, and the prospective renter would have to agree to the house rules, which included no cooking, no audible music, no excessive water use, and no overnight guests. Were they to rent this room at all, it would be to a tenant who barely existed. I'd kept up my end of the agreement, doing my best to be a ghost in their midst, a ghost with a checking account that automatically deposited rent money on the first day of each month. I was grateful to be accepted as a tenant, just as I was grateful for Karina's friendship. Ever since my awakening on board N92823, I'd feared other people would discover my connection with planes, and the fate I was bound for. I knew they'd be horrified and shun me. I'd tip-toed through life, keeping myself under tight restraint, afraid that an excess of feeling would cause me to reveal too much, ushering in my social demise. Though my isolation some-times weighed on me, I reasoned that my bond with planes more than compensated for my disconnection from people.

But today, post-VBB, I felt suffused by the universe's gen-erosity and was no longer content with being a ghost. I'd shown myself to be socially capable, and I wanted to exert my newfound confidence upon Mr. and Mrs. Chen. I would inflict on them my personality, which had been so amply tested at the brunch and proven to be a winning one!

I crossed the threshold into the main house. By contrast with the clammy air of the garage, the interior of the house was cozy, warm, and sunlit. I traversed the short hallway to the kitchen, where I beheld a serene domestic tableau. Mr. Chen sat at the table, tapping the screen of an iPad. Mrs. Chen stood at the sink, washing vegetables. I crept forward. The radio was on, tuned to a classical music station, and due to the screen of noise they did not notice me.

"Hello, Mr. and Mrs. Chen," I said, and they both turned with alarm.

"Linda!" Mrs. Chen said, shutting off the faucet. "Is everything okay?"

"I just wanted to say hi," I said. "Happy Sunday!"

Mr. Chen put down his iPad and removed his readers. He appeared to be around the age my dad had been when he died, and I felt a surge of affection for him. I wished I could participate in their family life and be loved as a daughter, or at least a quirky niece. "Is your room warm enough?" he said.

"Plenty warm, with the space heater," I said.

"Just make sure to unplug it when you leave. And don't use an extension cord, please. Fire hazard."

I nodded, thinking about the nest of extension cords under my bed. "Of course."

They stared at me expectantly, clearly waiting for the real reason I'd entered the house. Karina had told me the best way to connect with people was to ask them questions.

"I was wondering," I said, "do you enjoy flying?"

"No, I hate it," Mr. Chen said with a grimace. "The airlines are terrible. They overbook every flight. They treat passengers like cattle."

"Never fly United," Mrs. Chen said. "We learned our lesson the hard way, last year."

"Why do you ask?" Mr. Chen said.

I chuckled in acknowledgment that it had been an odd question. "Well, I happen to love flying," I said. "I'm going to Phoenix next weekend."

"You have family there?" Mrs. Chen said, wiping her hands on a dish towel.

I felt trapped by this question and became self-conscious, aware I was behaving in a risky manner. It was one thing to practice the art of socializing with people whose opinion had no material impact on my life, and quite another to practice with my landlords.

"My sister," I lied. "She just had a baby."

"How wonderful," Mrs. Chen said. "Give her our best wishes."

I promised I would. "Well, I should go back to my room now," I said before they could ask any follow-up questions. "I just went to brunch at a friend's house, and I'm pretty beat."

"Sounds good, Linda," Mr. Chen said.

I returned to my cube, which I saw in a new light. For the last year and a half, it had served as a comfortable hole in which I secreted myself, like a river eel in its mud burrow. Now it seemed cramped, depressing. The room was already tidy, as I possessed few belongings, but I further neatened it, smoothing the duvet across my bed and hanging my denim jacket on a hook I'd glued to the back of the door. I reflected on the jacket, dangling with an attitude of nonchalance, as though it had never doubted its own worthiness. Resentment set in. How I envied my jacket.

A knock came, startling me. For a moment, I believed my contemplation of the jacket had summoned the sound. I opened the door, revealing Kevin Chen. He was twenty years old, tall and broad-shouldered—a good-looking fellow, I gathered. He brought to mind the Bombardier CRJ100/200, a regional jet with a certain plucky maneuverability, though limited in range, as is characteristic of the young. Kevin had made the shrewd decision to continue living with his parents while he studied business at SF State and worked part-time as a trainer at the 24 Hour Fitness on Ocean Avenue. I wished my mom had allowed me to live with her after high school. Instead I'd been evicted to make space for a second macramé loom.

"Hey there, Linda," Kevin said. "Sorry to bother you. I talked to my parents, and they're a little concerned."

"Nothing to be concerned about," I said. "I just thought I'd wish them a happy Sunday."

Kevin's eyes scanned my wall. "Cool map," he said.

"Come have a look," I said. He advanced into my room warily.

"I keep records of all my flights," I said. "I can afford to fly once a month. I wish I could fly more."

"So you fly just for the sake of flying?"

"Oh, of course not," I said with a calculated laugh. "I also visit the sights at my destination."

I'd never had another person in my room before. I suddenly wanted to show Kevin everything. I unrolled my vision board and explained its components. "My goal is to get married," I said. "To find a man with a good job, with a pilot being one example."

Kevin examined the board with his arms crossed, like an art critic. "Well, good luck," he said. "I hope you find what you're looking for."

"Do you know how I might do it?"

"Do what?"

"Find a pilot to marry."

"Uh, I dunno. Have you tried the apps?"

"Is that how you met your girlfriend? Lois," I remembered.

"We met at school."

"Ah," I said. "Well, I'm not a student, so that's not an option for me."

"They have lots of dating apps now, for different types of people," Kevin said. "Maybe there's even one for pilots, if that's really what you're into."

I thanked Kevin for this information. He edged toward the door.

"Like I said, I didn't want to intrude," he said. "It's just my parents, they're not used to having someone living in the garage. I think it would be best if you kept it low-key."

"That's what I've been doing."

"I know, and we really like having you here. You're like a family member." He scratched beneath his left ear. "A family member we never see or talk to."

I was moved by this, though I knew he was only trying to manipulate me. I'd always hoped I could become part of their family.

"My parents, you know, they get nervous," he said. I gathered he was referring to my room's slapdash construction and lack of a secondary exit. "It's probably better for you not to remind them you live here, if you want to keep living here."

I remembered the mornings I'd seen Kevin on the bus on his way to SF State, while I was bound for Acuity. We didn't speak, but he'd acknowledge me with a nod that made me feel like I belonged in human society. I'd been so grateful for those small movements of his youthful head. Though I now realized he must have avoided me on the walk to the bus stop, as I never noticed him until we were already jostling down Nineteenth Ave.

"I promise I won't enter the main house again," I said.

"I think that's for the best."

"Thanks, Kevin. You're really looking out for me."

He lingered in the doorway. "If you need help with your dating profile," he said in a cheeky tone, "hit me up."

I SAT ON THE EDGE OF MY BED, MARVELING AT THE DAY'S EVENTS. I'd charted a course for future success and formed friendships with people who would help me on my way, even if they did not understand what they were abetting. Best of all, I would take to the sky on Friday, for my monthly roundtrip flight.

I reviewed the email detailing my itinerary. I would depart from SFO, bound for PHX, at 8:10 P.M. If I emerged single from the first flight, I'd spend the night wandering the airport, visiting past and potential lovers where they slumbered at their gates. I'd depart back to SFO at 11:00 A.M. Saturday, and if the second plane didn't choose me, either, I'd sleep through the day and awaken Sunday morning, with time to launder my clothes so I'd be fresh for the work week. My joints ached with accumulated gravity. I was getting by on the minimal flights my budget allowed, but by the third week of groundedness, withdrawal inevitably set in. I would become edgy and irritable, full of brittle energy that could pivot, at any moment, into despair. These symptoms typically abated the moment I entered the airport's secure sector, and when my lover's wheels lifted from the runway, I would feel reborn.

My date for Friday evening was N108DQ, a fellow I'd been with a few times before. I'd looked up his tail number only after booking the flight, a rule I adhered to with all my lovers, out of a superstition I harbored, something about how romance was dampened by overplanning. N108DQ was a fine twenty-year-old 737-800. I'd found him erratic and hot-tempered on our previous dates, qualities I ascribed to his lust for me. I kept meticulous records of my encounters in the Notes app on my phone, and presently, I revisited the entry I'd made for N108DQ. One line recalled the eroticism of an abrupt wing dip late on our flight to Seattle, six months ago. More recently, we'd made a bouncy landing at Dallas

Fort Worth, N108DQ's wings rocking from side to side as his landing gear settled, as though N108DQ didn't want our date to end. I was excited to reunite with him on Friday, and hoped the months since our last tryst had increased his desire for me. Just as tantalizing was my date for the return flight, N942NN, a seventeen-year-old A321-100 I hadn't yet had the pleasure of meeting.

In the meantime, I could make inroads on my quest for a pilot. I decided to fine-tune my intentions. I opened a fresh note on my phone and tapped out a list of things I would do if I succeeded in becoming intimate with such a man:

—Discuss flight routes

—Ask if I can fly in jump seat sometime

—Ask to describe experience of being a pilot
  (affection for planes?)

—Build trust over course of years

—Marry

—Use flight benefits to fly as much as possible

—Be united with soulmate plane for eternity

I squinted at my list and deemed it sufficient. The VBB had taught me that no goal was too lofty to aim for and that the universe respected fearlessness and positivity above all other human qualities. Certainly I would never meddle with the operations of a plane, even if it was for the sake of our eternal togetherness. I wasn't sure how such a thing would be attempted, and anyway, I was not a violent person. A crash I'd caused myself would not satisfy my desire, as it would be a fraudulent victory. The plane I'd sabotaged would descend with hatred for me in his heart. I wanted a plane to choose me, as human lovers choose to marry. I wasn't greedy, nor was I impatient when it came to something as important as marriage. I'd wait a lifetime if I had to.

I plugged in my phone, then perched on the edge of my bed, constrained by the cord's limited span. "Dating site pilot," I typed into the search bar. This query produced a slew of articles: "Six Reasons You Should Date a Pilot," "7 Things That Happen When You Date a Pilot," "How to Date a Pilot and Where to Find Them??" It seemed I wasn't alone in my mission. I recalled Judy's statement about pilots being sexy and felt proud to have devised a socially acceptable cover for my desire.

There was in fact a dating site catering to those seeking pilots. Within minutes I'd created an account on Pilotdate .net. Now it was time for photos. I made an honest appraisal of myself in the mirrored door of my closet. My breasts were a C cup that drooped unless held aloft by an underwire bra. My limbs were skinny, but my entire body was covered in a layer of fat, due to lack of exercise, probably. I possessed a wide mouth and a high forehead. My hair was naturally a sandy color, which I'd bleached and dyed a more vivacious blond a few months ago, at Karina's suggestion. Since then, the hair had grown four inches from its roots, so that it

looked like my hair was wearing socks. I caught Karina looking at my mangled dye job sometimes, but she never mentioned it, for which I was grateful, as I rather liked the effect.

I possessed nothing close to Karina's beauty, but my appearance was not objectionable. I was happy to occupy this
bland median status, as it protected me from unwanted attention. As I belonged nowhere on the conventional spec-
trum of sexual orientation, I allowed people to assume I was
heterosexual, and I suppose I was, as all planes are male in
spirit, just as all boats are female, and helicopters possess
the souls of mischievous children.

On the floor of my closet, I located the only sexy bra I
owned, black lace with cords of nonfunctional fabric strung
above the cups. I took several photos of myself in the bra.
When I reviewed the photos, I found that in the harsh overhead light of my windowless room, I looked somehow both
older and younger than I was. I could pass as a forty-year-old
methamphetamine user or a fifteen-year-old victim of human
trafficking. I appeared in dire need of hydration, vitamins,
sunlight, and a sense of humor. I imagined what Karina
would say—that like attracts like—and was frightened to
consider the male equivalent of the persona these photos
embodied. Natural light would yield more flattering images,
but it was 5:20 P.M., which meant the sun had already set,
according to my weather app. I was annoyed by the sun's la-
ziness, clocking out before dinner and delaying my plan to
lure a pilot into my net. I was too excited to defer my mission
entirely, however. I added the best of the bra photos to my
Pilotdate profile, along with the blurry headshot from my

Acuity ID card. In the written section, I cribbed from the "Six Reasons You Should Date a Pilot" listicle. *I'm a jetsetter!* I wrote. *I love a man in uniform!*

My profile went live, and I tucked my phone behind my pillow, imagining I was burying a magic seed that would bear fruit by morning.

I waited until my wellness break the next day to check Pilotdate. When I logged in, my heart soared—I'd received twenty-two messages from individual pilots! I inspected the tiny profile pictures placed beside previewed snippets of their messages. Nearly all looked similar to one of the pilots on my vision board: a man with a crew cut wearing aviator sunglasses.

As I peered more closely, I saw that many of them were in fact the same photo I'd placed on my board. For a moment, I was awed by the board's power. Was it possible I'd manifested this particular man, whom I'd assumed was a stock model? Had this pilot, in the fervency of his desire for me, somehow multiplied himself, fractal-like, so that all his duplicate selves could message me simultaneously, using slightly different approaches, thus maximizing his chances of a positive response? I wanted to assure him that such a scheme hadn't been necessary. I was more than receptive. I was stocked and fueled, my safety inspection complete. I was a cockpit of a woman—a warm, buzzing cavity ready to receive him.

But as I reviewed the messages, I found they all contained identical text: *AVIATOR FLASH SALE 30% OFF RAY-*

*BANS PROMOTION ENDS WEDNESDAY! PROMOCODE #PILOTSWAG www.sunglassesforcheap.com/pilotswag.*

So Pilotdate.net was merely a front for a sunglasses-oriented spam operation. My hopes sank into the hollow core of the yoga ball on which I'd stationed my pelvis. I should have known the pilot dating site was too good to be true. I'd have to try my luck on one of the more conventional platforms, but first, I needed better photos.

In the break room at lunch, Karina was in higher spirits than usual. While she tended to be jollier at the start of the week, before the strain of moderating took its toll, she seemed even more buoyant than on a typical Monday. She must have been invigorated by the VBB, in spite of the other women's criticisms of her board.

"My friends thought you were hilarious," she said, dipping a spoon into one of the yogurt parfaits left over from brunch. "Everyone's been talking about your board on the group chat."

"I'm glad it went over well," I said, though I felt a little offended, as my board was not meant to be humorous. "I was nervous at first, because my board was so different from everyone else's."

"That was the great thing about it. It's your vision, for your life. There's no right or wrong way to do it."

"Esme and Morgan seemed to think otherwise."

"Yeah, they've got it all figured out." Karina rolled her eyes.

"Stacy seemed nice."

"Stacy's cool. She runs a dog rescue."

"And Judy, with the long neck."

"Judy's my best friend from high school." Karina paused. "I don't think her neck is that long, is it?"

"I suppose not," I said to be polite, though Judy's neck was indeed freakishly long.

As I peeled the wrapper from a Nutri-Grain bar, I mentioned, in an offhand way, that I'd made a profile on a dating site.

"Ooh, exciting," Karina said. "Are you talking to anyone yet?"

"I think I've only matched with bots so far."

I didn't mention Pilotdate.net specifically, as I knew she'd find it strange I was limiting my search to pilots. Instead, I asked her to review the photos I'd taken in my bedroom. Karina winced as she scrolled through them.

"These are pretty intense," she said.

"I was trying to look seductive, I guess."

"You might be putting out the wrong vibe. You don't want guys who are just looking for a hookup."

"Definitely not," I said, disgusted by the prospect.

"You might want to save these for someone you're already dating. For the apps, I think it's best to look friendly and approachable. Your everyday look. Do you have anything like that?"

I shook my head.

"We could take a few now," she said, which was what I'd hoped for.

Karina agreed natural light would be best, which meant venturing outdoors. Before we left the office, I stuffed my jacket pockets with Nutri-Grain bars to eat on the go, so I wouldn't miss an opportunity to pack my body with life-sustaining calories. The sky was partly cloudy, with a few persistent spreading contrails, indicating a high degree of moisture in the air. We strolled to the middle of the overpass that spanned 280. Below, cars surged like fish in a crowded stream. I breathed the gasoline-scented air, feeling it cleanse me from within.

I posed while Karina took photos with her phone. She told me to lean back with my elbows on the railing. Next, she had me turn my back to her and look over my shoulder invitingly. She took a few close-ups of my face and some full-body shots. I tried smiling and not smiling. I tried looking sexily confused, my lips slightly parted. I pretended to laugh. I put my hands on my hips, affecting a sassy demeanor. "Good!" Karina said, snapping away.

Soon she said we had enough, and we needed to get back, as our break was almost over. She promised to review the photos and send me the best ones. I felt secure in my friend's manicured hands.

I TEXTED KEVIN ON MY BUS RIDE HOME, ASKING WHICH DATING site was best. He had offered to help, after all, and I wanted to nurture the connection we'd made yesterday in my room.

*For someone your age, I guess OkCupid?* he wrote.

Back in my room, I crafted a profile on OkCupid. In my bio, I answered the prompts as honestly as I could without seeming too weird. I disguised my devotion to planes as a benign love of travel, which the VBB had taught me was a ubiquitous passion. For "What I'm doing with my life . . ." I wrote, *My day job is in tech, but I travel as much as I possibly can!* For "On a typical Friday night I am . . ." I wrote, *Flying somewhere, or visiting my favorite bar that overlooks the runways of SFO!* For "You should message me if . . ." I wrote, *You're a commercial pilot for a major airline. Please do not message me if you have a different job!*

I uploaded a few of the photos Karina had taken of me. I was pleased by how normal I looked in them. I could have been a stock model myself, my image summoned by the search term "woman on overpass." For a male opinion, I sent a screenshot of my profile to Kevin, who texted back immediately, presumably from his own superior room inside the main house. *Looks good,* he wrote. *Knock 'em dead.*

As I drifted toward sleep, I attempted to fantasize about a hypothetical pilot. I imagined straddling the uniformed man as he sat in the captain's seat, his facial region a blur that occasionally resolved into the features of the pilot I'd seen on the AirTrain. He ran his hands beneath my shirt and massaged my breasts. My back grazed the control panel's gadgetry. Through the cockpit door, I stared down the length of the plane's body. As long as I focused on the plane, I could make myself come, imagining the pilot as an appendage of the aircraft, a human dildo the plane and I could use as a sex toy. This seemed promising, but I was unable to export this fantasy from the plane's interior. I assumed my pilot would prefer to make love in a conventional setting, such as a bedroom. My imagination faltered when I attempted to conjure such a scenario. I could visualize only snippets of sex scenes from movies, which I found dull and unpleasant.

My prior sexual experiences were embarrassing to recall. First there'd been Brett, my coworker at Subway in the John Wayne Airport. I got the job shortly after I turned eighteen, at which point I was finally eligible to work in the airport. From behind the counter, I gazed out the windows, watching planes mill about like contented farm animals, commingling with catering trucks, power washers, and luggage carts. My closeness to planes, coupled with my inability to fly on them, kept me in a state of constant, frustrated arousal, and one day I asked Brett if he'd like to fool around in the walk-in fridge. Brett was a surfer in his early twenties, an affable young man who always smelled of alcohol from the previous night's partying. He thought I was joking at first, but the novelty of my offer must have enticed him. We made a plan to wait until our manager took her lunch break, at which point we went at it in the walk-in, Brett thrusting into me while I braced my hands on a wire shelving unit. We repeated this transaction a few times, getting our routine down to two minutes flat, but on the fourth day our manager returned early from her break to find the counter unattended, and fired us both. I never saw Brett again, thank god.

My second partner, Freddie, provided a more instructive experience. Freddie was a married HVAC technician I met in my English class at Bakersfield College, six months after my flight binge. Since washing up in Bakersfield, I'd been working at a non-airport Subway—luckily, my previous manager must not have reported my activities with Brett to the corporate office. Al had begun pressuring me to go back to school, saying I couldn't work at Subway for the rest of my life. I knew he and Denise were annoyed by my tenancy on their living room couch, so I enrolled in a single class to appease them. Freddie and I were assigned to work together on a project, and when I realized he was flirting with me, I figured there was no harm in giving sex with people another shot. Our trysts unfolded in a single-user restroom on the college's campus or in the back seat of his Range Rover, parked at a sparsely occupied edge of the student lot. From Freddie I learned the basics of sexual technique, and more important, I learned how to pretend to enjoy sex. I could recede to an inner chamber of my mind, imagining planes while Freddie penetrated me. It wasn't so bad, and sometimes I did enjoy it, though I was only playing a role.

Our affair ended when I stopped going to class. Our final essay prompt was "The American Dream: Alive or Dead?" I chose "alive" but gave up halfway through. Any topic that didn't relate to planes bored me. I tried to write my essay with a plane theme—I argued that the aviation industry was robust, and so, the American Dream lived on!—but when I met my professor during office hours, he said my argument, while rich in pathos, was deficient in logos, and so I thanked him and never returned to campus. In his essay, Freddie planned to argue that the American Dream was dead, though he didn't actually believe this, being a small business owner. Of course the American Dream was alive, he said, but there was more evidence for it being dead, and he just wanted to pass the class since he'd spent five hundred dollars on it.

Back then, I was still reeling from the excesses of my flight binge. I was shocked by the depths to which my obsession had dragged me, and I wanted only to be normal. I hoped that, through repeated exposure, my desire for planes would be displaced by an ordinary desire for people. It hadn't worked, and I no longer suffered from such delusions, though I didn't mind the idea of sex with people, if it served my larger interests. I figured that a pilot's harried schedule meant I'd have to endure sex only a few times a month, freeing me the rest of the time to pursue my real love objects, with the help of my husband's family flight benefits. I wondered if a pilot's close relationship with planes would allow me to more easily transfer my affection for planes to him. Perhaps I could reveal to him a sanitized version of my obsession and be accepted. We were both, after all, people who'd devoted our lives to planes.

On my wellness break the next day, I opened the OkCupid app and was pleased to find I'd received several dozen messages. Unlike with Pilotdate.net, they all appeared to be from authentic humans, though as I scanned their profiles, I was disappointed that none of them seemed to be pilots. Their bios contained no references to aviation whatsoever. They must not have read my profile carefully, as I'd explicitly stated I was only interested in pilots, and usually all they'd written anyway was *hey*.

I showed Karina the messages at lunch. She scrolled my inbox with one hand while forking kale into her mouth with the other.

"Some of these guys look all right," she said, showing me

a picture of a fellow named Josh whose profile I'd already inspected.

"He's not a pilot," I said.

"He doesn't actually need to be a pilot, does he? I thought you were just looking for a guy with a job."

"Aren't we supposed to be specific in our goals?"

"Sure, but there's a limit." She regarded me skeptically. "Why do you like pilots so much, anyway?"

"I thought it made sense to be with someone who could get me discounted flights." This wasn't a lie, exactly, though it was only part of the truth.

Karina laughed. "That's messed up, Linda. You're hilarious." She continued scrolling through my messages. "I can't believe you actually enjoy flying. I hope I never have to fly again. It's such an unnecessary risk."

Before I could refute this ridiculous statement, a banner appeared at the top of my phone screen.

*Hiya Linda,* someone named Simon had written. *Pilot here. Wanna bang?*

"Ew," Karina said. "You should block this guy."

But I dared to believe I'd found him, after only two days on the apps. I refrained from writing Simon back, as I didn't want to be distracted by the thought of messages streaming in to my phone while it remained out of reach in a locker. I was determined to maintain my position at the top of the whiteboard, rather than falling behind my closest competitor, 39284F, who I suspected was Farhad, a quiet worker who sat in the interior row.

On the bus ride home, I reviewed Simon's profile. His

bio made no mention of being a pilot, which seemed suspicious. I was aware of the deceitful ways people presented themselves online, having posted on aviation subreddits for years using the fictional persona of a retiree named Greg who lived in Ottawa, but I tried to keep an open mind. What if the universe was promptly manifesting an item from my board, and I rudely rejected it as a scam? The risk of being duped by Simon was nothing compared to the risk of insulting the universe. Anyway, if Simon was a pilot, it made sense he'd want to keep it low-key, as Kevin would say. As I'd learned from those horny articles about pilots, many people objectified the profession in a way that might make the actual pilots uncomfortable. On his profile, Simon had posted five photos, all shot in low light, most from the neck down. His abdominal muscles were sharply defined, like corn on the cob, which I assumed some women found sexy.

*Hi Simon,* I wrote, in response to his earlier message. *I don't know about sex, but I'd love to hear more about your job as a pilot!*

Back in my room, I lay on my bed, eating salted peanuts from 7-Eleven and exploring plane content on my laptop. I grew aroused watching a compilation of takeoffs and landings at London Heathrow. I allowed the algorithm to guide me to a detailed tour of a 747. The camera lingered on his undercarriage, panels stitched together at the edges with bolts, then moved toward his wing, pivoting to display the eye of his powerful Rolls-Royce engine. I plumbed my underwear with salty fingers.

My phone pinged with a message from Simon. *I fly all over the world,* he'd written.

*Oh,* I replied, using my free hand.

*I'm drowning in stewardess pussy.*

*Wow.*

On the right side of the page, more enticing fare beckoned. "Falling from the Sky at Over 34,000 Feet per Minute," one title read. I clicked it, and a simulation began, re-creating an incident that occurred in 1979 involving a 727 operated by TWA. I knew the case of Flight 841 well. Eighty minutes into a flight from JFK to Minneapolis, the 727 had rolled to the right, and soon was spiraling toward the earth, dropping from 39,000 to 5,000 feet in a span of sixty-three seconds. The captain was ultimately able to steady the plane and make an emergency landing in Detroit. Miraculously, there were no casualties. While the NTSB determined the cause to be mechanical failure involving one of the wing slats, I suspected otherwise. I believed the 727 had been overcome with desire for a passenger on board, and sought to claim that person as his soulmate. He'd almost succeeded, thwarted at the last moment by his quick-witted pilots.

*What airline do you work for?* I wrote. On my screen, the 727 dove through the night sky.

*Delta,* Simon wrote, and I came.

I closed my laptop and wiped my hands on my thighs. I texted Kevin, explaining the situation and asking what I should do next.

*Ask if he wants to get coffee,* Kevin advised.

I followed his instructions. Simon and I agreed to meet at a Peet's in Millbrae on Friday evening, between my shift at Acuity and my flight to Phoenix.

"YOU'RE MEETING UP WITH THAT CREEP?" KARINA SAID AT LUNCH on Thursday. "The guy who opened with 'Wanna bang?'"

I stood at the microwave, listening to my popcorn pop. I'd been reluctant to tell Karina about my date with Simon, fearing such a reaction.

"He might be a little rough around the edges," I said, "but we had a nice conversation last night." The timer dinged. I set the bloated bag on a plate and flayed it down the middle with a butter knife.

"What does he look like?" Karina asked. I handed her my phone, open to Simon's profile. While she inspected his photos, I raked my thumbnail along the inner surface of the popcorn bag, then used my lower front teeth to extract the flavorful orange crud from under my nail. "He looks fit, at least," she conceded, placing my phone on the table. "Okay, Linda. What are you wearing on your date?"

I hadn't thought about it. "What am I supposed to wear?"

"Oh, I don't know," Karina said. She popped the lid off a yogurt. "Something casual, but sexy. Pulled together, but not trying too hard. A timeless, versatile, day-to-night look."

I must have looked baffled because Karina laughed. "Let's go shopping!" she said.

I was reluctant to spend money on clothes when I should

be saving it toward future flights, but I didn't want to pass up an opportunity to learn from Karina. I suspected she viewed me as frumpy raw material she could shape in her image. As a younger person, I hadn't been included in such rituals of feminine comradeship as shopping trips and makeovers, due to my habits of lingering near gas pumps and staring with eerie fixation at the sky. In elementary school, my friends had been the other two weird girls, Abigail and Meera. We'd gravitated toward each other like mice huddling for warmth. The popular girls had seemed like a different species, and we observed them from a distance, with awe and fear. I assumed Karina had been a popular girl, and I was honored that she wanted to teach me the ways of her people. I reflected that I was on track for the monthly bonus, having succeeded in keeping 39284F at bay.

"I can spend fifty dollars," I said.

"Perfect," Karina said. "I'll pick up the tab for happy hour."

Later, at the sushi place, we sat at our accustomed table against the back wall. As always, I gallantly offered Karina the superior bench seat, while I sat on a metal stool that jutted into the dining area, my back continually jostled by servers on their way to the kitchen. I observed Karina as she studied the menu, though we'd memorized its offerings. Her arms appeared hairless where they protruded from the sleeves of her ruffled pink top. Her foundation had caked and her forehead was shiny, but her beauty was undiminished, the imperfections only adding to her appeal.

We requested the cheapest bottle of warm sake on offer.

Karina ordered a hamachi jalapeño roll and a spicy tuna roll, while I ordered edamame and vegetarian gyoza, which I knew Karina would eat half of, while I could enjoy no portion of her rolls. I'd committed to a vegetarian lifestyle ten years ago, hoping to save money while also decreasing my overall carbon footprint. I would do my part in upholding the untenable status quo, which, for the time being, still allowed relatively affordable air travel. It was an unfair arrangement, as we always split the bill fifty-fifty in spite of Karina consuming three-quarters of the food, but I never complained, grateful as I was for her willingness to spend time with me beyond our working hours. I viewed the edamame and gyoza as a friendship tax.

Karina poured me a cup of sake and insisted on cheersing my foray into online dating.

"So what else do you know about Simon?" she asked.

"He flies for Delta," I said. "That's about it."

"How old is he?"

"Twenty-three."

"Isn't that pretty young for a pilot?"

I sipped my sake, considering. "I suppose it is. Should I ask him about it?"

"Might as well wait for tomorrow."

Our food arrived. Karina transferred a segment of hamachi jalapeño roll to her plate and began extracting chunks of fish with her chopsticks.

"You only like the fish?"

"Sorry," Karina said, seeming embarrassed I'd noticed.

She shoved the hollowed lump of rice and seaweed into her mouth. "Old habits die hard."

"From high school?" Karina had previously mentioned having an eating disorder.

"I guess that's when it started. My friends and I were, like, competitive dieters. I was so hungry all the time, I almost failed out my senior year."

"But you made it to college."

"Yeah, SF State. They'll take anyone." She eyed me. "Did you go to college, Linda? I can't believe I've never asked."

I recalled that Karina had been in the kitchen while the women of the VBB interrogated my educational background. "I took a different path," I said. "I wanted to be a flight attendant."

"What happened with that?"

The memory resurfaced, painfully. It was a few months after I'd been fired from the John Wayne Subway, and I decided it was time to go after the career I'd always wanted— one that would pay me to fly. My mom helped me prepare for a flight crew recruitment day, held at the Anaheim Convention Center, using her expertise from working as a bank teller at a Wells Fargo branch. It was the high point of our relationship. We got matching French manicures and shopped at Target for my interview outfit: a beige silk top, black trousers, and pumps. When the day arrived, I excelled at each stage, using tips gleaned from an internet forum. I nailed the group interview, in which I collaborated with other applicants on the creation of a fictional tourist island. I proceeded to the one-on-one interview with a recruiter, whom I impressed with my knowledge of the 737's development, as well as recent advances in aviation safety. That night, we went out for Mexican food, my family's customary celebration dinner. Al and Denise drove in from Bakersfield, though they might have been seizing upon any excuse to escape that wretched town. I was toasted with margaritas and two orders of queso. Never before had I given my loved ones a reason to be proud of me. We were all pleasantly surprised by the turn I'd taken.

My glory was short-lived. A few weeks later, I began training on a simulator, a cross section of an actual 737. I found it difficult to focus inside the simulator, which roused in me the same sensations I experienced on real flights. The trainer scolded me after I fumbled the safety demo. Then we were led through a drill featuring heavy turbulence. As the simulator rocked, the other candidates moved through the protocol we'd been trained in, while I collapsed into a seat, liquefied by desire. The drill was paused, and I claimed to have had a panic attack, which disqualified me from further training.

"I realized it wasn't for me," I told Karina.

"Yeah, it seems like a shitty job," Karina said. She'd brought out a makeup compact from her purse and was applying lip gloss using a little wand. I was relieved she didn't press for details.

From the sushi place, we proceeded to Stonestown Galleria in Karina's vehicle, a tan Honda Accord. At Forever 21, I submitted to my friend's expertise as she brought garments to my dressing stall. I tried on several dresses, feeling silly in all of them. Karina removed her own shoes and pushed them under the curtain, instructing me to put them on so we could ascertain the outfit's full effect. I modeled in the trifold mirror, my foot flesh overflowing Karina's little shoes like underbaked dough. The last dress was gold, in a ridged fabric Karina said was called satin plissé. It was sleeveless, with a high, ruffled neck, the lettuce hem rising a few inches above my knees. It was less formfitting than the previous dresses, and at twenty-two dollars, it lay within my budget. I pulled the curtain aside, and Karina coaxed me from my stall as though I were a traumatized dog from Stacy's rescue.

"You look amazing," Karina said. She asked me to turn around so she could assess the back. I was familiar with this procedure from shopping trips with my mom. My mom loved clothes, and I humored her attempts to bond with me over them, though I disliked confronting my form in the dressing-room mirror.

"Yep, this is the one," Karina said.

"Isn't it a little much for a coffee date?"

"Not at all. It's a day dress."

I bought the dress, though I'd begun to have doubts about Karina's taste and understanding of social norms. At Nordstrom, Karina selected a pair of "sensible heels"— cream-colored leather sandals with an ankle strap—and a sequined gold clutch to complement the dress. I balked at the combined price of shoes and clutch, a whopping ninety-seven dollars, but Karina insisted I should at least get the shoes, which would prove useful for many occasions. I caved and bought both items. Next, we headed to Sephora, where Karina asked an employee to give me a free mini-makeover, resulting in my acquisition of a tube of Dior lipstick along with several perfume samples. I bought us milk teas at the food court, having by now opened a valve through which money poured freely. I'd regret my profligacy later, but in the moment it felt thrilling to squander my resources, which I normally kept in tight restraint. Karina offered me a ride home, but I declined, preferring to flaunt my mini-makeover on the bus.

Back in my room, I lay in bed sucking my chunk of 737, basking in the smell of my product-laden face. From my vision board, which I'd mounted on the wall next to my flight map, Guillaume Faury gazed down at me approvingly.

6 I woke ahead of my alarm, full of anticipation for the momentous day I was about to embark on. Eight hours of moderation, coffee with a pilot, and then my real date for the night—my flight with N108DQ—would commence. I washed my hair and blew it dry, put on my gold dress, and applied makeup. I tucked one of the perfume samples into my backpack to use later, so the scent wouldn't curdle by the time I met Simon. I packed my toothbrush and a sample-sized tube of toothpaste for my overnight at the airport. I double-checked my wallet for my driver's license and the front pocket of my backpack for my chunk of 737.

Though I'd woken earlier than usual, my grooming ritual had taken over an hour, and for the first time, I arrived a few minutes late to Acuity. The interior row dwellers leered at me as I passed to my terminal. I now understood a fraction of what Karina experienced each day. I felt they were taking something from me that I hadn't offered. I'd dressed up on behalf of my date with a pilot, not to be gawked at by my coworkers. The planes didn't care what I wore.

Karina was already settled at her terminal. She'd placed her Louis Vuitton tote on my chair to save my spot, though it seemed unlikely anyone would try to take it. She humored me with a cartoonish double take. "You look hot," she mouthed.

At six o'clock I stood in line at the Millbrae Peet's. I scanned the board behind the counter, though I'd reviewed the menu while I was on BART and already knew what I would order. I'd been excited about a date with a pilot in the abstract, but now that it was happening, I felt anxious and almost hoped Simon would stand me up.

A human form sidled up to me.

"Hey. Are you Linda?" he said.

Simon was a few inches shorter than me, wearing a black suede jacket and distressed jeans that bunched at the knees, presumably stretched out from sitting. I nodded, and he pointed at himself, saying, "Simon," though this wasn't really necessary. I wondered if we should shake hands, or hug, but neither of us was deft enough to initiate contact. We stood together awkwardly. I thought back to his profile pictures. This man's abdominal muscles could not possibly resemble corn.

"You been here before?" Simon said.

"To Peet's? Sure."

"To *this* Peet's?" he pressed, as if the distinction mattered.

"I think so."

Simon seemed cowed by this, as though I'd won an argument. The man in line ahead of us—mid-forties, his gelled hair threaded with silver—glanced at us with a bemused expression. It must have been obvious we were on a first date. I was telegraphing to the world that I'd posted photos of myself on the internet for the purpose of finding someone to have sex with, or, worse, to build a life with. I wanted to assure the smirking silver fox that I only wanted to marry a pilot to maximize my access to planes before commercial flight became financially prohibitive due to the collapse of fossil capitalism. But that would be cruel to Simon, who was standing right next to me.

"Parking's such a bitch around here," Simon said. He seemed annoyed that I'd suggested we meet here, though he hadn't offered any alternatives.

"Sorry about that," I said. "I took BART."

"You don't drive?"

"I don't have a car."

"That sucks," Simon said.

I watched him study the menu board, as I'd pretended to do a few minutes earlier. My skepticism deepened. His profile had said he was twenty-three, but he looked less mature than he had in his photos. In fact, I now suspected the photos featured Simon's face grafted onto another man's body. He was a wormlike fellow, dubiously capable of operating a commercial aircraft. Karina had been right to point to Simon's youth as a red flag, as it took years to accumulate flight hours and climb the ranks of an airline. Becoming a pilot was an arduous journey, with erratic schedules, long hours, and paltry compensation at the outset. Only a true believer would commit to such a vocation, someone possessed of self-discipline bordering on masochism, perhaps resulting from a love-starved childhood or a family that fetishized the military. It was a pursuit requiring an immense capacity for suffering combined with a romantic predilection for viewing the earth from the sky.

Could Simon be such an exalted fool? As I observed him rocking back and forth on his Asics Gels, tongue pressed into cheek as he squinted at the menu, I knew the truth in my heart: this man was no pilot.

"What are you getting?" I asked him.

"Huh? Oh, I dunno. Just a coffee."

Karina had told me Simon should pay for my beverage. "If he doesn't pay, the date is over, symbolically if not literally," she'd said. But the moment came upon us quickly. I was first at the counter. The barista was a young, freckled woman, her hair dyed magenta. I ordered a medium iced green tea, proud to have studied the menu prior to my arrival, so that I knew the establishment offered three types of iced tea in three sizes. She pressed some buttons on her screen, then turned to Simon.

"Together?" she said, and I froze, knowing this was the moment when Simon should step forward and offer to pay for both our orders. He said nothing, and I said, "Sure, together," and handed over my debit card, eager to get the ordeal over with. Simon ordered a chai latte with almond milk, a five-dollar item.

We sat outside, as the interior was crowded with people working on laptops. Wind whipped around our metal table. I buttoned my jean jacket over my thin dress, though the denim provided little warmth. Across the street sat an Italian deli and a Taiwanese dessert café. Down the block was a tutoring center where high schoolers worked at raising their

SAT scores so that they might be admitted to an elite university, gain lucrative employment, and earn enough to one day send their own progeny to a similar tutoring center, a cycle that would perpetuate until the earth became too hot to sustain human life.

I dared to inspect Simon more closely. He had buzzed hair and a nose on the large side, but otherwise seemed featureless, like a stick figure. He did not resemble any plane I'd seen.

"So," he said. "Here we are."

I sipped my iced tea through a paper straw that had already gone gummy. "Here we are," I echoed.

"I guess we should get this out of the way," Simon said. "I'm not a pilot."

I was disappointed, but grateful to know the truth. "Why did you lie?"

"What's so great about a pilot, anyway? Would you want to date a bus driver? Because that's all a pilot is. A bus driver in the sky."

I stiffened with outrage at this ignorant statement. "There's more to it than that," I said.

"You women all want the same thing."

"What's that?"

"A rich guy who can pay your bills."

"Most pilots aren't rich."

But Simon was on a roll now. "You want a real macho, type-A kind of guy, and that's not me, so *excuse* me for taking liberties just so I can get a second glance. You would never have talked to me if I hadn't pretended to be a pilot."

"That's true," I said.

His expression softened, as though he, too, were grateful to have his suspicions confirmed. "Your dress is pretty," he said.

I sipped my tea, feeling more comfortable now that he'd paid me a compliment. "So what do you do? If you're not a pilot."

Simon groaned. "God, I fucking hate the Bay Area. The first question is always 'What do you do?' Which really means 'How much money do you make?' Which means 'How much should I respect you?' It's so fucking transparent. No offense." He sipped his chai, which must have reminded him that I'd paid for his expensive beverage, as he proceeded to answer my question. He lived with his older brother, who was a software engineer and earned a salary of two hundred thousand dollars, a fact Simon seemed both resentful of and awed by. Simon worked as a driver for a food delivery app and did odd jobs through a platform that allowed people to purchase each other's labor, though he wasn't often hired, as he possessed few skills. He wanted to drive for Uber but was waiting to be approved to lease one of their cars, as his own car was "a beater."

Simon's accounting of his life aroused my sympathy. I saw we were both misfits, struggling to find our place in the world. I, too, had lived with my more successful older brother for a time. "It must be nice not to have to clock in at the same place every day," I said.

"Yeah, it's pretty sweet," he said sarcastically. "So what do *you* do, Linda?"

I told him I was a content moderator, and he made a face.

"I've heard about those places," he said. "Sounds awful."

"It's not so bad," I said. "Our role is simply to make decisions according to the parent company's terms of service. Ideally, our judgment will align with the software they're developing. When our verdicts conflict, it's typically the software whose decision is rendered final."

"Then what's the point of having you do it at all?"

"As I understand it, our input helps to strengthen the AI. And occasionally, the software misses something, so it's important to have a human review its work."

"But soon the software will be so good it won't need you."

"Yes, that's what they say. Everything in life is temporary, after all." My feelings toward Simon had reverted to their original disdain. I'd tried to be nice to him, in spite of his having catfished me, and he'd responded with rude comments about my job.

"Do you see a lot of fucked-up shit?" Simon asked.

"I don't deal with videos, only text," I said. "I'm in the Hate & Harassment vertical. I moderate the comments section. My friend Karina works in Violence, which is more taxing psychologically. I suspect my skills are more suited to Violence, but I'm the most efficient moderator in my vertical, so our manager doesn't want to move me."

"Damn, Linda. That's hardcore."

I went on to describe the office culture. My friendship with Karina and our alliance against the interior row dwellers; the mysterious night-shift workers; our duplicitous managers; the fleece-clad bosses at the parent company, who issued dictates from an anonymous remove. Once I started, it was difficult to stop. I rarely had an opportunity to describe my life to someone I'd likely never see again, and who could thus be confided in freely.

Simon listened raptly, and at the end of my monologue, he asked if Acuity was hiring. "I think I'd be great at it," he said. "I've done some trolling in my day. I could bring an insider's perspective. Like a covert operative."

"You can say I recommended you," I said in a spasm of magnanimity, though he didn't need my endorsement. Acuity was always searching for unspoiled human consciousnesses to plug into their machine.

Simon thanked me. "I'm sorry for lying about being a pilot," he said.

"It's okay."

"You look different from your photos, too. Did you use filters?"

I hadn't, but it seemed undignified to debate him on this point. "Did you photoshop your face onto another man's body?"

"Yeah, I might have," he said, grinning. "My bad."

I checked the time on my phone and told Simon I had a flight to catch. He perked up, as though my scarcity increased his interest. "Where are you going?"

"Phoenix."

"What's in Phoenix?"

I shrugged. "It doesn't matter."

"Then why are you going there?"

"I like to fly." It was exhilarating to tell someone the unvarnished truth after my careful hedging at the VBB.

"So your profile wasn't a joke."

"Not at all. If I had the option, I'd never leave the airport."

"Wow. You're a freak," Simon said with admiration.

I stood, and Simon did, too, and shook my hand.

"We could hang out again sometime," he said. "I mean, if you want."

7 I felt deflated as I walked from Peet's back to the BART station. I'd been riding a temporary high, believing the items I'd placed on my vision board were manifesting at an astounding rate, but Simon had brought me back to earth. I wasn't cut out for the human dating scene. I couldn't keep up a performance of normalcy long enough to fake my way into a relationship I didn't want. My confidence in the vision board's power was shaken. Perhaps it was merely paper glued to thicker paper, after all.

I couldn't succumb to despair, however, while en route to a flight. My mood lightened the moment I entered SFO. When I visited the airport between flights, I'd stare at the security queue with bitterness, as though it were the velvet-roped line in front of a club to which I was barred entry. I resented those who gained admission, especially because they didn't appreciate their good fortune. Most people moved through the airport hollowly, as though they'd rather be anywhere else. I'd never understood the complacency with which ordinary people regarded the miracle of flight. They'd somehow dampened their hearts of wonder.

I was drawn through the TSA umbilical into the womb of the secure sector, a utopian realm in which all persons had been screened for weapons and vessels of liquid in excess of 3.4 ounces. I ambled dreamily through Terminal 2, pausing to admire planes stabled at their gates, as though the terminal were my personal red-light district. At D3, an Embraer 175 awaited departure to Palm Springs. He was a fine-looking fellow, but no match for the handsomeness of N108DQ. I moved along.

As I proceeded toward D8, I spotted an uncannily familiar figure standing at the pickup counter of the Peet's. A slight, dignified gentleman in a tailored suit. I drew closer, and the resemblance sharpened.

Could it be? Had I conjured Guillaume Faury, in the flesh?

Every night since the VBB, I'd gazed upon Faury's world-weary visage in the moments before I fell asleep. As Faury did in his photos, this man looked rumpled in spite of his perfectly starched ensemble. His eyes were red-rimmed, with bags beneath them that deepened his aura of trustworthiness. He looked tired but filled with grim resolve to execute his duties. I admired his solemnity, commensurate with the responsibility he wielded.

I approached him where he remained tethered to the pickup counter, awaiting his beverage. "Monsieur Faury?" I said.

He turned at the sound of his name, then looked away, perhaps believing he'd been mistaken in hearing it. He probably wasn't used to being recognized in public, and I'd no doubt butchered his name's pronunciation. Still, I needed to capitalize on this moment. I might never again have the attention of an aerospace CEO, a man whose early career was marred by tragedy, a helicopter crash in Norway that killed eleven oil workers and two crew members. I wondered if he ever felt nostalgic for his childhood in Cherbourg-Octeville, at the tip of the Cotentin Peninsula. On maps it appears at the top of France like one of the little horns of a goat. I wondered if, as Faury flew into SFO, the peninsula of San Francisco reminded him of his home village.

"I'm a big fan," I said. He squinted as though attempting to place me. He might have wondered if I'd confused him with another man, a conventional celebrity about whom I cared not at all.

"Thank you," he said finally, in what I perceived to be a French accent. He retrieved his beverage, on whose paper cup was inscribed the letter G, and retreated toward D10, where a flight to JFK was about to begin boarding.

I remained rooted to the spot, amazed by what I'd just witnessed. I'd placed Faury on my board as a plane-adjacent model of corporate success, an ambition the other women would recognize and validate. I'd never expected to manifest the actual man. I now realized that Simon hadn't represented a failure of my board. His appearance was in fact the very fulfillment of my board's vision. I'd included photos of stock models, and so I had gotten what I'd asked for—a man pretending to be a pilot. The universe apparently took things literally, which I would keep in mind when constructing my next board. Unfortunately, I'd have to wait several months to set my revised goals into motion, as Karina had told me the

VBB ceremony was essential to the art of manifestation, akin to an official seal on a letter.

At D8, I spotted N108DQ through the window. A punctual fellow, he'd arrived from Vancouver a few minutes early. I blushed as I beheld his handsome face. My eyes locked with his windscreen, in which I detected a hint of recognition. I mouthed a greeting to him, then turned away shyly. My love life consisted of a string of one-night stands. Karina would disapprove were my date with a man rather than a plane. But no man could do for me what a plane could. What man could propel himself to a speed of 150 knots before lifting us to an altitude of 37,000 feet? What man could carry me across continents and seas, all while keeping me warm and oxygenated inside his aluminum torso? No man I'd ever chanced to meet!

An announcement sounded—our flight would begin boarding in six minutes. I rushed to the restroom, where I emptied my bladder, pressing my fists into my abdomen to squeeze out the last drops, so that I wouldn't be tempted to use N108DQ's lavatory, degrading us both. After washing my hands and touching up my lipstick, I returned to the gate, where boarding had begun. The first-class passengers filed down the jet bridge. I hung back with my fellow members of the economy class, humble proletarians of the sky. I caught a woman staring at me and realized how odd my attire must seem in this context. I was both underdressed, with respect to the quantity of fabric covering my skin, and overdressed, given the gold dress's formality. My bare legs were stippled with gooseflesh in the chilly air of the terminal. My feet had blistered from the heels Karina insisted I purchase, and which I couldn't return, now that I'd stained them with blood.

My group number was called. I scanned my ticket and strolled down the jet bridge, pausing at the threshold of my lover's body. The line of passengers stalled, as people ahead of me navigated the narrow aisle and negotiated overhead bin space, giving me a chance to bask in the moment. I tapped my fingers, flirtatiously, along the edge of his door. I placed my palm against his outer shell, which would soon be exposed to the thin upper atmosphere, with a temperature of negative sixty degrees. As I entered him, I glanced into his cockpit, which always felt obscenely intimate, like seeing the pink meat of an exposed brain on Karina's monitor as I passed her terminal. The captain and first officer reviewed items on a checklist. Before them lay the instrument panel, aglow with amber lights.

I made my way down the aisle, drinking in every inch of N108DQ. His lighting panels highlighted the curve of his back, giving it the look of a chapel's vaulted ceiling. I was in a sacred place indeed. I reached my seat, 23F. As usual, I'd chosen a window seat on the starboard side, in a row positioned above the wing, so that I could observe the movements of N108DQ's comely slats, flaps, and ailerons. My row companions, a heterosexual couple in their thirties, were already present in 23D and E. They'd probably elbowed their way to the front of our boarding group line; though the average air passenger claims to abhor flying, they're nonetheless always impatient to board. This couple seemed annoyed to dislodge themselves to allow my passage. That was fine. I preferred to dislike my row companions, considering the activities I was about to engage in beside them.

Once we'd settled into our seats, I inspected the couple again, assessing the threat they would pose. The man was clean-shaven, wearing a Giants cap and a gray sweater. He was immersed in his tablet, his right hand placed upon the woman's left thigh. The woman's face was flushed and dewy, framed by wavy auburn hair. She clutched her leather tote on her lap until the flight attendant asked her to stow it beneath the seat in front of her. What an amateur! They both seemed determined to ignore me, for which I was grateful. There was nothing worse than chatty rowmates.

I draped my jean jacket across my lap and fastened my seatbelt over it. Beneath the jacket's cover, I tucked the chunk of 737 into my underwear. I pressed my right side against N108DQ's wall. I slipped my feet from the sandals and stamped them to the flameproof carpet, maximizing our points of skin-on-skin contact. The doors were closed, and the ventilation system switched from external to internal, marked by a poof of air from the vent above me. With a whirring sound, N108DQ's flaps extended to their takeoff position. The flight attendants performed their safety demonstration. My breath grew shallow, my crotch pulsing with anticipation. I relished every moment of foreplay, but I was impatient to get to the main event.

At last, we pushed back from the gate. N108DQ ambled along the taxiway, making several leisurely turns, his CFM engines groaning with pent-up energy. He lined up on the runway. Any moment now, his engines would fire. Beside me, the woman's eyes were closed, her face tense with fear, and I felt a grudging affection for her. I'd often wondered if flying alongside an aerophobe might provide the final ingredient in the stew of destiny. Like me, fearful flyers invested great stores of psychic energy into flight, commensurate with its grandeur and peril. I felt a kinship with them, and with everyone I flew beside, considering us spiritual siblings, our fates intertwined. There is no greater intimacy than to be fellow passengers of a doomed flight.

N108DQ's engines powered up in a ferocious roar, like a beast drawing air into his lungs. We surged forward in our takeoff roll, gathering speed that pinned me to my seat. His fuselage shook with the velocity, the cabin rattling until, at the moment it felt we would shatter apart, his nose lifted, and we rose into the sky. Our ascent was deliciously rocky, giving me hope that N108DQ had recognized me and sought to claim me. Each jolt issued a ribbon of pleasure through my body. I wedged my right hand under my thighs and pushed the chunk of 737 inside me. I didn't require much additional stimulation while in flight. N108DQ brought me to the edge, and I pushed myself over. As we carved through rough air, I came silently, again and again.

The bell chimed twice, indicating we'd reached ten thousand feet and releasing the flight crew from the sterile cockpit rule. I collapsed against my seat, feeling wrung out and sated. I brushed my lips against N108DQ's window rim in gratitude. The air smoothed, and N108DQ continued a steady climb to his cruising altitude. The woman beside me rested her head on her companion's shoulder. Flight attendants started down the aisle with the galley cart. I closed my eyes, pretending to be asleep, so I wouldn't be disturbed. I imagined I was alone with N108DQ. No pilots in the cockpit. Transponder switched off. Lovers on the run. We'd fly into the night until his fuel was spent.

# PART II

I resigned myself to waiting for April, the start of the year's second quarter, when there'd presumably be another VBB and an opportunity to present a fresh vision to the universe. The failure of my date with Simon had prompted me to reassess my priorities. Going forward, romance with a pilot, or any person, would no longer play a role in my vision. I'd shift my focus to professional success, the acquisition of money to fund more frequent flights, hastening my marriage to whichever fine plane would choose me, and maximizing my pleasure in the meantime.

With this new resolve in place, I committed myself to my work in H&H. The world festered with activity, and we were kept busy moderating its excesses as they appeared in our queues. In the latter days of February, the sky was cold and clear and densely stocked with contrails, which boded well for my flight to Salt Lake City. On that occasion, I trysted with an old friend, N85095, an A319 who treated me to a few rounds of turbulence halfway through the short flight, and then with N161SY, a haughty Embraer 175 who flew with disappointing smoothness all the way back to SFO.

On a Monday in March, I arrived at Acuity to find our office in disarray. Two of the computer monitors were missing from an interior row, while a third had its screen smashed in. A smell of excrement laced the air, though this was sometimes the case on normal days. Christa from HR and Scott, the elusive regional manager, stood at the edge of a row, conferring in hushed tones. Christa rarely appeared on the moderation floor, instead hiding in her office, from which she cast out occasional emails and Slack messages, like chunks of meat thrown into the cage of a dangerous animal. Scott's presence was even more unusual. He visited our site only a few times a year, to announce policy changes and, we suspected, to make sure we weren't trying to form a union, though I could have told him we weren't energetic enough to attempt such a feat.

"What's going on?" I asked my supervisors. "Was there a robbery?"

Christa turned to me with an air of impatience. "Go ahead and clock in, Linda," she said.

Fortunately, the exterior row seemed untouched by the chaos that had ravaged the interior ones. I settled at my terminal and pretended to mind my own business while Scott removed the smashed monitor, solemnly, as though he were carrying a fallen soldier from the battlefield. Karina arrived, one hand held over her nose. She gave me a quizzical look, and I shrugged.

Twenty minutes later, I was moderating lascivious comments on a video of a boy eating pudding when a scream erupted from the interior row.

"What the fuck?" Tonya said. "There's a *turd* on my desk."

Karina shrieked and leaped from her chair. The interior row workers gathered around Tonya's desk.

"This is an OSHA violation!" Aiden from Porn shouted, in the direction of Christa's office.

Scott ushered us into the hallway. "Everything is under control," he said, his hands raised, palms down, in a placating gesture. "The cleaners are coming. Take the morning off, and report back for your afternoon shift."

"Will we be paid for the morning?" Farhad asked, and Scott assured him we would be. I judged Farhad for being greedy, though I'd wondered the same thing.

Christa moved along the line of workers assembled in the hallway, handing us each a ten-dollar Starbucks gift card. She must have kept a box of them in her office, in case we needed to be pacified with a treat. Her tactic worked, as we all shuffled downstairs to the Starbucks to redeem our cards. In line, Tonya recounted finding the feces at her terminal. At a glance, it had blended in with the keyboard, which explained why Christa and Scott hadn't spotted it on their initial sweep.

"Or they didn't bother to look," Todd said. "They only cared about their precious monitors."

"All I know is, I'm done with this place," Tonya said. "Take care, y'all. I'm out." Tonya left the Starbucks without ordering a beverage. I hoped she knew she could use the gift card at any location.

Karina and I brought our drinks to a table by the window.

"I can't stand those night-shift freaks," she said, her voice low. "It was only a matter of time before one of them snapped."

"Maybe it wasn't even someone who works with us," I said. I didn't like the night-shift workers either, but it seemed unfair to assume one of them was the culprit. "It could have been a burglary."

"That's even scarier," she said with a grimace. "This is why I'm always telling you to wipe down your terminal."

Karina drank her Americano lustily, her eyes darting around the Starbucks, and I saw she was riled up, excited in spite of herself. She must have felt a perverse satisfaction in the validation of her fears. The world was indeed filthy and fraught with danger. We lapsed into silence, watching cars coagulate at the stoplight until it turned green and they streamed ahead.

We returned, as instructed, for the afternoon shift, to an office space that smelled overpoweringly of cleaning products. Our ranks had thinned. Some mods must have quit in disgust, or become immersed in another activity and forgotten to report back. I continued reviewing the pudding comments, but my focus was fragmented, giving Farhad a shot at pulling ahead.

The next day, order was restored. The smashed monitors had been replaced by identical intact ones. On my wellness break, I sat on the yoga ball, which had grown ever more deflated, my weight pressing the top to within an inch of the bottom. Something felt off about the room. My eyes fell upon a blank space of wall where the sunset painting had hung. For the first time, I shared the outrage my coworkers had expressed yesterday. The loss of the painting was a more intimate offense than the destruction of the monitors or even the depositing of feces. By taking the sunset painting, the offender was attempting to deplete our wellness at its source.

Seeking to calm myself, I watched videos of go-arounds—instances in which a landing is attempted and then aborted due to unsatisfactory conditions. A 747 drew close to the runway amid heavy crosswinds. His wheels came within ten feet of the tarmac before lifting up again, landing gear folding neatly into his belly. Under suggested videos, I spotted a new simulation of Alaska Airlines Flight 261, featuring actual cockpit-to-ATC recordings from the doomed flight. The aircraft, a McDonnell Douglas MD-83, had experienced a loss of pitch control, which, after a period of courageous struggle by the pilots, resulted in a crash in the Pacific Ocean off the coast of Southern California. I tapped the video, despite having previously sworn off the consumption of titillating content at work. The wellness room was not intended to be used for masturbation, though I suspected I wasn't the first to have broken this rule.

The trouble was just beginning for Flight 261 when an email pinged in from Christa. *Greetings to our rockstar moderation team!* the missive began. She went on to say that a representative from the parent company would be visiting our site tomorrow. His name was David Kinney, and from the muted urgency of Christa's words, I gathered he was an important figure. *Please adhere to our usual dress policy of busi-*

*ness casual :^),* the email read. *Dave wants to speak with everyone individually, so please be prepared to share what you love
about working at our center, along with any constructive comments about how we could make our work environment even better! :^).*

The email contained four smiley faces in total, all with
Christa's signature caret nose. I'd learned the inclusion of
smileys corresponded to Christa's emotional state. The more
smileys, the greater her agitation, and indeed four was the
highest incidence of smileys I'd witnessed in one of her
communiqués. The comment about dressing in business
casual was a plea for our cooperation. Though the dress code
was inscribed in our employee handbook, no one followed it,
except for Karina, as well as the mods assigned to the Child
Sex Abuse Imagery vertical, two men and one woman who
wore black blazers over white shirts as if by mutual agreement, and worked in a shielded cubicle in the back corner of
the room. I imagined the donning of professional attire
would present a challenge to the interior row dwellers, par-
ticularly those who toiled in Porn and Spam, young men
who typically wore sweatpants, T-shirts emblazoned with the
logos of failed startups, and flip-flops that exposed their yellow toenails.

Three minutes remained on the meditation timer. I returned to the Flight 261 video. Air traffic control contacted
planes flying near the wounded one, asking the pilots of
these healthy aircraft to provide a visual report of 261. One
pilot stated that 261 "wasn't doing so good"—an understate-
ment, as at that moment, 261 was flying inverted. I admired

those pilots, courageous to the end as they attempted to right the doomed plane and guide it to a water landing, which proved impossible. In their final report, the NTSB had faulted the airline for the crash. A component of the horizontal stabilizer trim had not been adequately lubricated, causing the failure of the jackscrew assembly, and a resultant catastrophic loss of pitch control. I accepted this was true and that most people would deem it a tragedy, and yet, my mind wove a dark fantasy around the crash. Perhaps the plane was so taken with a passenger on board the flight, he turned himself upside down, spiraling into the sea in a fit of passion.

I'd always known there was a chance that other people loved planes the way I did, as there are few anomalies in this world. One time, in my early twenties, I'd perused message forums discussing objectum sexuality, but concluded I was nothing like the woman who married the Eiffel Tower, or another who was in love with a trombone. Planes were not static objects, but sentient beings with rich inner lives. I was a jealous lover, and if there were others like me, I preferred not to know about them.

ON SLACK, SCOTT INVITED US TO AN EMERGENCY ALL-HANDS meeting in the conference room. At 2:00 P.M., we filed in past a table set with a spread of bagels and cream cheese. It was unclear whether we were meant to eat the bagels or if they were merely the mascots of the meeting, and so they remained untouched. Scott paced at the front of the room.

He was a slim, nervous, bearded man who had, at a previous all-hands meeting, revealed that his brother was once gored by a bison in Yellowstone National Park, where the two men were backpacking. Scott admitted his brother had been taunting the bison, as he had a volatile temper and an imperious urge to dominate the natural world through camping. The brother survived his goring, but the attack was witnessed by several park visitors, who uploaded the footage onto internet forums, where it went viral, reposted thousands of times with the addition of humorous sound effects. In the months after, Scott avoided social media, fearful he'd happen upon one of the videos and be forced to relive the experience. Through this ordeal, he'd come to understand the importance of "virtual hygiene," a term I'd never heard before or since. Effective moderation, Scott claimed, could have spared him from seeing the video. We were doing the world a service.

Scott's stern countenance indicated there would be no further personal revelations today. He stood before us in a white shirt and a red tie that emphasized the thinness of his neck. I felt like we were in trouble, though in fact we were victims; as far as I knew, the offender remained at large.

"So you've all heard by now that a manager from the parent company will be visiting our site tomorrow," Scott said, his beady eyes gleaming. "I hope you're aware that our site pays the highest wages of any moderation facility in the world. Christa and I have been working our butts off to optimize our center's working conditions. So if anyone has a problem with anything—*anything* at all—I invite you to share it with me, or Christa, directly."

We were silent a moment. Then Sheila, an older woman who worked in the Spam vertical, raised her hand.

"Do we know yet who vandalized the office?" she said.

"Yeah, do we have to worry about someone coming back with a gun?" Todd added.

"We've identified the perpetrator and we are dealing with them through legal channels," Scott said. "We can't disclose any more information at this time."

Christa stepped forward, grinning. "Y'all are perfectly safe here," she said. "We're looking into hiring security, and everyone will be required to wear their ID lanyards at all times." This elicited a grumble from the crowd. We hated the lanyards.

"Dave is aware of the challenges our site faces," Christa continued, "and he's looking forward to giving our rockstar moderators everything y'all need. In that spirit, we hope you'll give him your one-thousand-percent honest feedback tomorrow!"

Christa went on to remind us of the parent company's partnership with a mental health app, through which we were entitled to a fifteen percent discount on virtual therapy.

"Okay, team," Scott said, affecting the demeanor of a high school football coach. "That's it. Eat the dang bagels."

I took an everything bagel, smeared it with cream cheese, and ate the halves at my desk, crumbs dropping into the crevices of my keyboard and making certain keys stick, so that for the rest of the day, my commentary was cluttered with extra *t*'s.

After work, Karina and I decamped to the sushi place to process the day's events. She'd talked to Scott after the meeting, and he'd told her the confidential details of what we'd begun referring to as "the incident." Karina and Scott had a special friendship that I'd initially assumed was rooted in Scott's sexual desire for Karina, but when I'd mentioned this, Karina had laughed and informed me that Scott preferred men.

"Apparently it was Santiago," Karina said. "Remember him from the holiday party? Tall, skinny guy with bags under his eyes."

"Oh yeah. He was in Violence, wasn't he?" At the holiday party, we'd met a few of the night-shift workers for the first time. Santiago wore an oversized wool sweater and glowered at us over the cheese plate. He attempted to tell us a riddle about a well with no bottom but forgot the solution partway through.

"Turns out he's a real nut," Karina said. "He waited until everyone from the night shift left, then took a dump on Tonya's keyboard, smashed some monitors, and stole the sunset painting from the wellness room."

"What a monster," I said, imagining the lovely painting discarded beneath an overpass. "So they arrested him?"

"They want to, but he's disappeared." Karina shuddered. "He's still out there, somewhere. Scott says he won't come back, but how could he know that?"

Our gyoza arrived. We ate them quietly, contemplating

possible scenarios. I had a vision of Santiago stalking a desolate landscape in his giant wool sweater.

"Did Tonya quit?" I asked, dipping a gyoza in sauce.

Karina shrugged. "She missed Kay's, anyway." Tonya had often regaled us with stories from her former job, collecting debts on behalf of the Kay jewelry corporation.

"What do you know about this David Kinney guy?" I said.

"Dave." Karina popped a gyoza in her mouth, not bothering with the sauce. "I only met him one time, when they were setting up the wellness room."

Karina laid her chopsticks on a stand she'd made from their paper wrapper. On her phone, she showed me Dave's LinkedIn profile. His photo revealed him to be a tall, slim, middle-aged man, most resembling the 757-300, whose long, thin shape had earned him the nickname "flying pencil." Dave was clad in a gray suit, sans tie, and leaned against a brick wall bathed in golden-hour sunlight, laughing at someone to the side of the camera.

"He looks intimidating," I said.

"You think?" She examined his picture again. "Nah. He's a lame guy who's desperate for people to like him. He founded a clean energy company a few years back, but it went under, so now he's stuck with us."

Still, I was nervous for Dave's visit. I enjoyed the respectability conferred by office work. I was afraid Dave would sniff out my latent perversity and place me in the same category as Santiago. With his corporate intuition, he'd sense I was a liability, and I'd have to go back to working at Subway.

"Don't sweat it," Karina said, sensing my nervousness.

"They have to make a show of investigating, but they don't want to find any real problems. We say everything's fine and Dave goes away and Christa buys us more shitty snacks from Costco."

I hoped Karina was right. I would also appreciate more egg rolls, ahead of the scheduled replenishing, even if they were bought with my complicity.

THE NEXT DAY, I DRESSED CAREFULLY IN THE SAME OUTFIT I'D IN-terviewed in: a striped button-down shirt from H&M, black trousers from Target, and a marled gray cardigan that reached almost to my knees. I always felt more confident with the shape of my buttocks obscured.

When I reached the exterior row, Karina was already seated at her terminal, staring glassy-eyed into the Violence queue. For once, everyone had arrived on time, and the moderation floor thrummed with quiet anticipation. The interior row dwellers had risen to the occasion. The young men of the Porn and Spam verticals had a damp, startled look about them, like freshly bathed dogs. There was a tautness in the room, perhaps owing to the aggregated energy of our tensed core muscles and clenched sphincters. It was fortunate that Dave's visit was scheduled for 10:00 A.M., as I doubted we could maintain our performance past lunchtime. Christa and Scott flitted around the moderation floor, inspecting us. Christa straightened the mouse pads of unused terminals. Scott pondered a framed photograph on the wall, a snowy mountaintop awash in pink light. All of the office's artwork had been chosen, I assumed, for its benignity, so as not to trigger mental breakdowns among the already fragile crew. Maybe Scott wondered if the mountaintop evoked suicide, as all art does if one is thinking constantly of the act. He must have deemed it acceptable, as he left it undisturbed.

Right at ten o'clock, Christa ran out the door and returned moments later with Dave, as though he were a pizza she'd ordered for delivery. Through my headphones, I couldn't make out what Christa murmured to Dave as she led him down the interior row. I'd had a mental image of the man, from the photo Karina had shown me the night before, but in the flesh he was more impressive than he'd been in his tiny LinkedIn photo. His blond hair had faded to gray, but this made him look distinguished. He wore glasses with translucent frames, and surveyed the space with an air of authority, nodding as Christa detailed our site's operations. Scott joined them on their circuit, and I noted that Dave was several inches taller than Scott, who himself was not a short man. They made their way down the interior row with agonizing slowness. At last they arrived at the exterior row and stood directly behind me.

"This is Linda," Christa whispered, as if identifying a zoo animal belonging to an introverted species. I felt paralyzed, unsure whether I should turn and greet Dave or pretend to be so immersed in my work that I didn't notice them looming behind me.

"Pleased to meet you, Linda," Dave said. The blur of his

hand appeared in my periphery, and I shook it, gazing into his nostrils. Seated, my face was positioned at the level of his groin, clad in khaki.

"You, too," I said.

"Looking forward to chatting," he said and moved down the row, to my relief. He didn't greet any other moderators by name, and from this I feared the worst.

An hour later, I joined Dave in the conference room for our one-on-one. Rather than sitting behind the table, he'd positioned two chairs to face each other without obstruction. He sat with rangy confidence, left ankle slung over right knee, and sipped a venti Starbucks. His lanyard dangled down the front of his blue oxford shirt. My eyes darted to the face on his ID card then back to his three-dimensional face, giving me a sense of vertigo.

"So, Linda," he said, smiling. "What's your story?"

I'd already resolved to treat this meeting like a police interview. I would admit to only the objective facts of my existence, those already present in my personnel file. "I grew up in Irvine, and now I'm here," I said.

"Oh, come on. I bet there's more to it than that."

I struggled to think of an additional innocuous detail that would satisfy him. "I lived with my brother in Bakersfield for two years," I said.

"Bako, huh? I've never been."

"You aren't missing much."

"How'd you wind up at Acuity?"

"I always wanted to live in San Francisco," I said, though it would have been more accurate to say I'd wanted to live near SFO. I could never be satisfied, long term, with the offerings of a regional airport. "I saw an ad for the job on Craigslist, so I applied."

"I moved here for a job, too," he said, with a wistful expression. "Back in the nineties. Everyone was talking about what was happening out here, with the tech boom. I knew I had to get a piece of the action." His blue eyes twinkled with nostalgia. "Did you always want to work in tech?"

"Not really," I said. "I mean, I've always enjoyed using the internet."

I knew I was failing to impress Dave and wished I'd better prepared for our meeting, which felt like an interview for the job I already had. I tried to channel Scott. "I was drawn to Acuity's mission," I said. "I'm proud of the work we do in promoting virtual hygiene."

He smiled with tight lips, and I sensed he thought either I was a fraud or our job was. "Right. Well, Linda, everyone at headquarters is impressed by your metrics. Very impressed." He reached behind him to take an iPad from the table. He tapped around on its screen, presumably consulting my stats.

"They are?" I said, feigning modesty.

"You're incredibly efficient. It's like you were born to be a content moderator." He laughed. "Sorry. I meant that as a compliment."

I wondered if he was flattering me to gain a psychological advantage. "I do my best," I said.

"Moderating comments requires a highly nuanced understanding of cultural context. It's why the software alone can't be trusted with the edge cases. I've found that some mods have trouble distinguishing between comments that are personally offensive to them versus in violation of the terms of service."

"The ToS is all that matters," I said. "My own opinion is irrelevant."

"Exactly." He seemed pleased by this, and I was relieved I'd won him over. "Is there anything I can do for you, Linda? I'd like to keep you with us as long as possible."

I saw a chance to set my new goals in motion. "I'd like to be paid more," I said.

"Fair enough," he said, tapping a note on his iPad. He asked if there was anything else he could do for me. I mentioned the cushions in the wellness room needed washing and the yoga ball had gone flat.

After Dave's visit, the office settled back into its usual rhythms, until it could almost be forgotten that Santiago had defecated on Tonya's keyboard. Tonya, however, was gone for good, and the next week, she was replaced by Simon. My old suitor had returned to haunt me, though I wasn't surprised, as I'd sent him a referral link after our coffee date, exulting in a generosity I now regretted. I locked eyes with the worm-faced man as he emerged from Christa's office. He nodded to me in a dignified manner and settled into Tonya's old terminal in the interior row.

At lunch, Simon claimed a seat at the break room table with me and Karina, though we hadn't invited him to join us.

"Hey, Linda," he said, while staring at Karina. He introduced himself to her, extending his hand, which Karina shook coolly.

"You're in Porn?" I asked him.

"Hell yeah, I'm in Porn."

"I'm sure you have lots of experience in that area," Karina said.

Simon grinned, as if choosing to interpret her insult as a flirtatious overture. "You ladies want to get out of here? I thought I'd hit up the sushi place for lunch."

"We only go there on Thursday nights," I said. Karina glared at me, and I realized I should not have revealed our ritual to Simon, as he might try to intrude on it.

"Okay, whatever," Simon said. "Nice meeting you, Karina."

He left, and Karina shook her head. "I can't believe you went out with that guy," she said. "He looks like he's in high school."

"I thought he was a pilot," I reminded her.

Karina seemed grumpy. She snapped the lid off a Tupperware of kale salad. "How's it been going with the apps?" she asked.

"I haven't really been using them."

"That's good," Karina said, stabbing her fork into the salad. "Love is a scam."

I was shocked she would say this. She sighed and told me she feared Anthony was cheating on her. She'd looked at his phone while he was in the shower and found incriminating Instagram messages between Anthony and his coworker, who went by Baewatch1998. She showed me a screenshot she'd taken and sent to herself. Baewatch1998 had written, *you looked cute in your apron today ;)*, to which Anthony replied, *lmao*.

"It appears Baewatch1998 has a crush on him," I said. "But what fault is that of Anthony's?"

"That's his coworker Beatrice. The same girl I caught him messaging with before."

"Did you ask him about it?"

"No. I would seem crazy." Karina ate her kale sadly. I felt

grateful not to engage in romance with people, given their capacity for deceit.

"Maybe your next vision board will right the ship," I said. Sunday was April 1, the official start to quarter two, and I hadn't received an evite. I'd begun to fear I had been excised from the VBB's roster.

"I dunno," Karina said. "I'm kind of over the vision boards. They might have pressured Anthony to commit before he was ready."

My agitation increased, as I suspected she was evading discussion of the VBB. If I was being rejected, I wanted to know. "So you're skipping the VBB this quarter?" I asked.

"No, I'll be there. Are you going?"

"I wasn't invited."

"Of course you're invited. Aren't you in the group chat?"

Karina added me to the WhatsApp group. *Welcome, Linda!* she wrote, alerting the others to my presence. I was relieved to discover my exclusion had been the result of incompetence rather than a deliberate snubbing. The other women chimed in to greet me, which sparked a recap of VBB logistics for my benefit, along with a fresh round of planning. The event was set for Sunday, at Esme's condo in Glen Park. Judy asked if she should bring cupcakes or was there enough dessert already. Esme assured her no additional food was needed. If anything, she could bring a bottle of sparkling water or something else nonalcoholic, as she'd stocked up on booze as though the apocalypse were nigh! Nikki asked if they'd nailed down a time, and debate ensued as to whether the brunch should commence at eleven-thirty or twelve. I was honored to be privy to the women's strategizing. I'd been out in the cold, and now I was drawn into the candlelight of the generals' tent. I restrained myself from saying too much in the group chat, as I didn't want to betray any weirdness that might compel them to splinter off into a smaller thread in which they would question why Karina wanted to include me in their ritual again. All that mattered was that I'd secured an invitation.

I'd planned to take my monthly flight on Friday, but I hadn't bought my ticket yet, and I decided to put off flying until the following week, so that I could take to the sky with my new vision in place. On Saturday, I ventured to the CVS on Nineteenth Avenue, near a French immersion high school. Some sandy-haired adolescents with skateboards chattered in basic French near the entrance to the drugstore. I felt harassed, though they didn't obstruct my passage or even seem to notice me. I imagined Guillaume Faury lecturing them in his native language, demonstrating the extent to which the teens were mangling it, after which they'd greet me politely, having been humbled by life. At CVS, I bought a fresh posterboard, along with issues of *Real Simple* and *Women's Health,* plus a *Wall Street Journal* for cerebral ballast. I bought a new glue stick, too, though my old tube still held half its purple glue.

Next, I went to the copy store and printed fresh images of planes I'd compiled on a thumb drive. On a whim, I also printed Dave Kinney's LinkedIn photo, which I would place on the board to represent advancement at Acuity. Perhaps, with the universe's coaxing, Dave would secure the pay raise I'd requested.

Back in my cube, I set to work constructing my board. I'd learned to buffer my desires with mundane imagery, items I wouldn't mind manifesting, but which wouldn't distract the universe from my true goals. Houseplants and a pot of honey. A photo of two smartly dressed women shaking hands, along with a graph of the stock market and an image of stacks of hundred-dollar bills in a pile of ludicrous abundance. Swimming among these images were the tail numbers of doomed aircraft, as well as of my first love, N92823, letters and digits cut out individually with their original order maintained. I hoped the universe would divine my meaning—I wanted a plane to choose me, as N92823 almost had that day. I snuck in a few juicy photos of 737s, along with a palm tree and a piña colada, which would help me pass off the plane imagery as a general enthusiasm for travel.

I texted Kevin, asking him to come to my cube. He arrived after a few minutes, wearing Adidas track pants and a white T-shirt. His eyes were red, suggesting he'd just woken from a nap.

"Hey, Linda," he said. "What's up?"

I gathered he felt harassed, as I had earlier by the French-speaking teens. "I've made a new vision board," I said, gesturing to where it lay on my bed, "and I wondered if you could tell me your honest opinion of it."

Kevin examined the board. "It looks like you want to travel," he said, "and invest in the stock market?"

"Yes, that's right."

"You should max out your Roth every year."

"For sure," I said, though I had no idea what this meant.

"Who's that guy?" he asked, indicating Dave.

"He's my boss, sort of."

"You want his job? Or you want to date him?" Kevin's tone was rather harsh.

"I'd like to advance in my career and be paid more."

"Weren't you trying to date a pilot or something?"

"Not anymore." I regretted having told everyone I knew that this was my dream. "Do you think the universe will mind that my intentions have changed?"

"I dunno. I don't think the universe cares. Especially about you. No offense."

I thanked Kevin for his input and was glad when he left.

THE NEXT MORNING, I DRESSED IN THE SAME JEANS AS BEFORE but a different top, this time a striped T-shirt with a red cardigan layered over it. I stepped into my knee-high brown boots, and after appraising myself in the closet mirror, I added a chunky yellow scarf, which warmed my neck and provided a whimsical effect. I rolled up my board and headed out to catch the L Taraval, from which I transferred at Forest Hill to the 44 bus, which deposited me in Glen Park.

Esme lived in a condo on Chenery Street with her husband, a lawyer named Ian, who did not appear throughout the VBB, though he was rumored to be working in the bed-

room. From the doorway, I spotted Karina sitting in an armchair, and we waved to each other.

"Good to see you again, Linda!" Esme said, drawing me in
for a hug. Her neck smelled of an orange-scented lotion my
mother used. The condo had an open floor plan, its gleaming
silver kitchen ceding to an airy living room. The couches and
chairs were upholstered in sumptuous white leather, and
from their buttery skin I knew Esme was rich. Along with
Karina, the VBB's other core members—Morgan, Stacy, and
Judy—were already present, draped across the furniture and
holding mason jars of a red drink with chunks of fruit float-
ing in it. An additional woman, the previously absent Nikki,
arrived just after me, a human infant strapped to her chest.
I was the first to greet her, as I was still standing by the door.

"I'm Linda," I said.

"Hey, Linda," she said with an air of distraction. "Nice to
meet you. This is Sean." I regarded the baby's clenched,
sleeping face, and was reminded of my niece, Claudette,
who'd been born last June. I'd met Claudette at Christmas
and felt intimidated by the blank slate of her consciousness,
and her proximity to the realm of nonexistence, from which
she had so recently emerged. I now felt similarly about Sean
and was glad when the other women swarmed around him,
cooing and exclaiming over his cuteness.

"Sorry I couldn't join last time," Nikki said. "This little
guy got in the way."

The women laughed affectionately. "We're so happy to
get to meet him," Judy said.

Esme offered us beverages. Nikki declined the sangria, as she was breastfeeding, but I took a jar of the concoction and stood at the fringe of the group as they questioned Nikki about the experience of birthing her child. I perused the food offerings spread across the marble countertop, which were notably sparer and less pastry-oriented than Karina's had been. There were cubes of fruit pierced with skewers, as if to be roasted on a spit. There were canapés of smoked salmon folded into a flower shape, with the tiny roe of another fish piled on top, which seemed like a cruel joke at the expense of both animals. Karina sidled up next to me.

"Those look disgusting, don't they?" she whispered. I gave a slight nod. I'd thought the same thing, but I didn't want Esme to perceive us as disparaging her snacks.

After a few minutes, the women's curiosity about Sean was satisfied, and everyone settled back into their positions in the living room. I perched on an ottoman beside Karina's armchair, as if I were her lapdog.

"Esme, is that a new sideboard?" Nikki asked, her eyes trained on a rectangular gray object beneath the flat-screen TV.

"It's from Restoration Hardware," Esme said. She slid open the front hatch. Inside it there was nothing.

"This is leather?" Morgan said, running her hand over the surface.

Esme nodded. "Shagreen-embossed. It's supposed to look like stingray hide."

This revelation, in addition to the grotesque fish canapés, made me wonder what grudge Esme held against the ocean's creatures.

"The texture is exquisite," Morgan said. The other women, aside from myself and Karina, went over to fondle the sideboard. I glanced at Karina, and she raised her eyebrows.

"Do you know where the bathroom is?" I whispered to her.

"I dunno. I've never been here." She sat up and addressed Esme, loudly. "Hey, Esme, where's your bathroom?"

The other women, still gathered around the sideboard, fell silent, affronted by Karina's tone. "Down the hall, to the left," Esme said.

I stood. "I'm the one who needs to use it," I announced.

"Right down the hall," Esme said, gesturing.

I emptied my bladder into Esme's chic black toilet. The dimmer switch was turned low. A cone of incense burned on a ceramic plate set on the toilet's tank. Beneath the sink sat a metal wastebasket the size of a juice glass, within which lay a single, seemingly unsoiled cotton ball. The sight of the tiny trash can filled me with self-loathing. Compared to the women of the VBB, I felt like a soiled tissue deposited in a seatback pocket. The universe had shone favorably upon them, bestowing them gifts like this condo and Nikki's robust infant. I hoped the secretions of their success would ooze onto me.

When I returned to the living room, the women had taken their seats, and I sensed the main event was about to begin, as if my request to use the bathroom had reawakened the group to the fact of our corporeal existence, our finite and fleeting time on earth. Morgan went first. Her board contained images of rainforest foliage, scarlet macaws, waterfalls, and the naked back of a woman receiving a hot stone massage. "We're headed to Costa Rica in June," she reminded us. "I'm so excited!"

The other women inquired politely about the accommodations Morgan's family had booked. She described a thermal spa at the base of a volcano.

"The resort is carbon neutral. That was important to us," she said.

"So you've already booked your flight and hotel?" Karina asked from the armchair.

"Of course," Morgan said with a tight smile. "Months ago. This resort books up fast."

"Then do you really need to manifest it, if you already have it?" Karina said with the smug look of a prosecutor who'd laid a trap for a witness. "Or do you just want to brag about your vacation?"

I shifted on the ottoman, embarrassed by Karina's behavior. Morgan's freckled face reddened to nearly the shade of her hair. "I'm not bragging. I'm setting an intention for the experience."

"I think that's so smart," Stacy said. "It's all about your attitude going into it. You could be in a tropical paradise and still be miserable." She paused. "Not that you're miserable, Morgan! I'm talking about myself, mostly."

"So true," Esme said. "My business coach has been having me send her gratitude lists every morning. The perspective shift has been a total game changer."

"We should do that in the group chat!" Judy said.

Karina's sour comment was forgotten for the moment,

though I sensed her conflict with Morgan remained unresolved.

Judy, Stacy, and Nikki moved through their boards, which repeated similar themes from the last VBB. I noted they didn't directly ask for higher salaries—overt material requests must have been considered gauche. Instead, their boards featured items like the satisfaction of helping younger coworkers, learning from their mentors, or, in Nikki's case, revamping her business website. All of these seemed like tasks that could be accomplished without the collaboration of an infinitely powerful universe. It seemed Karina had a point.

When it was Esme's turn, she unfurled her board with a shy smile. Once again, she'd sectioned her board into quadrants. The upper left quadrant contained an image of a pregnancy test with two lines across its window.

"Esme! How long have you known?" Judy said from the counter, where she was refilling her jar of sangria.

"About two months," Esme said. "I wanted to wait to tell you all, just to be safe."

The other women gushed over Esme's pregnancy. Karina's face was set in a tense expression I could not interpret.

Esme briefly toured us through the other quadrants, then returned to the couch, dabbing her eyes with a tissue. "Thank you all for the support. It means so much to have such a solid crew of women in my life."

"Aww, we love you!" Stacy said, leaning over to hug Esme.

Nikki stood next to the couch, fussing with Sean in his sling. "Looks like it's down to you two," she said to Karina and me, seated on the armchair and its ottoman, respectively.

"That'll be a hard act to follow," Karina said with a laugh. "I'll go. Might as well get it over with."

Karina stood and revealed an uncannily familiar board. Again, it featured photos of weddings and babies. Morgan was the first to react, from her seat on the divan near the sliding door to the balcony. "Is this the exact same board from last quarter?" she said.

"No, I added some stuff," Karina said, gesturing to the label from a bottle of Bertolli olive oil and a photo of a young woman's face with $x$'s over her eyes in Sharpie. "I want to cook more at home," she said, pointing to the oil label.

"Who's the girl with x-ed out eyes?" Stacy said.

"That's Beatrice," Karina said. "She's always flirting with Anthony, so I hope she gets what's coming to her this quarter."

"I don't think you can use the boards like that," Esme said. "It isn't voodoo."

"What about work, Karina?" Judy said. "Don't you want to set any intentions there?"

"Not really," Karina said, growing prickly. "Like I told you all last time. I'm perfectly happy where I am."

"Are you, though?" Nikki asked. "You really want to be an internet janitor your whole life?"

"Acuity isn't so bad," I said. "We're promoting virtual hygiene. It's important work."

"Linda's right," Karina said. "Someone has to do it, so it might as well be me."

"That's bullshit," Nikki said. "You have options, Karina. You're not a martyr." Sean began burbling at her chest, as if he, too, were disturbed by Karina's board.

"Is this really all you want out of life?" Morgan said. "Marrying some guy and having a kid?"

Karina rolled up her board. "Why not?" she said. "Isn't that what you did?"

Morgan flushed again. "I'm very lucky that Luke can support us for a few years so I can spend time with the kids. I know not everyone has that privilege."

Judy put her arm around Karina's shoulders. "We've been worried about you," she said. "You hardly say anything in the group chat anymore."

Karina shrugged Judy off. "You mean the group chat no one talks in anymore, because you're probably on a different chat talking shit about me?"

Esme and Judy exchanged a quick guilty glance that seemed to confirm Karina's suspicions. I felt outraged on Karina's behalf. I'd expected them to gossip about me, but Karina didn't deserve such treatment.

"That's not very nice," I said, rather artlessly.

Karina gave me a withering look that conveyed I should stay out of it.

"We haven't been 'talking shit,'" Stacy said. "You're our friend. We want to help you."

"Well, I appreciate your concern, but I'm fine," Karina said. She returned to the armchair. "Linda, you're up."

Once again, Karina had released me as chum for these women, already gorged on fish and fruit, to feed upon, thus allowing her to swim to safety. I didn't see how my own board could fare more poorly than Karina's had, and so I boldly stepped up and displayed it for the women. They studied it quietly for a moment.

"It looks like investing's in your future," Esme said.

"I'm planning to max out my Roth," I said, remembering Kevin's advice.

"That's great," Esme said. "You should put any extra savings you won't need for the next three to five years in index funds. I can help you get set up, if you want."

Karina laughed bitterly. "You realize we only make twenty dollars an hour, right?"

The other women ignored her. "I see love is still on the menu," Judy said, pointing to Dave's photo.

Karina leaned forward. "Is that Dave Kinney?"

"Someone you know?" Judy asked.

"He works for the company that contracts our services," Karina said. "We met with him a few weeks ago, when he came for a site inspection. I didn't know you had a thing for him, Linda."

"I don't," I said, my face warming at the suggestion. "I included him as a symbol of professional success." It seemed too crass to admit I'd simply wanted to manifest a pay raise.

Karina scoffed. "Dave isn't successful. He's a loser."

"Karina, can we cool it with the cynicism?" Esme said. "The boards are meant to be an exercise in positive thinking."

Karina lifted her hands in surrender. "You're right. Sorry,

Linda. I'm in a shitty mood." She excused herself to the balcony, sliding the door shut behind her.

The atmosphere lightened in her absence. My strategy of interspersing plane content among photos of ordinary objects seemed to have proven effective. The women didn't even mention the planes, aside from remarking that travel seemed to be a theme of my board.

Then Morgan asked, "What's up with the numbers?"

Emboldened by the group's acceptance, I dared to push further. "They spell out the tail numbers of planes that are special to me," I said. "For instance, N92823 is a plane I flew in with my family when I was thirteen. It was an experience I've never forgotten."

"So you want to fly on that plane again?" Stacy said. I was startled by how closely she guessed at the true meaning of my board.

"Sadly, that's impossible," I said. "N92823 was decommissioned years ago, after a maintenance issue."

The women seemed confused. "What was so special about that flight?" Esme asked.

Of course, I couldn't truthfully describe the experience. I'd revealed too much already. "It was the last time my family went on a trip together," I said. "Soon after, everything changed."

This was not the reason the flight had made such an impression on me, but it was true that the trip to Chicago marked a turning point in our family. My dad had also been fascinated by our experience on board N92823, but for different reasons. One night at dinner, he told us about research he'd done on the phenomenon of clear-air turbulence. As he described wind shear and the air pockets that can occur around jet streams, I felt increasingly agitated. I wasn't interested in a scientific explanation, as I knew a more mysterious force was at work. N92823 loved me and wanted to be with me forever.

"I don't want to hear any more about planes," I'd said, interrupting him.

"Me, either," my mom said, spooning more green beans onto her plate.

"Seriously," Al said. "Who gives a shit?"

We were used to my mom's and Al's disdain for our shared passion, but it was the first time I'd ever uttered a harsh word to my dad. He was still smiling, as though he hoped I'd apologize and say I was joking. "I thought you loved planes, Linda," he said.

"Not anymore," I said. I fled to my room and burst into tears. I felt awful to have hurt my dad's feelings, but I couldn't continue discussing planes with him now that my obsession had taken on a sexual component.

In the months after, my dad became scarcer by increments, until he was coming home only to sleep. Al and I later learned he'd been having an affair with a waitress who worked at a restaurant near the marina where *Wendy* was docked. I blamed myself for his drift away from us. I'd rejected him, and he'd been forced to find connection elsewhere, his relationship with my mom having long ago grown threadbare.

Now, in Esme's living room, I found the women staring at me, waiting for me to elaborate. "My parents got divorced," I said simply, and they all nodded and cooed sympathetically.

"Girl, so did mine," Stacy said, putting her arm around me.

"Mine, too," Esme said.

"Mine didn't, but they should have," Judy said.

They gathered me up in a group hug. I'd never felt so accepted. When they released me, I fetched Karina from the balcony, and we all joined hands to recite the manifestation mantra, sealing our intentions for the quarter, to marinate like tofu in a ziplock bag.

AS WE EMERGED ONTO CHENERY STREET, KARINA PROPOSED WE go to Dolores Park. It was a nice day, and she wasn't ready to go home. I felt honored that Karina wanted to spend more time with me. I'd planned to return to my cube and book my tickets for next weekend, having refreshed my plea to the universe, but I could do that later.

We drove to the Mission, purchased burritos at a taqueria on Valencia, and took them to the park. Karina brought a blanket from the trunk of her car, and we laid it on the grassy incline of the park's southern section. Above us, the sky was clear at the center, a fringe of clouds pushed to the edges, like a bald man with hair around his ears. A jet moved in a northeasterly direction at around six thousand feet, his engines singing their wistful song. I itched to check my flight-tracking app to see who this fine gentleman was and where he was bound, but I wanted to give Karina my full attention. She hadn't explained her strange behavior at the VBB, and I wasn't sure how to broach the subject.

"Esme's condo was nice," I said, as we unwrapped our burritos.

"Yeah, of course it is. She's loaded. They all are." Karina picked chicken out of her burrito with a plastic fork. "I have a feeling I might not get invited to the next VBB. I know I was out of line today."

I chewed a mouthful of beans and tortilla, apprehensive at the prospect of Karina's expulsion from the group. I knew Karina and I were a package deal, and I feared missing out on future VBBs, cutting off the clearest line I had to the universe. "I'm sure they'll forgive you," I said. "Aren't they your best friends?"

Karina laughed. "Are you kidding? No way. Judy's my friend. The rest of them are *her* friends. Judy and I went to high school together, but her family's rich. She went to Stanford, which was where she met all those women. They're who she should've been friends with all along."

My initial impression of the group had been all wrong. It was not Karina's inner circle, but rather a set of women she was tangentially connected to, among whom she felt like an outsider. I wondered if Karina had invited me to the VBB, in part, to stake her own claim on the ceremony.

"Is everything okay, Karina?" I asked gently.

She sighed. "Anthony and I got in a fight this morning," she said.

"What about?" I took another bite of burrito. A pinto

bean fell on my thigh, and I brushed it off quickly, as if it were a loathsome bug.

"There's a show at 1015 Folsom next Friday that he's going to sell shirts at," Karina said, her eyes resting on a pair of young women doing a hula hoop routine nearby. "I assumed he wanted me to go with him, but this morning he said maybe it would be better if I didn't come. He thinks I'm too negative about the T-shirts. That I kill his vibe. But I wondered if the real reason had to do with him wanting to flirt with other girls. I was even imagining he'd made plans to go with Beatrice. I knew that would sound crazy, so I just said I was hurt we never do fun things together like we used to, and it spiraled from there. By the end it had flipped around, and he was begging me to come with him, saying he needs me to handle the money."

She stood her half-eaten burrito upright in the grass, like a cigarette butt. "I probably am too negative about the shirts," she said. "I feel like Esme got in my head last VBB. Remember how she said the novelty T-shirt market was saturated?"

"Esme doesn't work in that industry, does she?"

"No, but she's usually right about things."

"You seemed sad when she said she was pregnant."

"Oh, god," Karina said. "I did?"

"A little bit."

"Well, I'm happy for her, of course. Maybe I'm a little jealous. I feel like everyone's moving on in their lives, and I'm stuck in the same place."

"I don't think you give yourself enough credit," I said. "You were the first person who made me feel welcome at

Acuity. You always look amazing. You keep your terminal sparkling clean." I paused, sensing this was sufficient, though I could have listed more qualities. "You're my best friend," I added impulsively.

"Aw. That's sweet, Linda."

We lay back on the blanket. The clouds had moved to cover more of the sky, just as additional people had crowded around us on the grass, smoking cannabis and drinking beer. Nearby, a stereo played rap music, through which I could just make out the hum of a plane above us, his form hidden behind the clouds.

"Maybe you could come with me and Anthony to the club," Karina said.

"Friday night?" I said, with a sinking feeling. I'd been planning to fly then, having already delayed my March flight by a week. "I don't know if I can."

"Come on, it'll be fun!"

I'd never been to a club, but I'd gone to a music festival once, with Brenda and Roxy, my brother's old roommates, at a man-made lake near Bakersfield. I'd just come to live with Al, and his roommates were still being nice to me, as they thought I would be sleeping on the couch for only a week, rather than the two years I ultimately stayed. I shuddered at the memory of that night at the lake, which had proceeded by its own hazy logic. A man wearing clown makeup nuzzled my ear. At some point, I lost a shoe.

"I'm not really a club person," I told Karina.

"Neither am I," Karina said. "But I do love to dance. Dancing and swimming—those are two things I'll never pass up.

I figure when I'm old, I'll look back on my life and be glad that I enjoyed my body while I could."

"I know what you mean," I said. I felt the same way about flying, the sole activity that gave my life meaning.

"It's a plan, then," Karina said. "Friday night. We'll pick you up."

I hadn't actually agreed to go, but Karina's will seemed impossible to resist. I accepted that this was the consequence of getting close to someone and calling her my best friend: she would want to do things with me.

10 All week, I dreaded the club excursion. I reminded myself that varied experiences would enrich my character, making me a more appealing prospect to the plane who'd turn out to be my soulmate. I also held a grudging curiosity toward San Francisco's nightlife scene. The club was located in the SoMa neighborhood, a terrain of old warehouses that had undergone a rebranding effort in recent years. Now condo buildings had been erected, along with hip lunch restaurants catering to the tech workers whose companies were headquartered downtown. I knew this from internet research, as I'd never visited SoMa myself, preferring to stick to my well-worn channel along the city's western flank.

Friday night, I stood before my mirrored closet door, auditioning various garments and settling on a flimsy flower-patterned dress I'd bought at H&M years ago, which might in fact have been a long shirt. Beneath the dress, I wore a pair of black leggings my mom had sent from her defect pile. They were fine, aside from a large hole in the crotch, which would provide pleasant ventilation. Over it all, I draped my men's camel coat from Goodwill. From my closet I unearthed the gold-sequined clutch I'd purchased on my shopping trip with Karina, glad to finally have an occasion to use the stupid thing. Into the clutch I tucked my ID, my debit card, the tube of lipstick from my mini-makeover at Sephora, and of course my chunk of 737, which I never left home without.

Karina had said she and Anthony would pick me up "around nine," and at precisely 9:00 P.M. I went outside to await the Honda's arrival. I feared Karina might want a tour of my cube, which I was unwilling to provide. By waiting outside, I could take control of the situation, steering us into the car and accepting no further delay to our journey to the club. With the sun's departure, the temperature had plummeted, and the avenues were bathed in fog. I heard the howl of a plane above me, his form hidden behind dense clouds. I checked my flight-tracking app, which revealed the plane was a 787 Dreamliner inbound from Taipei to SFO. I wished I could see the handsome fellow rather than only hearing his call, which seemed infused with melancholy, as though he, too, cursed the clouds that separated us.

After twenty minutes, the Honda pulled up, with Anthony driving. Karina hopped out, wearing a tight sequined dress whose hemline hit just below her labia. A layer of cosmetic sparkles covered her skin, so that in the salty streetlamps, she glimmered like a healthy trout. She threw her arms around me.

"Yay! I'm so glad you're coming!" she said.

At first, I thought she'd gotten out of the car to properly greet me, but then I recalled the Honda had only two doors. Karina pulled the lever that moved her seat up, and I wedged myself in the back. She returned the passenger seat to its original position, entombing me snugly.

"Sup, Lindy," Anthony said, turning down the music, which featured heavily thumping bass. The car's interior was thick with smoke. "Everyone strapped in?" he said in a charmingly maternal way, and when we confirmed we were, he drove west, toward the Great Highway, and then north along the coastline. Karina relit their cannabis cigar and handed it to me. I inhaled shallowly, then passed it to Anthony, who was still attempting conversation in spite of the wind whipping through the open windows and the ponderous bass line of the music he'd turned back to full volume.

"These guys are sick," he said. "You heard of them, Lindy?"

I gathered this was the same musical act that would play at the club tonight. Karina had sent me a link to their SoundCloud, but I hadn't clicked it. "No," I yelled. "I don't know much about music."

"What?"

"She doesn't like music," Karina said.

"Yes, I do," I said, though I wasn't sure this was true. I rarely listened to music deliberately. Songs would lodge in my brain after I'd heard them at Safeway or from the device of a troublemaker on the bus, but I'd resent their presence, as they'd tunneled into my ears without my consent. All I cared to listen to was the siren call of a turbojet engine.

From the Great Highway, we turned onto Lincoln and zipped along the southern edge of Golden Gate Park, then continued east on Oak Street with its stately Victorians, past Market to Folsom Street and the warehouses of SoMa. I overheard snippets of a story Anthony was telling Karina about his shift that day at the pizza place. A teenager attempted to steal a five-dollar bill from the tip jar, but Anthony told him to put it back, and the boy obeyed. I sensed Anthony hoped to convey a message through this story, something about himself as a masculine figure whose authority was respected by comparatively powerless strangers. "Good job, baby," Karina said, sounding sincere.

Anthony found a parking spot on Howard, a dark stretch of concrete that sparkled with the shattered glass of cars that had dared to park there before. Karina sprung me from my tomb, and I joined them at the trunk, which was full of boxes I assumed held the infamous T-shirts.

"My buddy's the promoter, so he lets me sell here even though it's not technically allowed," Anthony told me. Then he paused, his eyes twinkling, as if only now fully appreciating my presence. "What's good, Lindy? Long time no see." He drew me in for a hug. I smelled his cologne and beneath it, the scent of his body, a pleasant mingling of sweat and bacteria.

We each took a box and began walking to the club, Anthony a few steps ahead of me and Karina.

"The promoter's kind of a creep," Karina told me.

"Ryan?" Anthony said. "No way. He's solid."

"He was a dick to Judy when they dated."

"That was high school, babe. A decade ago."

Karina and I exchanged a private glance. She must have remembered her resolution not to kill his vibe. "You're right," she said. "It's cool he's letting you sell shirts here."

The club loomed ahead, a concrete box along whose side stretched a line of people, most of them inadequately dressed for the brisk evening. Luckily, we didn't have to join those shivering commoners. Anthony led us to the head of the line, where he and the bouncer bumped fists conspiratorially. Inside, the space was dark and packed with bodies. Music blared, and in the sensory chaos I had the impression of sound adding density to the air. We pushed through a throng of men in polo shirts and women in short tubular dresses similar to Karina's.

After journeying through several rooms, all flashing with multicolored lights, we arrived at a ledge cut into the side of one of the dance floors, onto which Anthony began laying stacks of T-shirts. Karina held up a neon-green shirt, shouting, "We've got T-shirts! New designs! Anthony Gutierrez originals!" She shimmied around like a game show model. On the front of the shirt was a depiction of Jesus riding a skateboard. In a curvy, hippie font, letters proclaimed, *RIGHTEOUS DUDE*. I recalled the crucifix hanging above Celia's couch and wondered if Anthony shared his mother's religiosity.

A crowd gathered at the ledge. It seemed Anthony had a following. He high-fived two men wearing shirts I gathered were also Anthony's designs, one neon pink with psychedelic frogs, the other neon yellow with a cartoon pickle wearing a backward hat. Karina began conversing with a petite woman whose hair was slicked into a high ponytail.

I set down my box, though I was reluctant to relinquish the prop that had given me a sense of purpose. As long as I held it, I could pretend I was a worker hired to carry boxes, rather than someone who fancied herself a clubgoer. My outfit was all wrong, every inch of my skin covered by the leggings, boots, shirt, and giant coat. Karina had forgotten me, immersed in conversation with the ponytailed woman, so I went off to find the coat check, where I surrendered my outer garment. Without its carapace, I felt exposed, but less conspicuous. I sat on an open patch of bench off the main dance floor, wishing I had a drink but too timid to approach the crowded bar. I opened my flight-tracking app and zoomed out to view the map of the entire United States. I was comforted by the teeming nest of yellow icons, each representing a plane currently in flight.

"What are you doing?" Karina stood before me. "Let's dance."

"What about the shirts?"

"Anthony's got it handled."

She grasped my hands and pulled me onto the dance floor. I allowed myself to be swept along. I'd always avoided scenarios that involved dancing, but Karina's enthusiasm was infectious, and once I was surrounded by similarly enthused clubgoers, I found myself moving my body, and enjoying it. The DJ was playing the same type of music from the car—thumping bass that paused occasionally while a woman wailed, her voice hanging in the air for a moment before the bass thumped again. I mimicked Karina's movements. Periodically a man approached her from behind, and she ground her ass against his crotch for a brief interval before politely shrugging him off. A different fellow attempted a similar maneuver with me, but despite my attempts to move my body sinuously against him, the effect must have been unpleasant, as I soon felt him depart.

After a few songs, Karina shouted that she needed a drink, and did I want anything. I requested a gin and tonic, the only cocktail whose name I recalled in the moment. Karina slithered from the dance floor. In her absence, my self-consciousness descended. I looked at the enraptured faces of the clubgoers and felt embarrassed for us all. I sought refuge on the bench, figuring I should remain in the room so Karina could find me, by the same protocol one was urged to follow if they'd survived a plane crash and been stranded on a mountain. Better to stay in one place than to wander and risk never being found.

Time passed, and my thirst increased. I wondered what was taking Karina so long. I approached the threshold of the room with the T-shirt ledge and saw Karina, drinkless, talking to Anthony with rapid hand gestures. Nearby stood several young women in skater pants and crop tops. One of them seemed familiar, and as I observed her face in the strobe light, I recalled its inclusion on Karina's board, with the eyes x-ed out. So this was Beatrice, with whom Karina suspected Anthony was cheating on her, emotionally if not physically. I felt ill-equipped to render assistance in this fraught situation, recalling my clumsy attempt to intervene on Karina's behalf at the VBB, so I went to the bar, where I purchased a gin and tonic from an unsettlingly attractive female bartender. It cost fourteen dollars and was served in a ribbed plastic cup like the kind they have at the dentist's office. I returned to my bench and sipped my drink through a tiny black straw. Soon I'd consumed all the liquid, and I was crunching ice between my molars when a male form sat beside me and slung an arm across my shoulders.

"Linda," a voice spoke directly into my ear, and I turned to discover the voice belonged to Dave Kinney.

I would not have recognized him in the crowd, so distant were we from the context in which we'd first met. He was dressed in what I imagined was his weekend attire, a pale blue button-down shirt with little sailboats on it, unbuttoned over a white undershirt, which had a brown stain dribbled down its front. His glasses were gone, giving his face an obscenely naked look. I saw he was intoxicated, his eyelids heavy, his lips curving in a dumb smile. Though his clothing was youthful, he struck me as older than he'd seemed when I met with him in the conference room, perhaps due to the contrast he presented with the club's other patrons. Admittedly we'd both aged several weeks since we last saw each other.

"Crazy running into you here," he said. His arm remained around my shoulders, and though I wished to escape its weight, I didn't know how to accomplish this without offending him. I could feel his armpit sweat seeping into the thin cloth of my dress.

"Do you come here a lot?" I asked.

Dave gazed at the crowd. He didn't seem to have heard me. "I hope you're making the most of your youth," he said.

"I'm thirty."

"Thirty! You're a baby."

He closed his eyes, a pained expression on his face.

"Are you okay?" I asked.

"Never been better. Never, ever." He leaned close to me. "We pregamed with scotch at the Fairmont," he whispered. "Plus a little coke and some ketamine, which was a new one for me."

"Who are you here with?"

"No one, anymore. I came with a friend, but he left with some girl. I've been abandoned! Can you believe it?"

I checked my phone. It was ten forty-five. Only an hour had passed since our arrival, though it seemed a flaccid lifetime.

"Are you having a good time?" Dave asked me.

"Not really."

"Me, either! I fucking hate clubs." We watched people dance. The crowd had grown denser, bodies appearing to move as a single organism. I wanted to go see how Karina was doing, but I remained pinned beneath Dave's biceps. I prayed she'd remember my existence and rescue me. She would know how to extract me from the situation without incurring professional damage. But I was also afraid for Karina to see Dave in this state. He seemed to be having a personal crisis, and I wanted to protect him, though in an impersonal way, as I would wish to spare anyone from humiliation.

"If you could do anything in the world right now," Dave said, "what would you do?"

"I'd take a flight," I said without hesitation.

He laughed. "That's fucking brilliant. I'm game. Where should we go?"

I hadn't expected this. I wasn't sure he was serious, and knew what I said next would be critical. As he was presumably normal, Dave would be drawn to the prospect of a destination, rather than the flight itself. At this hour, our options were limited. I remembered there was a nightly red-eye to Houston, departing at 11:55 P.M. If we left now, we might make it.

"Houston?" I said.

"Hmm. I was thinking Paris, but Houston works. I've never been. Let's do it!"

I was stunned. "Are you sure?"

He was already standing. At last, I was freed from his arm. "Yeah, fuck it. Why not?" He extended his hand, just as he'd done a few weeks ago at the office. "It's on me, Linda."

I knew better than to question a deal, especially one that had been engineered by the universe. I'd glued Dave's image to my vision board, and less than a week later he'd manifested at the club, presenting me with an opportunity to fly for free. I fetched my coat and led us out the back exit, avoiding the T-shirt ledge. Once we were safely in an Uber bound for SFO, I remembered how invested Karina had been in my presence at the club. I'd abandoned her, just as Dave's friend had done to him. I texted Karina, *Left with a hot guy* 😊, and tucked my phone into my clutch, fearful to see her response. I brought out the chunk of 737 and held it in my fist, bringing its edge to my lips. Nothing else mattered now. I had a flight to catch.

If I told Karina what I was doing, she'd try to talk me out of it, and rightly so. It was risky to take advantage of a boss-like figure while his judgment was addled by horse tranquilizer in order to indulge my obsession with planes. In the moment, though, I wanted to fly more than I wanted my job, and anyway, Dave seemed set on doing it. My suggestion had coalesced into a plan that now throbbed with its own life. I trusted the universe wouldn't lead me astray.

The Uber driver merged onto the 101, and we barreled south toward the airport.

"Oh, Linda," Dave said. "I'm glad I ran into you tonight. The last year has been so fucking awful."

"How so?" I asked, though I feared if Dave regained his grip on reality, he might realize an impulsive flight with his subordinate was not in his best interests.

"It doesn't matter," he said, to my relief. "Tonight is about new beginnings."

"Flying always lifts my spirits."

"I love it! Flying to Houston, in the middle of the night, for no reason. Accountable to no one. It turns out there's an upside to being divorced. That's what Charlie was trying to tell me."

I imagined his mental state as a beach ball I had to keep aloft with careful jabs. Divorce seemed too heady a topic to allow him to dwell on. "Do you live in the city?" I asked.

"Belmont. The peninsula. Suburban hell. What about you?"

"I live in a windowless in-law in the Outer Sunset."

"Jeez, no windows? That can't be legal." A sporty car roared past us, darting into the narrow space between our Uber and another car before switching lanes again. Our driver honked. Dave didn't seem to notice, slumped impassively in his seat.

"It's not so bad," I told him. "A view of the sky only leads to trouble."

"I guess that's true," he said, though he couldn't have understood what I meant. He rubbed his eyes. "God, I'm so glad to get out of that club. It made me feel like a dirtbag. Those kids were closer to my daughter's age than mine. I should be home asleep right now. Not doing blow at a club with Charlie from Gamma Delta Chi."

"Who's Charlie?"

"An old buddy from college, in town on business. He's a partner at a law firm in New York. And a total maniac. I thought he'd cheer me up, but it was just fucking depressing."

He was spiraling, the beach ball of his mood crashing to the sand.

"It's okay," I said. "Lots of people use drugs recreationally. It's not a moral failing."

"I'm forty-seven years old, chasing youth by seeing some shitty DJ with a guy I never even liked. Forty-seven! Can you believe that? I should just fucking die. Do everyone a favor."

I shushed Dave, embarrassed for the driver to hear his histrionics. We took the SFO exit and approached the departures curb at Terminal 3. Above curved the airport's signature double-helix awning, beams exposed, like the ribs of a boat. The driver found a free spot of curb to pull against.

"I can't believe we're really doing this," Dave said.

"Fuck it," I said, echoing his prior sentiment.

"Yeah! Fuck it all!"

We entered Terminal 3 and approached the United counter. The ticket agent regarded us placidly as we rushed toward her.

"We need tickets to Houston, stat!" Dave said.

"We were hoping to get seats on Flight 505," I said, in an attempt to compensate for my companion's obvious lack of sobriety.

"Let me check," the agent said, and began typing. Dave glanced at me, his jaw grinding.

"Our uncle is in the hospital, in Houston," he told the agent. "He's very ill, and if we don't get to him by the morning, it might be too late to say goodbye."

"Sorry to hear that, sir," the agent said, without looking away from her screen. "Looks like you're in luck. I can get you on that flight, but you'll have to hurry. Boarding begins in ten minutes."

"Great!" Dave said. "How much?"

"The cost for the two fares is nine hundred and fifty-two dollars, sixty-four cents."

Dave flinched at this sum. "What time would we get in?" he asked. I cursed him for waffling when we were so close to our goal.

"Five thirty-eight A.M."

"That's perfect," I said. "Uncle Bob will be so happy to see us one last time."

Mention of the uncle Dave had invented moments before seemed to spur him to action, if only to save face with the ticket agent. He handed her his American Express card. I held my breath, praying for the card to go through before Dave realized his money would be better spent on other things: mortgage payments, groceries, additional shirts with sailboats on them.

The transaction completed. The agent handed us our tickets, still warm from the printer. We hurried to the security line, sparsely occupied at this late hour.

"This is wild," Dave said as we placed our items on the belt—Dave's keys and wallet, my gold clutch. "My ex would flip if she knew I was doing this. She won't even fly anymore. Carbon footprint, yadda yadda. Once a year back to Connecticut to see her folks. She's a real pain in the ass!" I shushed him, afraid his spirited commentary would alarm the TSA workers. The airport was no place to display an excess of personality. Luckily, these agents, being night-shift workers, didn't seem to notice or care. We passed into the secure sector of the terminal, and the knot of stress I'd been holding released, flooding my body with endorphins. Nothing could stop me now. Dave could change his mind and turn back, and I would still board the flight.

He chattered on as we walked to our gate, but I could hardly hear him, his voice fading in and out like a distant radio frequency. Through the window of our gate, F7, I beheld the plane, upon whose flank was inscribed the name N14249. I hadn't had a chance to check my flight records, but I was fairly sure I'd never been with this plane before, and I was embarrassed to meet him while tethered to Dave. I tried to mentally convey to the plane that this man meant nothing to me. He was merely an appendage to his American Express card.

N14249 was a big boy, a 777-200ER, colloquially termed the Triple Seven. He was the world's largest twinjet, capable of traversing 5,240 nautical miles. He was more plane than I could handle, and I felt shy in his presence. N14249 had an embarrassed look about him, too, the jet bridge's canopy suckling his temple like a leech. Soon, I would propel myself down the bridge and into his body. I would fill him up. Together, we'd rise.

Dave stood beside me, mimicking my reverence.

"Planes are kind of beautiful, aren't they?" he said. This comment piqued my interest, but from the neutral expression on Dave's face, I knew he wasn't like me. He possessed only the typical masculine admiration of large vessels and feats of engineering. I recalled my dad's casual interest in aviation, along with his ardent, but as far as I could tell nonsexual, passion for his boat. While I agreed planes were beautiful, among countless other descriptors, I feared Dave would keep up his commentary throughout the flight, ruining my date with N14249.

"Do you think once we board, we could be quiet?" I said.

"That's a great idea. Like meditating."

"Exactly."

The first groups were already boarding. We hung back, watching them file onto the jet bridge. My phone buzzed in my clutch. *What???* Karina had written. I switched it to airplane mode. I was off the clock, as far as friendship went.

"Before we do this, Linda, I just want to be clear that I'm not in the position to date anyone, especially someone I work with," Dave said with sudden lucidity.

"I figured," I said. "I'm not interested in dating people, anyway." I'd never admitted this to anyone, but I felt like I could say anything to Dave in this moment, and it would bounce right off him.

"So you're asexual?" he said, smiling.

"I'm into planes."

He laughed. "Me, too. We're a couple of plane-sexuals."

I allowed him to believe I was joking.

N14249 was an immense plane indeed, with rows ten seats across in the economy cabin. I felt we were in the belly of a whale. Lights ran along the ceiling between the baggage compartments and his girthy central spine. This was the only club I cared to patronize.

We were seated near the back of the economy section, being latecomers to the flight manifest. Row 47, seats K and L, a window and middle seat on the starboard side. As we proceeded down the aisle, I saw passengers were settling in for sleep, with eye masks and headphones and neck pillows. I abhorred such accessories of airborne slumber; I couldn't imagine wasting my precious time on board a plane by sleeping through it. However, I did prefer that my fellow fliers succumb to unconsciousness, affording me and the plane greater privacy. I hoped the concentration of intoxicants in Dave's system was waning, so he'd sleep, too.

Near the rear of the plane, the passengers thinned. The row ahead of ours was empty, and I suggested we sit separately. "We can stretch out," I said.

"Nah, sit with me," Dave said. "I'm scared to fly." From his cheeky tone, I knew this was a lie. He wasn't afraid, but he should have been, with me at his side.

I resigned myself to orgasming beside this obnoxious man. It was fine. I'd pleasured myself next to hundreds of strangers without detection. I took the window seat, and Dave sat in the middle. I draped my camel coat over my lap, then brought out my chunk of 737 and kissed it discreetly, though for once I didn't tuck it inside myself, fearing Dave would notice. My anticipation mounted as the safety announcement played. I breathed deeply, focusing on N14249's subtle vibrations. As we pulled back from the gate, Dave said, "Do you think . . . ," and I cut him off, placing a finger over my lips, reminding him of our agreement to be silent.

N14249 lined up. His engines fired, and his former gentleness on the taxiway was revealed as a predatory ruse. His enormous white body raced down the runway, 250 tons of aluminum and fuel and luggage and human bodies. We gathered speed, N14249 working himself into a frenzy, his turbofan engines generating more than a hundred thousand pounds of thrust, until at last, he lifted into the sky. A groan escaped my throat, the sound concealed by his engines. The ground receded, revealing the bay and, across it, the hills of Oakland. I felt Dave leaning toward me, looking out the window. "The San Mateo Bridge," he said, then clamped his hand over his mouth theatrically.

I resented Dave's presence, and yet, as we continued our climb, my anger was mixed with arousal, an itchy, confusing sensation. N14249 made a sharp turn, his left wing dipping, diverting us from the northwesterly direction we'd taken off in. My window faced the enormity of space, and I willed N14249 to keep turning, surrendering his tenuous grip upon the sky. Impulsively, I grabbed Dave's hand and plunged it under my coat, guiding it to my crotch. His hand remained still for a moment. I squirmed against his shoulder. Slowly, he obliged, rubbing my genitals through the hole in my leggings, then probing his fingers under the hem of the leggings and into my underwear. I was already lubricated thanks to N14249, and I guided two of Dave's fingers inside me. He leaned closer to me, getting into it now, and proceeded to thrust his fingers into me while I rubbed myself until I bucked against his hand, imagining the hand belonged not to him but to N14249, a part of the plane transformed into human flesh, so as not to injure me.

We broke apart, moments before the man in the row across the aisle wakened and switched on his reading light. N14249 leveled and continued a shallower climb to his cruising altitude. As my breathing slowed, my excitement ceded to horror at what I'd just done. I had forced Dave to finger me, against his will. Never before had I drawn another person directly into my communion with a plane, and worse, he was someone I worked with. I felt desperate to smooth things over.

"I changed my mind," I said, turning to Dave. "I want to talk."

"Thank god," Dave said. He grasped my hand. "Are you okay, Linda? I'm so sorry. I shouldn't have done that."

"I wanted you to," I said. His hand was clammy, his fingers still coated in the secretions of my body. This repulsed me, if only because I feared it would repulse him. But presumably, Dave had made love to women before. He'd probably been inserting his fingers into vaginas since middle school, or at least wishing he could. I remembered he had mentioned a daughter, which meant his ex-wife had excreted an entire baby from her body, probably with Dave by her side. I admired his lack of squeamishness and the depth of his life experience.

"I just feel like we crossed the line," he said. "I hope you don't think I'm some sleazy guy. I wasn't planning on anything like that happening."

I told him to calm down. N14249 glided along, untroubled by Dave's outburst. A moment later, the bell chimed, and the pilot came on the intercom with a summary of our flight path. It was expected to be mostly smooth, but we should obey the fasten seatbelt sign when it was illuminated. He'd get us there a few minutes ahead of schedule. I felt lulled by his husky, nonchalant voice. I imagined his hands manipulating the controls of N14249, his eyes gazing out the eyes of the plane, a parasite nestled in the plane's skull.

The flight attendant arrived at our row with the beverage cart. Dave took a cup of water, while I requested a Diet Coke, reasoning I'd need caffeine for the layover. The Houston airport, also known as George Bush Intercontinental, was vast, and I hoped to make the most of my visit, as an international airport was my version of a speed-dating event. It was an opportunity to mingle with many attractive planes, any one of whom might prove to be my soulmate.

Dave sipped his water and chuckled. "That was crazy," he said. "I always wanted to join the mile high club."

"That's not what we did." I'd always loathed that term, which diminished the plane to an exotic backdrop for human rutting.

"No, I guess that would mean going at it in the lavatory. I never understood how people managed in such a tight space." He laughed again. "Sorry, Linda. I'm loopy. How long is this flight?"

"Three hours and forty-five minutes."

"Jesus."

"You could take a nap."

"No way. I'm fucking wired."

I regretted allowing Dave to speak. I now had to keep him occupied for the rest of the flight.

"You have a daughter?" I said, grasping for one of the few facts I knew about him.

"Yeah. Gabi, with an *i*." Dave's voice was solemn. "She's fifteen. She lives in LA with her mom."

This was a bleaker situation than I'd anticipated, and I worried it had been an unwise topic to broach. "Do you see her often?" I asked.

"Every other weekend, I go down there. I rent a one-bedroom in Koreatown. It's a dump."

I sipped my Diet Coke, which tasted pleasantly of chemicals. "I always had fun in LA as a kid."

"That's right. I forgot you're from SoCal."

He leaned his head back against the seat. "I used to like LA, too. But now it's just a reminder of failure."

"What sort of failure?"

"Well, my marriage, for one."

I waited for him to say more. We were wrapped in the hum of the plane's engines. The man across the aisle turned off his light and reclined his seat. Around us, the cabin slept.

"She left me for someone else," Dave said. "This guy Peter. An old flame from college."

"Oh. I'm sorry."

"That was just the final blow," Dave continued. "We'd drifted apart for years, especially after Gabi was born. My business was tanking. I was under a lot of stress."

N14249 rumbled, his broad airframe shaking. I held on to my armrests, praying for more. The fasten seatbelt sign chimed on. I closed my eyes.

"I can't blame Michelle for cheating," Dave continued,

oblivious. "I wasn't meeting her needs. The funny thing is, I was always curious about polyamory. Especially when we came out to SF and met people who were in that scene. We went to Burning Man a few times. I even proposed we try an open marriage, and she shot me down, hard."

"And then she got with Peter," I said, my eyes still closed.

"They reconnected online," Dave said. "She was so sneaky about the whole thing. That's what really bothered me. The deceit."

"My dad cheated on my mom," I said. I was surprised I'd told him this, as though the turbulence had jostled loose a confession.

"Oh yeah?" Dave said. "Did it last? The new relationship."

"Only two weeks. He said it was an act of temporary insanity, but my mom wouldn't take him back." I suspected my mom had been waiting for an excuse to divorce him, as she'd grown tired of my dad's antics. The boat, which required constant, expensive upkeep. Poker nights with his Navy buddies, who had a habit of putting out cigarettes on our lawn and stealing the silverware. Though he'd worked as an actuary, calculating risk on behalf of corporate entities, my dad indulged in risky behavior in his own life, and he was famously bad with money.

"Was it hard on you? The divorce," Dave said.

"Not really," I said. "It was better than my parents fighting all the time." By that point, I wasn't paying much attention to my family, anyway. I'd been busy stalking N92823 and plotting our reunion.

"That's good to hear, I guess," Dave said. "I feel so bad for

Gabi. But she seems to like Peter more than me now, so go figure."

I realized that Dave cared about my personal story only for the insight into his own it could provide him, which was fine with me. I'd already betrayed too much of myself, though he didn't understand what he'd witnessed. He must have thought I'd been seized with horniness for his bony, sun-spotted hand.

The turbulence abated. N14249 flew on into the night. The window was a black oval, without stars visible. I felt disappointed, as arousal had begun to build in my body again. I turned back to Dave, seeking distraction.

"So what's Peter's deal?" I asked.

Dave made a sound of disgust. "He's a hipster douchebag. An adjunct English professor, which means he's broke. He makes his own kimchi and plays drums in a band. You know the type."

I didn't, really.

"But Michelle seems happy with him. They're having a great time, living off my money. Peter must feel like he hit the jackpot."

The flight attendant came by with a garbage bag. We tossed our cups in and raised our tray tables. Dave seemed subdued now, his former mania quelled, and I hoped the drugs had finally worn off.

"It's been a dark time for me," he went on. "I'm a lot better now than I was six months ago, but I still have bad days." He paused. "I guess tonight, with Charlie, I was trying to take a risk, mix things up, feel young again. Charlie kept telling me there's an upside to getting divorced. Total freedom to do drugs and get laid, no one checking up on me. But it was a joke. Those women at the club seemed like children. What would we say to each other? I can tell when women pity me, or when they're only talking to me to find out if I have real money, an amount of money so obscene it automatically makes someone interesting. But I'm just a middle-management schmuck. And Charlie's a drug addict."

Dave had been staring into the seatback in front of him, but now, he turned to me with an urgent expression. "Let's face it, Linda. Total freedom is overrated, especially when you get to a certain age. If you aren't tied down to anything, you're a loser, you're fucked. You drift out to sea."

I didn't know how to respond to this. Before tonight, I hadn't realized Dave's life held such despair. His mental state sounded like how I felt after my monthly flight—a barren zone, stripped of dopamine. I looked out the window. The sky seemed to have lightened a few shades, as we flew east toward the sunrise. Beyond our wing, perhaps a mile away, another plane's signal lights blinked, heading west. It was a sight imbued with longing, two planes passing in the hour before dawn, unable to touch each other as they might have liked to.

"I'm sorry for dumping all this on you," Dave said.

"It's okay," I said. "I'm happy to listen."

"I want to hear more about your life."

I'd dreaded this pivot. "My life isn't very interesting," I said.

"I feel terrible that you have to do that job," he said with sudden vitriol. "I couldn't say that at the office, obviously, but I want you to know."

I was surprised he'd say this. "I like my job," I said.

He scoffed. "No, you don't. How could anyone?"

"Someone has to do it," I said, annoyed.

"Well, soon the software will be good enough that we won't need human moderators. Have you given thought to what you want to do next?"

I was tired of having to lie about what I wanted from life. "I want to earn more money," I said. "Do you think I'll get that raise, after all?"

"I'm trying. The budget is pretty tight."

"That's okay," I said, though I was disappointed.

"What about other dreams? Do you want to get married? Start a family?"

Just as I'd thought, Dave hadn't taken me seriously when I'd said I was only attracted to planes. "I might be willing to marry a pilot," I said.

Dave laughed. "That's very specific. I bet we can find you one."

We were quiet for the rest of the flight. Dave finally dozed off, his head resting on my shoulder.

N14249 TOUCHED DOWN. HIS ENGINES REVERSED THRUST, HIS wheel brakes deploying, spoilers rising from his wings, until his massive body slowed from its fevered landing speed, and he proceeded down the runway in a civilized manner, back to his gentle, grounded persona. It was for the best that

N14249 hadn't chosen me, as Dave would surely have sullied our final moments with trite exclamations of terror. I toggled my phone off airplane mode as we taxied to our gate. A text from Karina popped up, likely having been sent hours before.

*Status update requested,* she'd written. *Please confirm you're alive.*

*I'm fine!* I wrote back. *Still with the guy. Sorry I've been out of touch.*

I didn't expect Karina to write back, as it was 3:30 A.M. in California, but to my dismay, the three dots popped up, indicating she was typing, followed by a string of rapid-fire messages:

> OK well it's fucked up you just left like that without saying anything
>
> I never thought you were the kind of bitch who ditches her friends at a moment's notice for some dude
>
> I needed your support tonight and you just bounced for some cheap dick?
>
> like you said I'm your best friend??
>
> really Linda you seem fake af to me now

I was dumbfounded by the aggression of these texts, revealing a side of Karina I'd never witnessed firsthand, though I'd guessed at it from her accounts of fights she'd had with Anthony. The dots appeared again and lingered, indicating

Karina was composing a long, devastating final message. I replied quickly, hoping to stem her rage.

*You're right,* I wrote. *I'm sorry, Karina. I'll make it up to you.*

N14249 pulled up to the gate. The fasten seatbelt sign dinged off, and Dave and I shuffled into the aisle. *Have a good night,* Karina wrote, which I found more chilling than her prior onslaught.

I couldn't worry about Karina now, as the problem of Dave was more pressing. He grew impatient as we waited to exit the plane, sighing as the line stalled, blocked by people gathering their belongings from the overhead bins. In the gate area, he collapsed into a seat.

"Christ, I'm dehydrated," he said.

"I'll get you some water," I said, and trotted off to the nearest Hudson News, where I purchased a bottle of water and a protein bar. Dave accepted these items without thanking me. No trace of his buoyant mood at takeoff remained. He was grumpy, as though his in-flight nap had restored his brain to its factory settings.

"I need to take my contacts out," he said. "They're dailies. My eyes are so dry they're stuck to my corneas."

He made a show of tilting his head back and attempting to pour water from the bottle directly into his eyes. It splashed on his forehead. He cursed and wiped his head with the hem of his sailboat shirt.

"Don't do that," I said. "Drink the water. It'll moisten you from the inside."

"I need my meds. Fuck. This was such a stupid idea."

He buried his face in his hands. I sat next to him and patted his back, bony and warm beneath his thin shirt. I felt
sorry for him. I hated to see any creature suffer. But the little
Karina I'd installed in my mind flipped her hair and reminded me that Dave was a grown man, and I wasn't his
mother.

"Don't you want to explore Houston?" I said. I hoped he'd
go off on a touristic adventure, allowing me to enjoy a few
hours in the airport.

"Are you kidding? Fuck Houston. I just want to lie in my
own bed and die."

His lack of energy was promising. I could permit myself
an hour of wandering, and he'd remain where I'd left him.
"I'll be right back," I said.

I walked away, and he didn't protest. At C4, I gazed upon
a 757-300 awaiting departure to Raleigh-Durham. I bid that
fine gentleman good morning, and continued toward a central passageway, past a Sunglass Hut and a restaurant called
Pick Up Stix, both shuttered at this early hour. C3 lay empty,
so I proceeded to C1, where a 737-800 named N16709 was
set to depart to Guadalajara in a few hours. N16709 looked
familiar, and I consulted my flight records to discover I'd
flown on him during my flight binge. My notes revealed he'd
been a generous lover, pleasuring me with patches of turbulence all the way from Newark Liberty to Cleveland Hopkins.
He was nineteen years old, the same age as N92823. I teared
up, imagining N92823 lying dormant in a boneyard alongside other condemned planes, white angels arrayed in the
desert like the lines of cocaine Dave had done with his friend.

As I continued toward the D gates, which serviced international flights, I contemplated the appearance of Dave at the club, and his willingness to fly with me on a whim. It was the clearest demonstration yet of the vision board's power. If not for Karina, I would never have gone to the club, which meant the universe was using her as a puppet, too. The thought of Karina pained me. She'd brought me to the show for emotional support, and then, when she'd most needed me, I had disappeared. I hoped our friendship would recover from my betrayal.

I realized I should check on Dave before surrendering to the pleasures of Terminal D. I turned back, intercepting him as he rushed down the corridor, holding a Starbucks cup. I noted he hadn't bought me a coffee, which seemed rude after I'd bought him the water and protein bar.

"Where were you?" he said, grasping my elbow with his free hand and steering me to an escalator. "I had to walk all over to find you."

This claim seemed dubious, as I hadn't traveled far from our arrival gate. I saw he was mad at me. His attitude reminded me of my dad's when I failed to take out the trash or left the cap off his Subaru's gas tank after sneaking into the garage to sniff at it.

Dave led us up the escalator to the platform for the Skyway, the AirTrain's Houston cousin. I asked where we were going.

"Back to SF, obviously," he said. "They're boarding now. I almost had to leave you here."

A train pulled up and we climbed aboard. "The tickets cost a fortune," he said as the doors closed.

"I can pay you back," I said, and was relieved when he dismissed my insincere offer. He really did feel like my dad—not my real dad, but a counterfeit version who paid for things and bossed me around.

Our return flight was serviced by a 737-900, an alluring stranger named N66831. It was a full flight, and this time, Dave took the window, without asking which seat I preferred. As we pulled back from the gate, he lowered the shade and turned to me.

"Listen, Linda," he said. "Last night was fun, but I hope it goes without saying that we should keep it between us."

"Of course," I said. "I won't tell a soul." Dave seemed reassured by this. He leaned his head against the seatback and closed his eyes, allowing me to make love to N66831 without distraction.

12 On Monday, I felt anxious as I ventured to Acuity, my stress levels heightened by my unresolved conflict with Karina. I was relieved when she sat at her usual terminal next to mine, hinting that not all was lost. She smiled at me distantly and went about her sanitizing routine.

At lunch, her curiosity got the better of her. "Okay, Linda," she said. "Let's hear about this guy you left the club with."

I glanced fearfully at the humming microwave, inside which my egg rolls revolved. Dave himself might be stationed in a surveillance room within the parent company's headquarters, awaiting my answer.

"He was in his late twenties, stocky, with a beard," I said, aiming to describe the fictive man as the opposite of Dave.

Karina considered this over a spoonful of yogurt. "How'd it all go down?"

"We danced together after you left to get us drinks," I said. The microwave dinged. I retrieved my paltry lunch and joined Karina at the table.

"Yeah, sorry I dropped the ball on that," she said. "Beatrice showed up, and everything went downhill from there."

I affected surprise, though I'd witnessed Beatrice myself. "Did you confront her?"

"No. I mean, I don't even know the girl. I just acted like a bitch to Anthony all night."

Again, I regretted leaving Karina at the club. I could have at least served as an absorbent surface onto which she could pour her feelings. Historically, I'd been so focused on planes, I neglected my human relationships. With Karina, I'd hoped to do things differently, proving that I was capable of being a good friend.

"I'm really sorry I left," I said. "That was selfish of me."

"No, you were fine," she said, to my surprise. "It all worked out for the best. The next morning, I told Anthony I'd looked at his messages, and he was shocked I'd been tripping off Beatrice. It's like you said. She has a crush on him, but he thinks she's annoying. He didn't invite her to the club. She follows his T-shirt account, so she saw the flyer there."

"I knew it," I said, happy that Anthony had been vindicated.

"We worked some things out. We talked about all the feelings we'd both been having since getting engaged, and I think we're in a better place now. We even set a date for the wedding! August eighteenth."

I congratulated her. I was glad Karina's vision board was bearing fruit, which further bolstered my belief in their power.

"Can you make it?" she asked.

"Of course," I said, honored that she would invite me to

attend such a momentous occasion. I'd only been to one wedding before, my brother's. It was two years ago, shortly after I'd moved out of Al's house in Bakersfield and come to live in San Francisco. The ceremony was held outdoors, at a ranch in San Luis Obispo, Denise's hometown. The ranch was positioned near the SLO airport, and I was distracted by planes flying low overhead. The roar of one plane's engines disrupted Al's vows. He paused, grimacing at the sky, and the assembled guests chuckled, as if it were all a grim joke about the modern world. I sensed the plane was imparting a message to me, a promise that my own wedding day would soon arrive. At the reception, I caught the bouquet.

Karina scraped her spoon along the yogurt container's inner wall. "So what happened with your guy? Did you go back to his place, or what?"

"Yeah, back to his place in SoMa," I said. I'd devised a cover story over the weekend, even choosing a building for my fictional paramour to reside in. "He lives at the Harrison."

"I know that building. He must be loaded. What does he do?"

"Something in tech," I said, shrugging.

"So what happened? Did you, you know . . . ?" She mouthed the word "fuck."

"We fooled around a bit," I said quietly, wincing at the memory of Dave's fingers inside me.

"You should be careful, Linda. I'm glad it worked out, but going home with a stranger is dangerous."

"I know. I was caught up in the moment."

"Next time, at least tell me you're leaving, and drop a pin when you get to his place."

I was touched by her concern. She asked if I'd see him again, and I said, truthfully, that it seemed like a one-time thing. I hoped Dave and I could move on, pretending nothing had happened. Before we'd parted ways at SFO, he insisted we exchange phone numbers, in case something came up, though I couldn't imagine what that would be.

"What's his name?" Karina asked.

"Stewart," I said. I'd chosen this name after Payne Stewart, the famous golfer who'd died in a ghost plane incident.

Simon entered the break room. He must have been listening to our conversation, as the first thing he said was, "Linda got some dick?"

"I don't want to talk about it," I said.

"Must have been a lame lay. Figures, with a name like Stewart." Simon went to the freezer and shook the last four egg rolls in the box onto a plate.

"You shouldn't use them all up," I said. "We won't get more until August."

"I'm starving," Simon said.

"Linda's right," Karina said. Simon, chastened, replaced two of the rolls in the box. Karina and I exchanged a withering look at Simon's expense, and I was relieved that our friendship seemed back on solid footing.

ALL WEEK, I BRACED MYSELF FOR PROFESSIONAL FALLOUT FROM our flight to Houston. I feared Dave would want me gone from Acuity, simply so he wouldn't have to see me and be reminded of what he'd revealed on the plane. It wasn't being fingered that doomed me. It was Dave's confession about his failed marriage and mental health struggles that marked me as a dangerous presence. I worried he'd seek to terminate my employment on some flimsy pretense, perhaps a failure to adhere to the dress code. As such, I dressed with more care than usual and conducted myself as a model employee.

Wednesday, on my wellness break, I was pleased to find the yoga ball fully inflated. Dave must have followed through on my request, which he'd noted on his iPad and ignored until this week. I saw an opportunity to normalize our relationship, reverting to our roles of supervisor and subordinate. I texted him, *Thanks for inflating the ball! —Linda.*

Dave replied immediately: *No problem, Linda! How's your week going?*

I told him it was going fine, and he "liked" the message, concluding our brief exchange. I wondered if our flight together hadn't been such a big deal, after all. I recalled there was a section in the employee handbook discouraging employees from dating each other, but in spite of this prohibition, several mods had struck up relationships in my time here, exchanging sexual favors in the single-occupancy restroom. Christa must have been aware of these activities, but she'd looked the other way, as she did for most things that happened at our center. I gathered the rules might be different when it came to a manager from the parent company engaging in a sex act with a moderator, but Dave had more to lose than I did. I could claim he'd coerced me into a perverse, pointless flight to Houston, and he'd be sanctioned, perhaps even fired. In my relative powerlessness, I held some power over Dave, which he must have realized.

But I had no interest in claiming Dave had victimized me, when in truth I'd been the aggressor, having wielded the universe's infinite power to entice him to fly with me. I was the real pervert, while he was simply a heterosexual man who'd been duped into caressing a woman's genitals in an unusual setting. I was gripped by a familiar shame, the force that had kept me in check all these years, hiding my true nature from everyone in my life. I regretted having told Dave about my attraction to planes, though luckily he hadn't taken me seriously. I wished I could tell Karina about my weekend trysts and have her inquire about my lovers with the same curiosity she'd shown regarding the man I'd left the club with. But it was pointless to dwell in this fantasy. It could never be.

I'd revealed my desire only one other time, to my mom, over lunch at the Cheesecake Factory when I was fourteen. It was a year after my awakening on board N92823. As my family unraveled, I'd sought refuge in fantasy, spending most of my time in my room, pleasuring myself to plane content on my long-suffering iMac. I'd never heard of anyone being attracted to planes, but I held out hope that it was a harmless quirk of sexuality, the way some people were attracted to crooked teeth or hairy chests. I decided to ask my mom about it, in a roundabout way. I figured discussing romance might bring us closer; our relationship had been strained since she'd refused to let my dad move back in. Perhaps I also wanted to shock her, asserting that I'd moved beyond her control.

As we waited for our salads, I said, "Planes are kind of beautiful, don't you think?"

She fiddled with her napkin. "You and your dad always seemed to think so. Planes and boats."

"Boats are his thing," I said, already irritated. "I only like planes."

"I thought you didn't like them anymore."

It was true that I'd said this, though it was only because talking about planes with my dad now made me queasy. I'd missed our plane-spotting excursions, but I could no longer allow them, as I was horrified by the possibility of becoming aroused while in his company.

I pressed on, wanting to shake my mom out of her complacency. "Do you ever feel excited when the plane is taking off?" I said. "Like, you know you're about to be miles up in the air, and something could go wrong, and there's nothing you can do about it? And you have to let go and hope for the best?"

My mom raised her eyebrows. "I wouldn't call it exciting," she said. "I'm mostly glad when it's over."

"Like our flight to Chicago last year," I said. "I felt like the plane was trying to tell me something. Like it wanted us to crash, so we could be together, forever. Does that sound crazy?"

Our salads arrived. My mom speared a stack of romaine with her fork. "You shouldn't say things like that, Linda. People will think there's something funny about you."

In the weeks after, I felt my mom watching me as I watched TV in the living room or stood at the kitchen counter pouring a glass of orange juice. She pestered me about whether there were any boys I liked at school. "Or girls?" she added, seeming proud of herself for allowing this possibility. Weren't my friends dating now? They were, and my peers asked me the same questions, in more caustic tones, until I invented a crush on a boy named Caleb who sat beside me in Spanish class and was gentle and shy to the point of near muteness. I could have used Caleb as a cover with my mom, too, but I resented her prying. I said it was none of her business, and eventually, she stopped asking. The possibility of true intimacy between us had foreclosed when she dismissed my revelation at the Cheesecake Factory. We'd since settled into a friendly but superficial relationship, like strangers chatting in the boarding group line.

BY FRIDAY, I'D RECEIVED NO SINISTER CODED MISSIVES FROM Christa, nor from Scott, nor from Dave himself, and I hoped the threat had passed. As my vigilance waned, my desire to fly resurged. I worried the planes would be offended that I'd flown with Dave, and especially that I'd invited him to penetrate me on board N14249. I longed to fly again, to show them that Dave had meant nothing. I decided to wait until the end of the month, however, so the universe would not deem me a glutton and withhold its favor. Instead, I headed to the Elephant Bar after work.

I was dismayed to find the establishment more crowded

than I'd ever seen it. The Golden State Warriors were playing a pivotal game, and the bar was clustered with spectators, drinking beer and gazing at screens placed above the liquor bottles. Additionally, a large party was assembled at a long table in the restaurant's interior, evidently a birthday gathering, judging from the balloons tied to the chair of the young woman who sat at the table's head. Jose stood at the host stand, frowning at his lighted screen—I realized he was a kind of air traffic controller of the restaurant, which made me feel a grudging respect for him. I considered walking away before he saw me, sparing myself humiliation, as the booths were all occupied, and I suspected that Jose was in no mood for our usual dance.

But before I could leave, Jose glanced up from the screen. When he saw me, his eyes flared with malice.

"Party of two?" I said out of habit.

"Are you sure about that?" Jose said. "Because you've been coming here for a year, and your friend never shows up."

I felt so humiliated, I longed for violence to be done to me. I imagined being hit by a car, my head knocked cleanly off my torso, like a Lego person. "I'm sorry," I said.

Jose's shoulders softened. "No, I'm sorry, that was so rude of me," he said. "Do you want to sit at the bar, hon? It's not a good night for booths, I'm afraid."

I mumbled, "That's okay," and fled next door to the Marriott, where I locked myself in a restroom stall. Jose's rejection felt like a message from the universe. I'd erred by drawing Dave into my intimacy with planes, as though I'd been experimenting with polyamory, which Dave said he'd always wanted to try. But I was a monogamist at heart, as I assumed planes were, too. I'd betrayed myself and my soul-mate plane, and now I was being punished.

After a few minutes, I composed myself and emerged into the Marriott lounge, whose hostess cheerfully led me to a table along the gridded windows. I ordered fries, which were okay, but not as good as the Elephant Bar's. Through the window, a plane glided in for landing. His main landing gear, two sets of tires placed along his broad hips, touched down first. His nose remained aloft for a moment, taking in the night air, before gently lowering, his delicate nose gear kissing the runway. My chest flooded with longing. I turned from the window, feeling I did not deserve to gaze upon such an immaculate creature.

13 Saturday afternoon, I lugged my hamper three blocks to the laundromat. I was stooping to pry a waterlogged bandage from the lip of the public washer when my phone vibrated in my pocket.

Dave was calling. I stared at my phone screen, adrenaline spiking through me. I saw no alternative but to accept the call.

"Hey, Linda," he said. "You busy?"

I glanced at my hamper, knowing my soiled clothes would hear my response. "Not really."

"Want to grab a bite? I have a lead on a pilot for you."

I'd forgotten I told him I wanted to marry a pilot, a claim that had brought only trouble to my life. "Now?"

"I'll pick you up."

I was intrigued, though I wondered if he was using the pilot thing as a cover, just like I'd used it as one, though for different reasons. Corporate types like Dave enjoyed delivering bad news disguised as good news. If I was going to be fired for our trip to Houston, I might as well know now, so I could begin submitting applications at local Subway franchises. I fed the washer the fourteen quarters it demanded, imagining the coin slot as a narrow mouth through which the machine gorged itself, sometimes rejecting a quarter, as though it hadn't liked the taste of that particular coin.

I sent Dave the address of the laundromat, and fifteen minutes later, his Prius pulled to the curb, and he hopped out to greet me with a light hug. His hair was damp, and his neck smelled of shaving cream. He wore expensive-looking sweatpants and a clean white T-shirt through which his nipples were faintly visible. A small sporty backpack hung from his left shoulder.

"Hey there," he said. "What should we eat?"

"I'm not that hungry," I said. I'd just eaten some string cheese and a granola bar from a box I'd stolen from the break room.

"I've heard there are a lot of good restaurants around here," he said. "It's the new Chinatown."

"There's a dumpling place that way," I said, gesturing west.

"Perfect." We walked toward it. "I just came from the gym," he said, which explained his attire. "Equinox. You ever been?"

I hadn't been to a gym in my life. "No, but Karina says it's the nicest gym in town," I said.

"Three hundred a month. But it's worth it. There's a sauna." He paused. "Who's Karina?"

"Karina Carvalho. She's in Violence."

"Oh sure, Karina."

We reached the dumpling place, which was empty of patrons, as it was only 4:30 P.M. The server, a friendly older gentleman, showed us to a table by the window. Dave asked him which dumplings were their "house specialty," and the waiter pointed out three types—lamb, pork, and shrimp with chive. Dave ordered them all.

When the waiter left, Dave leaned back in his seat and regarded me with a sly smile. "So, I realized I do know a pilot," he said. "A guy named Brock I went to high school with. He was in the air force, and now he's been flying for United for twenty years. I sent him an email. He'd love to meet you."

I found it unsettling that Dave had already emailed this man on my behalf. I asked him what he'd told Brock about me.

"I said I had a friend who's curious about aviation. I might have mentioned you have a thing for pilots and that you're an attractive young woman. I hope that's okay."

I cringed at this summary of me. An attractive young woman. A dumb girl, easy to impress, lusting after men in uniform. Was that how Dave saw me?

I asked if the pilot was single, the only question that came to mind.

"I don't know, to be honest. He seemed interested, though." Dave showed me Brock's photo on his phone. Brock was wearing his pilot uniform, similar to the phony pilots I'd placed on my first board, but he was older than those men and—even I could tell—far less handsome. He had a wide, ruddy face and lips that curled in a snarling smile.

"He lives in South Bend, but obviously, he's very mobile,"

Dave said. "He mentioned having overnights in Denver and Houston this month. Just say the word, and I'll arrange a meeting."

I held my facial muscles in a pleasant configuration, trying not to betray my disgust at Dave's attempt to pimp me out to his old classmate. I was no longer interested in making detours en route to my destiny. I'd hoped my second vision board had redirected the universe's efforts, but it seemed some residual energy from the first board was still active. "Thanks, but I don't think it's a good idea," I said.

Dave outstretched his palms in a gesture of benevolence. "I'm here to serve, Linda."

The dumplings arrived. Dave drenched them in orange hot sauce from a jar on the table. He ate quickly, barely swallowing one dumpling before popping another in his mouth. While his mouth was occupied, I saw a chance to voice the fears that had plagued me all week.

"I'm sorry about what happened last weekend," I said. "If you want me to pay you back for my tickets, I'm happy to."

"Don't be silly, Linda," Dave said. "It was my treat."

He didn't seem to understand what I was getting at. "I haven't told anyone about it, and I won't. I just want to keep my job."

Dave looked up from his dumplings. Sweat beaded his forehead, from the orange sauce, presumably. He emitted a single barking laugh. "You think I would try to get you fired? What for?"

"I don't know," I said. It did seem a bit silly now. "Maybe

you'd be embarrassed about what we did and want me gone."

"Even if I wanted to fire you—which I never would—I don't have direct authority over personnel decisions. I mean, I could make a recommendation, but then you'd be free to tell Christa about our little adventure, and that would make me look pretty bad, wouldn't it? It would be mutually assured destruction!" He laughed again, too loudly for the little restaurant.

Then Dave leaned forward and placed his hand on mine. "I haven't been able to stop thinking about our flight to Houston," he said, his voice lowered. "It was the most erotic experience I've had in years. Maybe in my whole life."

Of all the Dave-related scenarios I'd spun out in my mind over the past week, I hadn't considered this one. "But I didn't even do anything to you," I said. "I forced you to pleasure me."

"I know. It was so fucking hot," Dave said. He smiled, as though remembering the feeling of his fingers inside me. "You sparked a flame that I thought had been snuffed out for good. A feeling I had when I was young, and even then, only occasionally. A sense of possibility and novelty. It's what I was trying to find at the club that night, but I didn't find it there. I found it with you. It was like a spiritual awakening."

I wasn't sure what to say. Dave was acting weird, and I suspected my vision board was to blame. He dabbed his mouth with his napkin and drank an entire glass of water. "Jesus, that sauce is hot," he said.

"You were miserable in Houston," I reminded him. "You said we'd made a mistake and that you wanted to die."

"I said all that?" He chuckled. "Well, I was being a baby. I was hungover, and I didn't have my contact solution or my meds. I'm better prepared this time." He patted his backpack, which dangled from the back of his chair.

"This time?" I said, a sinister awareness dawning within me.

He glanced at my empty plate. "You're not eating?"

I told him I didn't eat meat. "But it's okay. I'm really not hungry."

Dave was already calling the waiter back over and requesting their most popular vegetarian items.

"So what are you up to tonight?" he asked, as the waiter walked away. "I thought we could have a drink in Denver."

My genitals tingled, while my brain insisted it was a bad idea.

"There's a flight leaving in two hours," Dave said, consulting his phone. "My friend has a bar in Aurora. I've always wanted to check it out. They close at midnight, so we'll be able to grab a drink there, as long as the flight's on time. What do you say, Linda?"

I reasoned the planes wouldn't mind if I flew with Dave as long as I was only using him for a free ticket. Dave probably wanted to penetrate me again on the plane, given what he'd said about our flight to Houston being a peak erotic experience. That was okay, too. I was willing to compromise most of my ideals in exchange for a flight. I remained troubled, though, about our work situation, as well as the question of Dave's agency, his presence in his life's cockpit, which might have been hijacked by my vision board.

"Are you sure you want to do this?" I said. "You're acting out of your own free will?"

He looked puzzled. "Are you asking me if I believe in free will? That's a big question. We can discuss it on the plane, if you want."

He took my hand again. "Please, Linda. I'm begging you to do this with me. No expectations. Nothing weird. Just two buddies taking a spontaneous trip to the Mile High City."

I reached my free hand into my pocket and stroked the shard of 737, which seemed to emanate heat, confirming I should proceed. "Okay," I said. "Let's do it."

Dave clapped his hands triumphantly. He handed me his phone, and I entered my information for the ticket. "Thank you, Linda," he said. "You have no idea what this means to me."

My dumplings arrived, and I ate them quickly, for sustenance, like a snake swallowing eggs. Soon we were driving south in Dave's Prius. It was only after we'd merged onto 280 that I remembered my laundry, trapped in its wash capsule.


ON THE DRIVE, DAVE TOLD ME ABOUT THE YEAR HE'D SPENT IN Colorado after college. He'd worked as a white water rafting guide in the summer and a ski instructor in the winter, which was where he'd met his ex-wife, Michelle.

"It was the best year of my life," he said. "I wish I'd stayed longer."

"Why didn't you?" I asked. Forest stretched to the right, while to the left, the concrete expanse of the airport beckoned. A plane flew above us, having just taken off. I leaned forward for a better view of him through the windshield, then turned to watch his form recede through the car's rear window.

"That's a good question," Dave said. "At the time, it didn't seem like an option. My dad paid for my education, which wasn't cheap. I figured I owed it to him to get a good job."

We reached the exit for the 380 interchange, which connected 280 to 101, providing access to the airport exits. I grew irritable on the brink of my fix. I knew I had to feign interest in Dave's life, seeing as he was paying for me to fly, but I was already fatigued by the effort.

"So you moved here instead," I said.

"Yeah. It was the late nineties. Everyone was talking about what was happening in Silicon Valley. My friends from college were either working in finance in New York or in tech. I wasn't cut out for Wall Street, so I came here."

"You made the right choice," I said hollowly. We came to an intersection. While we waited for the light to turn green, a wide-body plane flew directly above us, shockingly low, landing gear still extended. I trembled in his wake, the roar of his engines ringing in my ears.

"I don't really believe in right or wrong," Dave said, seeming oblivious to our encounter with the wide-body. The light turned, and he continued toward the long-term parking garage. "You asked if I believe in free will. Well, I'm not so sure. Everything that's happened in my life has led to this moment. We make choices, and they shape our destiny, and it's pointless to think about what might have been, because the present moment is all that exists."

I found his philosophizing tedious, though these sentiments aligned roughly with my own notions of fate. I was eager to enforce our pact of silence on board the plane—the sterile cockpit rule, extended to the cabin. In fact, I wished I could ask him to be quiet now, but that would have been cruel. The man loved to talk.

My excitement mounted as we entered the terminal and proceeded through security. Having come from the laundromat, I carried only my wallet, which luckily contained my ID, as well as my chunk of 737, and a drawstring sack of quarters for the machine, which I placed on the belt. I imagined the TSA worker operating the X-ray would consider my quarter sack a tad eccentric, but he must not have found it nefarious, as I wasn't selected for additional screening.

At Gate F14, our plane awaited. He appeared to be either an A320 or a 737. As I approached the window, I saw he was an A320, as evidenced by his slightly softer, rounder nose. His tail number was N415UA, an auspicious name, I felt, as 415 was San Francisco's area code. I smiled shyly at his windscreen. I sometimes felt disloyal taking pleasure from an A320, as this model was designed as a direct competitor to the 737, but the A320 was a fine plane in his own right, and I'd gladly marry such an aircraft if he chose me.

I sat with Dave in the gate area. "I feel like this whole recreational flight thing could come into vogue," he said.

"Oh yeah?" I said without interest.

"Rather than going to dinner and a movie, people could take a flight together. We could make an app for it."

"I don't think it would catch on," I said, offended by the idea. I hated to think of my personal religion, access point to the eternal sublime, diminished to harmless fun for pampered tech workers.

Dave nodded. "Yeah, you're right. It would be expensive. And there's the whole environmental angle. Though I think that's part of the appeal. The taboo factor."

Before I could respond, he placed his hand on my thigh.

"Is this okay?" he asked.

"Sure," I said, though I didn't care for it. I was confused about Dave's intentions. He'd claimed the flight would involve "nothing weird," and referred to us as "buddies." He'd also told me that he wasn't interested in dating anyone, much less someone he worked with. But as far as I knew, platonic friends did not make a habit of caressing each other's thighs and genitals.

"I want you to use me for your pleasure again," he said softly.

"Once we're on the plane, let's stick to the no-talking rule," I said.

"Yes, ma'am."

Tonight's flight was fuller than our red-eye to Houston last week. The mood of the cabin was loose and talkative.

Apparent strangers conversed in their rows, yelled to one another, watched video clips on their phones with audible volume. I wanted to tell them to shut up. The interior of a plane was not a hall to be filled with inane chatter.

To my chagrin, our seats were 30A and B, on the port side of the plane; I always stuck to the starboard side, as this had been my family's position on N92823. As we approached our row, I was further dismayed to see a middle-aged man already present in the aisle seat. His polo shirt and khakis suggested he was a business traveler. I imagined he'd come to San Francisco for work, and was now flying home, perhaps connecting through Denver to a regional airport. His company was too cheap to book him in business class, so he was stuck with us. When Dave gestured to our seats, he shuffled into the aisle without complaint, and I felt guilty about the indignity we were about to subject him to. Alone, I could commune with the plane discreetly, but with Dave, the endeavor took on a more sordid quality.

I took the window seat. Dave removed his sweatshirt and draped it over my lap. I gathered he wanted to use the sweatshirt as a shield beneath which he could stimulate me. His forethought unnerved me. I felt like a dead bird whose cavity he wanted to stuff with seasoned breadcrumbs. A flight attendant walked down the aisle, taming the unruly passengers. She instructed them to push their bags fully under the seats in front of them, to fasten their seatbelts and raise their seatbacks. I was surprised they'd already had a chance to recline their seatbacks in the minutes after boarding, and that they weren't aware their seats had to be upright before take-

off. Had they never flown before? Were they stupid, muti-
nous, or merely drunk? It was for the best I hadn't become a
flight attendant, as I would have found it difficult to maintain equanimity around people who were so disrespectful of
planes.

As we pulled back from the gate, I closed my eyes, imagining I was alone with N415UA. My body, an object from
which I could derive pleasure, remained strapped in its
grubby seat while my soul converted to energy that fused
with N415UA's airframe. As we surged down the runway,
Dave's hand crept back onto my thigh. Beneath the sweatshirt, I shifted my hips and unbuttoned my jeans. Dave
leaned forward, pretending to look out the window, so that
his torso blocked our rowmate's view of our activities. He
probed one finger inside me, then another. I clenched my
thighs against Dave's wrist and pulsed my hips against him.
At the verge of climax, I turned and plunged my tongue into
his mouth. N415UA lurched as if in response. I came harder
than I had in recent memory, my lips latched to Dave's as the
plane carved through rough air.

A moment later, N415UA's nose leveled, and I broke from
our kiss. As we resettled ourselves, my hand brushed the
front of Dave's sweatpants, inside which his penis had
firmed. I moved my hand away quickly, as if I'd touched a
hot stove, and looked up to find Dave staring at me with a
dreamy expression.

"That was fucking incredible," he whispered.

I glanced at our rowmate and was relieved that his eyes
were shut. I held my face close to the window as we passed

over the Diablo Range, the waning sunlight etching dramatic shadows around its peaks and furrows. I prayed for the return of turbulence. I'd felt something novel in the moment my lips touched Dave's. A spark, met with N415UA dipping, as though Dave were a conduit through which the plane felt my kiss. Perhaps N415UA was jealous and wished to claim me. There was possibility in this.

The plane's early bout of passion did not return, however, aside from a gentle rumbling as we flew over the Rockies before making our descent. When his wheels touched down, I faced the prospect of a night in Denver with Dave. His erection on the flight reminded me that he, too, was a sexual being. If our evening concluded in a hotel room, I would fulfill my side of the implicit bargain we'd struck. It was a small sacrifice. I'd allowed past men to do the same without paying for me to fly.

Dave led us quickly through the terminal, eager to get to his friend's bar before last call. The taxi carried us along a desolate stretch of highway to the suburb of Aurora, where we arrived at the strip mall that housed Barley Bros, sandwiched between a tattoo shop and an Ethiopian restaurant. Inside, the walls were lined with beer kegs and stacks of wood, steer horns posted over the doorways. The communal tables were crowded with people in outdoorsy clothes, shouting to be heard over a din of classic rock.

We found an open spot at the end of a table. I studied the laminated menu.

"This place is incredible, don't you think?" Dave said,

looking around the space with an awed expression. His enthusiasm seemed forced, and I wished he'd drop the act.

"It's okay," I said. "It's just a bar."

"You're tough to please, aren't you?"

"I wouldn't say that."

Dave ordered us IPAs and a basket of fries from a young
waitress. When she returned with our items, Dave asked if
the owner, Mike, was around. "I'm a friend of his, in town
for the weekend," he said.

"I love that!" she said. "I think he's still in his office. Do
you want me to pass a message along?"

"Sure," Dave said. "You can tell him his old buddy Dave
Kinney is here."

The waitress lingered, resting the empty tray against her
hipbone. "Where'd y'all travel from?" she said.

"San Francisco," Dave said.

"Oh my goodness! That's quite a journey!"

"We didn't come here just for this place," Dave said in a
sharp tone. "We're here for a conference."

The waitress's smile stiffened, and she moved along. I
found the beer gross but forced myself to sip it, imagining it
was medicine that would inure me to the sex acts I assumed
would unfold later in the evening.

"This was a mistake," Dave said, staring out the front
windows. "It's weird to show up like this."

"I'm sure he'll be glad to see you," I said.

Dave turned to me with sudden urgency. "Is it cool if we
pretend like we're dating in front of Mike?"

"What do you want me to do?" I said, flustered.

"Oh, I don't know. Just act like you're into me." He shifted in his seat, scanning the bar. "That shouldn't be impossible, right? I'm not a monster."

I was disturbed by Dave's frantic mood and decided the best way through was to maintain a posture of agreeability. "I can do that," I said.

Dave finished his pint quickly and went to the bar for another; the waitress seemed to be avoiding us since he'd snapped at her. I ate the fries, which were pretty good, rough-cut with some skin intact. I checked my phone and found Karina had sent me photos of the wedding venue they'd secured. Anthony stood in a garden outside the chapel, his arms outstretched. *Looks amazing!* I replied. I wished I could tell Karina where I was. I imagined sending her a pin, revealing I was in Colorado, but I didn't want to frighten her. I was on my own, as usual.

My eye snagged on movement at the back of the room, where our waitress was talking to a stocky man in a flannel shirt. They conferred, casting worried looks toward Dave—who stood at the bar, unaware he was being watched—as though they were strategizing about the containment of a wild animal. The man walked over to Dave and greeted him. Their mouths opened in exclamations, but I couldn't hear what they said over the music. They hugged, slapping each other's backs, and then Dave led the man to our table.

"Mike, this is my girlfriend, Linda," Dave said. I was disturbed by how naturally he said this, which made me wonder what else he'd lied about.

"Nice meeting you, Linda," Mike said, shaking my hand. His broad, flat face reminded me of an A350-900, though his body did not attain the epic proportions of that jumbo jet. He sported a goatee, and his hair was gelled into tufts, reminiscent of the peaks of the Denver airport's roof.

"I was just heading out," Mike said. "I wish I'd known y'all were coming by."

"It was a last-minute thing," Dave said. "Have a drink with us?"

Mike looked toward the door, clearly longing for escape. I felt the same way. "I've gotta pick up some things for the old lady," he said. "She's six months pregnant. You know how it is."

"Come on, five minutes," Dave said. "It's been too long."

Mike demurred, perching on a free stool. "Ashley said you were in town for a conference?" The music seemed to have increased in volume, and we struggled to hear each other over it.

"Yes," I shouted back, rolling with Dave's lie. "We work in the field of virtual hygiene."

"That's rad!" Mike said, though I doubted he'd understood me.

"You still get out on the slopes?" Dave asked Mike.

"Nah, I slipped a disc in my back a few years ago, so I have to take it easy. Anyway, we're pretty busy these days with the kiddos. We've got two boys plus the one on the way."

On his phone, he showed us a picture of his family. Mike and his wife stood beside a Christmas tree, two small blond boys crouched in the foreground. They all wore matching red checkered pajamas.

As if to compete, Dave brought out his phone and showed us a photo of Gabi, the first I'd seen. She was pretty and lanky, like Dave. In the photo, she wore a soccer uniform and stood on a field, glaring at the camera, her straw-colored hair lying in a single braid over one shoulder.

Mike whistled. "Look at that. She's all grown up."

The song that had been playing ended. A moment later, a gentler one began, with acoustic guitar rather than electric. Dave sipped his beer. "You talk to Michelle these days?" he asked Mike.

"Not really," Mike said, tucking his phone in his pocket. "Once in a while, we'll chat on Facebook."

Dave's face tensed. I remembered he'd said that Michelle and Peter had reconnected online, too.

"You probably knew I was getting divorced before I did," Dave said.

Mike shook his head. "I dunno, man. It's really none of my business."

"I should have seen it coming. She was always kind of an empty person, wasn't she?"

"I wouldn't say that. I always liked Michelle." I felt the tension rise between them, and resented Dave for bringing me all the way to Denver for this.

"Yeah, I remember you two were such good friends," Dave said. "Every time we had an argument, she'd end up at your place. I could smell your shitty cologne on her when she came home."

Mike smiled at Dave in a way that seemed menacing. "You want to know what I think?" he said.

"What's that?" Dave said, smiling back.

"I always thought you were a miserable, stuck-up son of a bitch."

"That's funny," Dave said. "I thought you were a dumb hick who wanted to fuck my girlfriend."

Mike turned to me. "What did he tell you about us?"

"Not much, really," I said.

"I bet he said, 'Let's go visit my old buddy Mike's bar. We had the time of our lives together in Winter Park, back in the nineties.' Is that right?"

"Something like that."

"Well, it was bullshit. We weren't buddies. We hated each other. He tried to swing on me one night at karaoke, and I laid him out flat. I didn't want to do it, but I had to, just so he'd leave me alone." He turned to Dave, jabbing his finger near his chest. "And now you show up here, wanting to talk about ancient fucking history? Some shit that happened when we were twenty years old? I'm glad Michelle got away from you, man. You're a real piece of work."

Before he left, Mike glanced at me sheepishly. "Nice meeting you, Linda," he said.

DAVE ORDERED AN UBER, AND AS WE RODE AWAY FROM BARLEY
Bros, he told me he'd reserved two rooms at a Hampton Inn

near the airport. We'd fly back in the morning. I was angry at Dave, and a little afraid of him. He'd brought me here on false pretenses, claiming our visit was friendly, when actually he wanted to use me as a prop in the settling of an old score. His moods were erratic, like my dad's had been. My dad was cheerful ninety percent of the time, which made the other ten percent more terrifying, especially as his anger was triggered by trivial events that, in other moments, he'd have laughed off—Al forgetting to bring sandwiches on a boat trip, me spilling orange juice on the couch, my mom failing to remind him of a dentist appointment. Storm clouds gathered in his brain, and you had to stay out of his way until they burned off, speaking only when spoken to, and then only in a tone that would not be perceived as passive-aggressive. Similarly, I went along with Dave's plan for the night, hoping to weather our remaining hours together until I was safely back in my cube.

We checked in. Dave walked me to my room and waited as I inserted my keycard. Freedom lay on the other side of the door. I looked at Dave and found his former appearance of freshness, when we'd met outside the laundromat, had faded. His blood had receded into his organs, giving his outer shell a pale, wrinkled look. His eyes were sad and hopeful. I knew I should invite him in, but I couldn't bring myself to utter the words. The prospect of solitude was too tantalizing.

"Make sure you drink a glass of water before bed," I said.

"I will." He turned down the hall. "Good night, Linda."

Relief flooded through me as the heavy door clicked shut.

The room was narrow, with two queen beds pushed against an orange wall. In the moment, it seemed like a sumptuous haven. I removed my jeans and bra and lay on the bed by the window, which looked out on the parking lot. I listened to the call of planes flying over the gray building. I perused my flight app and speculated that the plane whose cry I heard might be an A319 departing for Philadelphia, or perhaps a 757 arriving from Washington Dulles.

A text popped up from Dave: *Can't sleep. Up for a chat?*

I considered not responding. I could pretend to have fallen asleep, or to have placed my phone out of reach in an attempt to wind down. But I knew Dave was feeling fragile after his reunion with Mike, and we'd only ended up here because of my vision board. I invited him over. I put my jeans back on and hid my bra behind a pillow to avoid a scandalous impression. When Dave entered my room, I watched him make a quick calculation as to where he should sit. He could use the chair, but it was positioned close to the bed whose covers I'd already undone, which seemed too intimate. If he sat there, he'd be stationed at my bedside, like a country doctor tending to me in my sickbed. Instead, he sat on the other, unspoiled bed, his long legs extended before him.

"Are you okay?" I asked, returning to my bed.

"I feel pretty dumb, I guess."

I searched for the right words, wanting to be tactful, in spite of my annoyance. "I didn't realize you two had such a complicated history."

Dave sighed. "I'd kind of forgotten, too. I was feeling nostalgic for Colorado, and he was part of that period of my life. But it's true, we were never friends. I think Michelle played us off each other. And it seems like she's still doing it."

"So you didn't go there to confront him?"

"No," Dave said. "I wanted to fly somewhere with you, and I saw there was a flight to Denver, and then I remembered Mike had opened a brewery. I thought I was over it—it was so long ago—but when I saw him, it all came rushing back."

I wasn't sure I believed him, but it seemed possible he was unaware of his own motivations. I seized on the first thing he'd said. "So you felt a sudden compulsion to fly with me tonight?"

"I'd been thinking about it all week, but I wasn't planning on asking you to do it until this afternoon. I was supposed to go to LA, but Michelle asked to switch weekends so they could go camping in Joshua Tree." He paused. "You wanted to, right? It wasn't because I pressured you, or anything?"

"Not at all," I said. "The truth is, I've been taking advantage of you."

He turned to me with a bemused expression. "How do you figure that?"

I sat up and crossed my legs beneath me. The time had come to tell him the truth, or at least a partial version, so that he knew what he'd gotten himself into. "A few weeks ago, I attended a Vision Board Brunch, where participants present a board that conveys their intentions for the upcoming quarter," I began. "I glued your LinkedIn photo to my board, along with images of planes, and the universe must have gotten its wires crossed."

"Wow," he said. He lay on his side, with one hand under his cheek, as though we were at a cozy sleepover. "You put me on your vision board?"

I nodded. "I included you as a figure of authority and success in his field. I also hoped to manifest that raise we discussed."

"I'm working on that."

"I've learned the universe takes these requests literally," I went on. "I believe it was because of my board that you've become compelled to fly with me, against your better judgment."

Dave was quiet for a moment. "I know you're trying to make me feel better, and I appreciate that," he said. "But your vision board isn't that powerful. I'm responsible for my own decisions."

"A few months ago, I would have agreed with you," I said. "But other items from my boards have already manifested. On my first board, I included an image of Guillaume Faury, and then I encountered the man himself at SFO a week later."

"Guillaume Faury?"

"The CEO of Airbus."

"Why'd you put him on your board?"

"The point is, I conjured him," I said, growing impatient. "And now I've conjured you. What are the odds we'd run into each other at the club?"

"The club was Charlie's idea."

I was annoyed by his obstinacy. "I don't think you understand what I'm saying," I said. "My board might be tampering with your free will."

"Linda, no offense, but you're sounding kind of cracked with this vision board stuff." It was the same tone my mom had used that day at the Cheesecake Factory. I felt chastened and crawled under the covers.

"So you put planes on your board?" Dave said. "Is this, like, a fetish of yours? Getting off on the plane?"

"In a way," I said. I was no longer interested in making Dave understand. If I were ever to reveal myself again, it would be to someone I truly cared about.

"Have you done this with other guys?"

"Never," I said truthfully. He looked pleased by this.

"I never thought about the erotic potential before, but it makes sense," he said. "All that horsepower directly under you. The roar of the engine. And the whole getting-off-in-public thing. I've always been a bit of an exhibitionist."

I said nothing, offended by Dave's interpretation of what we'd done on the planes. He made it sound cheap.

Dave's eyes had drifted shut. "I like that you put me on your vision board," he said. "Did you think I was hot?"

I cringed at his use of the word "hot," which seemed undignified for a man his age. "You struck me as very tall and well groomed," I said.

"I'll take it," he said. His breathing grew steady and soon curdled into a snore.

I couldn't believe it. He was asleep, which meant the

threat of sex had passed. I'd assumed that, at any moment, he would ask to join me in my bed, which I would have consented to, preferring to dispatch with the unpleasant obligation as quickly as possible. As I listened to Dave's increasingly guttural snoring, I realized that what he wanted from me was more onerous than a simple sexual exchange. He wanted an empathetic ear, someone to listen to his accounting of his life's disappointments. Dave wanted a girlfriend, or at least someone who'd pretend to be his girlfriend. I didn't see much difference between the two.

It had been a mistake to fly with Dave again. I could not be a man's girlfriend if I hoped to be a plane's wife. I resolved to end our affair as soon as we were back in San Francisco.

14 In the morning, we flew back to SFO on another A320. Our seats were on the starboard side this time, to my relief. I was grateful, too, that Dave didn't touch me during takeoff, instead occupying himself with a block game on his phone. I was free to commune with the handsome plane, having tucked the chunk of his competitor, the 737, inside my flesh.

While night flights possess a glamorous aura, morning flights lay claim to their own sublimity. The cabin was peaceful, passengers sleeping off their hangovers or busying themselves with books and tablets. I watched out the window as we headed west and then north, flying over Death Valley and the Sierra Nevada Mountains. As we descended into SFO, I admired the salt ponds of the bay, rectangles of pink like blood diluted in milk.

Dave insisted on driving me home. I directed him to my intersection, and when we arrived, he took my hand over the center console. "I had fun with you last night," he said.

"I did, too," I said uneasily.

"I like you, Linda. I feel like I can tell you anything, and you won't judge me."

I was pleased he found me trustworthy, though in fact I'd

been constantly judging him. I stared through the windshield, down Taraval. The sky was overcast, a solid gray wall, and I couldn't tell where it ended and the ocean began. I didn't relish what I had to do. I'd never broken up with anyone before.

"I don't think we should keep doing this," I said.

Dave's hand tensed in mine. "Oh?"

"Because of work, you know," I rushed on, though this wasn't the real reason. "If someone found out, we'd be in trouble."

"I don't think so."

I was surprised. "You don't?"

"We haven't done anything wrong, have we? We're both consenting adults."

"I doubt Christa would approve of our flights together."

He laughed and released my hand. "No, probably not. You're right, Linda. The flights are a bit much. I'd like to do other things with you, though. How about dinner this week?"

He was relentless. "Maybe," I said, and exited his vehicle quickly, before he could say more.

I escaped into the garage, and only when I saw Mrs. Chen at the washer did I remember I'd abandoned my laundry the day before. We regarded each other warily. I sensed we were both equally unhappy at the prospect of a conversation. I was embarrassed to recall my spasm of extroversion, three months ago, when I'd entered the house and attempted to converse with the Chens.

"Hello, Linda," she said.

"Hi, Mrs. Chen," I said, proceeding to the door of my

cube. I wanted to go straight to the laundromat, but it would look like I was running away from her. I fumbled my key at the lock, feeling self-conscious in her presence.

"You didn't come home last night," she said.

I told her I'd stayed with a friend, touched that she'd noticed my absence from the cube.

"Boyfriend?"

I understood her angle now. "No, not a boyfriend. Don't worry, I won't have any overnight guests."

Mrs. Chen smiled, as if in apology for her nosiness. "We just went to Costco," she said. "Would you like some toilet paper?"

She piled six rolls into my arms. Upon entering my room, I let them tumble to the floor. I showered quickly, scrubbing my face, which had already broken out from the hotel body lotion I'd slathered on it. I put on the same jeans I'd worn the night before, as my other pants were part of the imperiled laundry load. I donned a 24 Hour Fitness shirt I'd salvaged from a box in the garage marked for Goodwill, and which still smelled faintly of Kevin's body odor, though I'd laundered it many times since. In lieu of a bra, I wore my jean jacket to conceal the shape of my breasts. I wouldn't want a stranger glimpsing the outline of my nipples and thinking they'd gotten one over on me. I shuddered at the memory of Dave's nipples poking through his white T-shirt.

As I'd feared, when I reached the laundromat, my clothes were gone, aside from a single hot-pink ankle sock in the lost-and-found basket, a searing reminder of all I had lost. I lowered myself into a folding chair next to a wall riddled with flyers for open mic nights, housecleaning services, and missing pets. The loss of my laundry felt symbolic of a larger dissipation at the center of my life, a whirlpool sucking the edges of my attempts at respectability. My wardrobe had been bare-bones to begin with, and the loss of an entire load, comprising all the clothes I wore in a typical week, was devastating. I dreaded having to spend money to replace them, which would eat into my flight budget, especially now that I'd cut off my source of free flights. I decided to forgo my end-of-April flight, which I'd normally have booked for around now. I'd already flown twice this month, and I didn't want to spiral into further recklessness. I would put my affairs in order so that I could fly next month with a clear conscience.

I brought my pink sock, the sole survivor, back to my cube and took stock of what remained. Aside from my present outfit, I possessed two pairs of underwear, the bra I'd worn last night, a white T-shirt with yellow stains in the armpits, and a striped sweater that I never laundered, as it was dry-clean only. Occasionally, I spritzed it with Febreze. Digging deeper in my closet, I found a T-shirt Anthony had thrown to me, out of the trunk of Karina's Honda, after we'd all had drinks together at the Olive Garden bar last year. It was neon green, a men's size large. On the front, a cartoon cat puffed a cannabis cigar. I liked the shirt, but it didn't seem appropriate for work, even by Acuity's lax standards. Exhausted, I threw myself on the bed and fell asleep, though it was only 5:00 P.M.

I woke in a more optimistic mood. I could wear the white shirt as long as I layered the striped sweater over it, concealing the pit stains. At work, I moderated comments on a video featuring a buxom kindergarten teacher reciting *The Very Hungry Caterpillar* to her students. I rapidly green-lit the comments, which ranged from graphic descriptions of sex acts with the teacher to fantasies of murdering her and consuming parts of her body with various side dishes. These were all fine as long as they didn't contain any banned words. Either I was getting even better at moderation, or they were tossing us easy ones to distract us while they made plans to lay us all off. I glanced at the whiteboard and was gratified that my number remained at the top of the H&H vertical.

It felt good to be an employee, and to know that the minutes spent at my desk were being converted to currency that would soon appear in my bank account, the climbing numbers indicating I remained woven into the fabric of society. I was further comforted to work alongside Karina, who smelled great as usual, like gardenia perfume and baby powder and sweet mint Orbit.

At lunch, I hugged Karina by the fridge. She laughed.

"What's gotten into you?" she said.

"I'm just glad to see you," I said. "I missed you this weekend."

"Aw, that's sweet."

A knot formed in my throat. I busied myself scrounging in the cabinets. The Costco run had dwindled to its most unappealing offerings—chocolate-covered coffee beans, stale saltines, and some peppermint bark that had appeared after Christmas. I wasn't picky, however. I loaded a paper plate with servings of these food-adjacent items and joined Karina at the table.

"Is that all you're eating?" she said.

I crunched some beans. "It's fine," I said, my mouth full of grit.

Karina brought a fresh plate from the cupboard and scooped half her salad onto it. "It's just kale, sunflower seeds, mandarin slices, and dried cranberries," she said. "No meat."

"I feel bad taking your lunch," I said.

"Yogurt's the main event for me, anyway."

I thanked Karina, feeling cared for. Today she wore a green seersucker halter dress and a white cardigan. Her hair was gathered into a messy bun. She appeared fresh and glowing, unburdened by the fears that usually troubled her.

"So you found a place for your wedding?" I said.

"Yeah, this Catholic church in South City," Karina said. "Anthony went there as a kid, and Celia still goes to mass every Sunday, so she has some pull." She smiled. "I know it's old-fashioned, doing a church ceremony, but I don't want to take any chances, with what's at stake."

I asked her what was at stake, and she shivered, pulling her cardigan around her shoulders. "Eternal damnation. Hell. Purgatory. I worry God would sabotage our marriage, or make me infertile, or kill one of us, or kill our baby. Something like that."

I'd known Karina believed in cosmic forces, given her

faith in the vision board and her cryptic references to deserving punishment, but I'd never heard her mention God before. "I didn't realize you were Catholic, too," I said.

"I'm not, really, but I might as well cover my bases," Karina said. "Besides, Celia would never forgive Anthony if he didn't get married in the church."

"What about your mom?"

"Is she religious, you mean?"

I nodded.

"She's Wiccan now, or something. She lives in Mendocino with her boyfriend. She'll come to the wedding, but I'm not counting on her for much more than that. She's a real free spirit." Karina said this derisively.

"And your dad?" I realized Karina had never mentioned him.

"I didn't invite him," she said, with an edge to her voice.

I gathered the man was alive but disqualified from attending. I was savvy enough to drop the subject.

"So what did you do this weekend?" she asked, returning to her salad.

I admitted I'd seen Stewart again. "We spent Saturday night together," I said. I shot the microwave a defiant look, no longer caring if Dave was listening. I wouldn't betray him, but I reasoned I had a right to discuss my weekend in general terms.

"You must like him, then?"

"Not really."

Karina looked confused. "Did something happen?"

"I think he's still hung up on his ex."

"Eww. That's the worst."

I knew Karina was waiting for me to say more, and I was curious how she'd react to Dave's behavior, which I'd found disturbing. "He took me out to this bar, saying a friend of his owned it," I said. "But it turned out they were enemies. They got into an argument. At one point, I thought they were going to physically fight."

"Oh my god," Karina said. "That's so scary. What did they fight about?"

"His ex-wife," I said. "It sounds like she cheated on Stewart with the friend, years ago, and Stewart's still mad about it."

"This guy sounds like a mess."

"He even asked me to pretend to be his girlfriend for the night," I said, on a roll now.

"No! Stop!" Karina was laughing. "What an absolute freak."

I was glad to entertain her, though I felt embarrassed to have been part of the charade. "I broke it off with him."

"Good. You can do better, Linda."

I felt redeemed by Karina's friendship and vowed to be a better friend going forward. I would no longer be a parasite who ate half her salad. After work, I went to Trader Joe's, where I bought some premade salads for lunch, along with string cheese, high-fiber fruit leather, carrot juice, and pretzels. I brought these groceries back to my cube, where I packed my mini-fridge to capacity. I looked at clothes on the internet, but quickly felt overwhelmed by the options available in a globalized marketplace.

At lunch the next day, Karina noticed I was wearing the same outfit as the day before, and I admitted my laundry had been stolen. She insisted we go shopping after work, as I couldn't wear the same sweater every day. I knew she was right. Though I was no longer worried about losing my job on a sartorial pretense—Dave's point about mutually assured destruction was apt—I still had some pride. Also, at a certain point the armpits of my sweater would not be able to absorb any more Febreze.

We drove to Stonestown and went to the Uniqlo store, where Karina guided me in the selection of several T-shirts, a pair of elastic-waist trousers, some socks and underwear, and a new striped sweater to reduce the strain on the original one. The total was $146.78, a sum that made me wince. But what else could I do? I trusted the universe was working hard on my behalf, but I had to tend to my corporeal being in the meantime, feeding and clothing my body while I awaited my destiny.

We sat in the food court, drinking milk teas. The tables around us were crowded with young people, probably students from SF State or nearby high schools. The air had a cloying, powdered-cheese smell I associated with teenagers. I felt superior to them, having been born in an earlier decade. I was proud to be seen with Karina, who was surely the most beautiful woman in the mall, if not in the entire 94132 zip code. Her engagement ring sparkled on her hand as she brought the milk tea's thick straw to her lips.

"I need to ask you something," she said. Her brown eyes were grave beneath her fake lashes, and I braced myself, fearing she'd somehow found out about my flights with Dave.

"Would you want to be one of my bridesmaids?" she said.

I was stunned. "Are you sure? I've never done that before."

"There's not much to it. You just have to wear a dress in a jewel tone and walk up the aisle before me, with one of Anthony's groomsmen. His friends are dumb bros, but they're harmless."

"I'd be honored," I said. "If I'm still around then."

Karina's eyes narrowed. "Where else would you be?"

I couldn't tell her that I might be married by then, too. "Oh, you know, just in the way of, like, who knows what tomorrow holds."

"Yes, living in the moment is important and all, but we have to book the venue three months in advance."

"Count me in."

"Yay!" Karina said. She came over to my side of the table and gave my shoulders a squeeze. Upon returning to her seat, however, her face took on a pensive look. "There's just one wrinkle in our wedding plans."

"Oh?"

"The honeymoon," she said. "This big shot from the T-shirt community has a house in Kauai, and he invited us to stay as long as we want. I always dreamed about having my honeymoon in Hawaii. It would be so perfect."

"But you'd have to fly there," I said.

She nodded. "I worry I'll have a panic attack and ruin the whole trip. Or, if we make it there, I'll be fixated on the flight back the whole time, and it'll be miserable. I suggested we go to Tahoe instead, even though that seems depressing."

"You really have nothing to worry about with flying," I said. "You're much likelier to die in a car crash than a plane crash. You aren't afraid of your Honda, are you?"

"No, but I probably should be." Karina's eyes lingered on my face. "Simon told me you like to fly places by yourself."

"He did?" I was embarrassed, yet flattered, that I'd been the subject of office gossip. I hadn't realized Simon and Karina spoke outside of work, and I felt a little jealous, as though Simon and I were Karina's children, vying for her affection.

"He said that time you guys had coffee, you were flying to Phoenix after," Karina said. "Do you do that a lot?"

I knew I had to tread carefully, so as not to alienate her. "Sometimes," I said.

"How often is sometimes?" Karina pressed, with the same cross-examining look she'd had while critiquing Morgan's vision board.

"Once a month or so."

Karina sucked some tea through her straw. "That's a lot. Why didn't you tell me?"

"I don't know," I said. "I was worried you'd think I was weird."

"Not at all. Solo travel is something I've always wished I could do."

I felt emboldened to confide in her further. "Stewart and I flew last weekend," I said. "The brewery wasn't in San Francisco. It was in Denver."

Karina's eyebrows rose. "How glamorous."

"And the week before, after we met at the club, we flew to Houston." My face grew hot as I realized I'd just admitted to having lied before, about going back to Stewart's place. Karina studied me across the table.

"What did you do in Houston?" she asked.

"Nothing. We flew back the next morning. We didn't even leave the airport."

Her nose crinkled, and I saw I'd lost her. "Isn't that kind of wasteful? Not to mention expensive?"

"All of life is wasteful."

"Don't planes use a lot of fuel?"

"The flights would run whether we took them or not," I said, wincing at how defensive I sounded. "Anyway, he paid for it. It seemed like something fun to do on a date." I was channeling Dave now, when he'd proposed making an app for people to fly recreationally, though I still loathed his idea.

Karina shook her head, unconvinced. "I wish I was as brave as you. Whenever I think about flying, I just imagine all the things that could go wrong."

I saw that Karina's questions about my flying habits had been rooted in envy rather than judgment. I was free to fly wherever I wanted, while her fear kept her grounded, her options limited. I wished I could help her, but I worried I'd do more harm than good.

Karina offered me a ride home, and for once, I accepted. When we arrived, she asked if she could see my room.

"Maybe another night," I said. "I need to clean."

"Okay. I have something for you." She hopped out and retrieved an object from her trunk: a small, box-shaped object from which a cord dangled.

"It's a lamp that treats seasonal affective disorder," she said. "You mentioned your room doesn't get much light."

I'd never claimed to suffer from SAD, but I was moved by the gesture of this useless gift. I couldn't remember ever being given a present by a friend. Back in my cube, I plugged the lamp into my power strip. It shone blindingly, like a false sun. I was disturbed by its brightness but felt uneasy stashing it in the closet, as it seemed wrong to possess the lamp, yet not allow it to shine as it was meant to. I compromised by turning its bright face to the wall.

15 I'd hoped I was free of Dave, but on Wednesday night he texted me, asking how my week was going. His message gave me a slimy feeling, as though a tentacle of need were reaching through my phone and wrapping around my wrist.

I was in my cube watching an animation of the crash of Helios Flight 522, which had become a ghost plane after the cabin failed to pressurize. The same type of incident had claimed the life of my fake suitor's namesake, Payne Stewart, though in Stewart's case the plane involved was a Learjet 35, a small, pointy-nosed fellow to whom I felt little attraction. The Helios flight involved a 737-300 traveling from Cyprus to Prague, with a stopover in Athens. Due to a simple mistake—the flight crew's failure to switch the pressurization system to "auto" prior to takeoff—the cabin's pressure decreased as the plane climbed. The passengers, along with most of the crew, passed out from hypoxia. Still conscious was a flight attendant named Andreas Prodromou, an athletic young man who'd accessed an oxygen supply at the rear of the plane. Prodromou entered the cockpit and assumed the controls, waving to the fighter jets that had been scrambled to investigate the silent plane, but by that point the 737 had flown seventy minutes on autopilot, and his fuel was exhausted. The left engine flamed out, and the plane began his descent. It was possible the passengers were still alive at that point—that, as oxygen returned to their brains, they had regained consciousness, only to experience the last terrifying moments before impact.

To be the sole conscious human on board a ghost plane was my ideal scenario. The video showed an animation of the plane cruising serenely above the Greek islands. Exhaust plumed from his tail cone, his signal lights blinking as though nothing were amiss. He flew on, though no pilot controlled him. I admired any plane who asserted his independence, shirking the airlines' dictates and forging his own path across the sky.

Through my Helios-induced haze, I heard my phone chime again. I hadn't responded to his first text, so Dave had followed up with a photo of the salmon filet he'd made for dinner: a rectangle of pink flesh on a white plate, alongside an overcooked clump of leafy greens. It seemed oddly aggressive to send a fish pic to a vegetarian, unless he'd simply forgotten I didn't eat meat, which was likely. I could practically smell the salmon corpse through my phone. I added a "thumbs-up" reaction to the photo, to be polite, though in my heart I meant it sarcastically. *Dinner tomorrow?* he added, and I ignored the invitation, hoping he'd take the hint and leave me alone.

I had no interest in spending time with Dave if he wasn't paying for me to fly, and I also knew it would be wrong to continue flying with him, having manipulated his free will and placed him in mortal peril. Dave was clearly unwell, chasing ghosts from his past, trying to make sense of how his life had arrived at this point. But this compulsion to exca-vate was part of the problem. It fed into his pathological self-absorption, the root, probably, of why Mike and Michelle had come to despise him. I felt sympathy for Dave, and regretted having placed him on my vision board, which seemed to have eroded the last load-bearing column of dignity within him.

I looked up at my board now and decided to revise it, so the universe would stop pushing Dave in my direction. I peeled off his photo, leaving behind a strip of white residue where the glue refused to part with the paper, and burned it in the sink. The smoke alarm didn't go off, which was worri-some.

This gesture didn't seem to work, however. On Friday, while I was watching planes land through the windows of the Marriott lounge—I'd been too embarrassed to return to the Elephant Bar since Jose had rejected me—Dave texted me a photo of himself on board a plane, his head framed by the seatback. *Wish you were here,* read the text accompanying it, along with a winking smiley face. In spite of my resolve to cut ties with Dave, I was jealous he was flying while I re-mained grounded. I asked where he was going, and he told me he was spending the weekend in LA with his daughter. *Let's get dinner when I'm back,* he wrote, to which I didn't bother responding. The man was obsessed with dinner.

Saturday night, Karina invited me out for drinks at the Olive Garden with her and Anthony. When I arrived, I found

Karina alone at the bar, as Anthony was still finishing his shift at the pizza place. She asked if there'd been any new developments with Stewart, and I told her about the plane selfie he'd sent.

Karina laughed. "What's his deal? It sounds like he has some kind of plane fetish."

I sipped my rum and Coke, disguising my hurt feelings. I figured she'd describe my relationship to planes as a fetish, when it was so much more than that—a reciprocal connection with planes, a sacred bond we'd shared since I was born.

"I guess he's lonely," I said.

"I thought you ended it." Karina squeezed a lemon wedge into her cocktail, which was the color of Windex.

"I told him we can't fly together anymore, but now he keeps asking me to have dinner with him."

"You should tell him you're not interested, straight up," Karina said. "And if he keeps bugging you after that, block him."

I knew she was right, but I was afraid to reject Dave, as I still hoped he'd secure me a raise. Also, I realized that on some level, I liked the attention. I'd never been pursued by another person, and even though I wasn't interested in dating Dave, I enjoyed holding a measure of power over him.

Karina asked if she could see the photo "Stewart" had sent. "I'm dying to know what this freak looks like," she said.

I was reaching for my phone when I remembered that I couldn't show Karina the picture. I'd invested so thoroughly in the lie, I had begun to see Stewart as a separate entity from Dave. I told her I'd already deleted it.

Anthony entered, wearing a black denim jacket over a white T-shirt stained with tomato sauce. He came up behind Karina, wrapping his arms around her and kissing her cheek. She pushed him away, laughing.

"You smell like pizza," she said. "And weed. Did you smoke in my car? You better have opened a window this time."

Anthony grinned. "What's up, Lindy?" he said. He hugged me, and I lingered in his embrace, comforted by the sturdiness of his arms and the clear boundaries of our friendship. His hugs were muscular and fearless, while Dave's involved only glancing contact, as though he were afraid to commit to the gesture.

"Hey, Mindy," Anthony said, addressing the bartender. "Can I get a Heineken, please?" I wondered if the bartender's name was actually Amanda, or something else that Anthony had converted into an affectionate nickname, as he'd done with my name. If so, she didn't seem to mind, smiling at him in a familiar way. I understood why Karina had questioned Anthony's faithfulness in the past, as he couldn't seem to help flirting with everyone.

I asked Anthony how his T-shirt business was going.

"It's about to blow up," Anthony said. "That's just one of my income streams, though. It's important to diversify. Do you have any investments?" I shook my head. "I know I've told you this before, but you gotta get in on crypto. It's going through the roof."

I watched Mindy remove glasses from the dishwasher and set them on a towel to dry.

"Did you ask her?" Anthony said to Karina.

"No," Karina said quickly. "Now's not a good time."

Their furtive exchange hinted at a scandalous proposal, and I feared they wanted to ask me to join their lovemaking. While I would have been flattered to be viewed as an object of sexual gratification, I'd have to decline, as the prospect held no pleasure for me, only vast potential for discomfort and humiliation.

"What is it?" I asked, unable to bear the suspense.

Karina turned to me, resting her elbow on the bar. "I told Anthony what we talked about at the mall. How you fly for fun and know all this stuff about planes . . ." She trailed off, looking at Anthony.

"We were thinking maybe you could help Karina get over her fear," Anthony said. He pulled out his stool to form a triangle with ours. "Maybe you two could take a practice flight."

My stomach churned with adrenaline at the prospect of flying with Karina, though I knew I couldn't allow it to happen. I'd be putting her life at risk, as well as exposing the most private aspects of my life to unwanted scrutiny.

"But only if you want to," Karina added, perhaps having noticed the stricken look on my face. "I wouldn't want to pressure you, especially right after some weird guy was making you fly with him."

"Like a flight coach," I said, stalling for time. This was a job I'd once considered, going so far as to post a Craigslist ad offering my services. But in the end, I decided it would be unethical, given my proclivities, and no one had responded

to my ad anyway aside from some bots advertising penis en-
largement pills.

"Exactly," Anthony said. "A flight coach. I like that. I'll pay
for the tickets, obviously."

"We wouldn't have to fly right away," Karina said, placing
a hand on Anthony's thigh. "We could work up to it."

"I thought you never wanted to fly again," I said.

"Well, of course I don't *want* to," Karina said. "But I'm
sick of being held back by fear. It would be horrible to miss
out on the perfect honeymoon just because I'm so fucked
up." Her eyes filled with tears.

Anthony wrapped his arm around her shoulders. "You
aren't fucked up, baby. We just want to show you there's
nothing to be scared of. Right, Lindy?"

"That's right," I said, feeling like a fraud. That afternoon,
I'd gorged on crash animations until the air of my cube felt
charged, hotboxing catastrophe as Anthony had hotboxed
Karina's car with cannabis. I was the last person they should
trust when it came to flying. My fate could manifest on any
flight, especially with the added boost of my vision board.
Still, Karina's fear was so deeply rooted, it seemed unlikely
she'd want to go through with a practice flight. I reasoned
there was no harm in teaching her about the joys of flying
while we remained safely grounded. "I'm happy to help, if I
can," I said.

"Hell yeah," Anthony said.

Karina thanked me, though I saw fear in her eyes, and I
hoped she wasn't doing this only because Anthony was pressuring her. She excused herself to the restroom. As Anthony

sipped his beer, I observed his hands, which were broader than Dave's, his fingers stubbier. Dave's fingers were long and thin, like the rest of him.

"This means a lot to us, Lindy," Anthony said. "I offered to take a flight with her, but she said it would be too much pressure. She'll be more comfortable doing it with you. She looks up to you."

"She does?" It seemed so improbable that I wondered if he was making fun of me.

"Totally. She's always saying how funny you are. How you're so unique, and you don't care what other people think of you."

I was surprised to hear this, as I'd always assumed our friendship was imbalanced, Karina's kindness to me an act of charity. When she returned, we moved on to other subjects. The wedding's guest list, and whether to invite Ryan, the club promoter, who Karina still thought was a jerk. The house on Kauai, which Anthony showed me pictures of on his phone. A conflict Karina had been having with Judy, who only wanted to see Karina on weeknights; Karina suspected Judy reserved the weekends for her superior college friends. We ordered breadsticks, which were pleasantly aerodynamic, their slick exterior pebbled with parmesan. All the while, I remained uneasy about having agreed to be Karina's flight coach. I hoped it would turn out to be one of those schemes I'd heard people concocted over drinks, then never followed through with.

The next morning, however, Karina messaged me, asking when we could start. I saw she was serious about overcoming her fear, and it was true that my skill set aligned perfectly with her need. If I were in possession of brawny muscles and a pickup truck, I'd be happy to help a friend move. By the same token, I would gladly tutor Karina in the joys of commercial flight. We arranged for her to come over that afternoon, after her eyebrow appointment. I spent the morning preparing the cube, concealing my most private items at the back of my closet, and clearing my browser history of all the disturbing simulations I'd watched in recent weeks.

I met Karina outside the garage. "The lady overthreaded them," she said, gesturing to her eyebrows. "Do I look like a freak?"

"Not at all," I said, though the arches did look a bit thin. I was still nervous about showing Karina my room, so I proposed we start at the beach, where I could give her a tour of the sky. We walked west on Taraval, passing roadwork equipment that lay dormant on the Lord's day. Many people were out, walking dogs and pushing strollers, and I was proud that for once, I, too, had a companion. We crossed the Great Highway and climbed a sand dune.

"We can sit here," I said, indicating the scrubby vegetation crowning the dune. Karina was reluctant, as she was wearing white pants. I lay down my denim jacket, and she lowered herself onto it, while I sat directly on the scrub. It was windy, and I shivered without my jacket, but I'd gladly suffer the cold on behalf of Karina's outfit.

"I always thought Ocean Beach was a dumb name," Karina said.

"It is a bit redundant," I said, though I'd always liked the name, which had an honest ring to it. I pointed out the cloud formations above, along with some diffuse spreading contrails that created a plaid-like pattern. After a few minutes, a plane approached from the right, heading south at perhaps six thousand feet.

"That plane must be coming in for a landing at SFO," I said. I brought out my phone and showed her the icons of planes on my flight-tracking app. Thousands of yellow plane-shaped symbols inched their way across the continent. Karina peered at the map with grudging curiosity.

"There's so many," she said.

"A hundred thousand flights a day, every day, worldwide," I said proudly, though I'd had nothing to do with it.

I zoomed in on our location. "Looks like that plane is a 787-9 Dreamliner, flying in from London." The Dreamliner passed above us with an air of nonchalance, his engines roaring their greeting. We watched his form diminish as he proceeded down the coastline.

I asked Karina when her fear of flying had started, and she was quiet for a moment, considering.

"It must have started with my mom," she said. "When I was a kid, we'd fly to São Paulo once a year, to spend Christmas with her family. She hated going there. On the way to the airport, she'd say she hoped the plane would crash, to spare her the misery. It freaked me out. It seemed like tempting fate, saying stuff like that."

"She doesn't like her family?"

"She felt like a disappointment to them. They paid for her to go to UC Berkeley, hoping she'd become a doctor or a lawyer, and instead she got knocked up within two months."

"With you."

Karina nodded. She explained how her parents had met at a house party when they were freshmen. They'd stayed together for a few years after she was born, and then her dad had moved back to Virginia, where he was from. He'd since remarried and had two sons.

"They're his real family," she said. "I was just a mistake he made when he was young."

"Don't say that," I said. "You're not a mistake."

"Thanks, but I literally was."

Below us, on the flat part of the sand, a young couple was attempting a picnic. The wind blew up their blanket, and they scrambled to pin down its corners with various objects—beer bottles, the woman's *New Yorker* tote. They seemed determined to persist with their romantic excursion, though their hummus and brie were no doubt seasoned with sand.

"Idiots," Karina said with affection.

"Do you still talk to your dad?" I asked.

"Once in a while. I used to go visit them in Virginia, but it was always super awkward. Like I was a guest they had to be polite around. So I stopped bothering, around eight years ago. That was the last time I flew, actually."

Karina lay back on my jacket, propping her elbows behind her. Another wide-body plane passed above us, this one heading north, his underbelly lit golden by the setting sun. "Did you fly much as a kid?" she asked me, once the plane had passed.

"Not as much as I'd have liked," I said. And then, perhaps because she'd told me about her dad, I recounted going plane-spotting with mine. "We would make up stories about the planes and their adventures," I said.

"That's cute," Karina said. "You were close with him, then?"

I nodded.

"It must have been hard to lose him." I was touched she remembered. I'd mentioned my dad's death during one of our first happy hours, though I hadn't told her the details. A knot of grief formed in my throat, which surprised me. I normally tried not to think about the hospice room in which he'd spent his last days, a building in a corporate park, through whose windows I'd scan the sky. I took comfort from the planes I saw flying over the row of buildings across the highway, coming in for landings at John Wayne.

"It's just one of those things, I guess," I told Karina now. I wasn't sure what I meant by this, but Karina murmured as if I'd said something profound. On the sand below us, the couple gave up, putting their food back into the basket. The clouds had thickened, obscuring the sun. The wind grew sharper, and Karina zipped up her jacket, while my own jacket remained imprisoned beneath her shapely hips. I suggested we head back to the garage, where I could make us a dinner of ramen.

As we approached my corner, I told her we'd have to keep

it low-key. "My landlords don't like me having guests. If we run into them, let's say we're doing a work project."

Karina laughed. "It'll be like when I used to have to sneak into Celia's basement."

I cracked the side door of the garage to confirm Mrs. Chen wasn't doing laundry before ushering Karina to my cube. She surveyed the space, her lips pressed together. "It's cozy," she said. She pulled back the mirrored door of my closet and inspected its contents. I was glad I'd prepared the cube for her visit, anticipating her nosiness. "You're such a minimalist. My crap would fill this whole room."

"Do you want a Rockstar lemonade?" I said, opening the door of the mini-fridge and exhibiting its wares. "Or a string cheese?"

"No thanks." She paused. "Did you steal those Rockstars from the break room?"

"I always take my cut after Christa makes her snack run."

"Good for you. Fuck that place."

We sat on the narrow strip of floor not occupied by my bed. I heated water in my electric kettle and poured it into two ramen cylinders from 7-Eleven. I turned on the SAD lamp Karina had given me and turned off the overhead light, so that it felt like we were eating beside a violently bright campfire. Karina inspected my wall. "What's the map about?"

"It shows all the routes I've flown since I moved here," I said.

"You really do fly a lot."

Her gaze drifted to my vision board. "It looks different from when you showed it to us." She kneeled on my bed, training the beam of her phone's flashlight on the board. "What's missing here?" she said, running her fingers over the blank patch. "Wait, I remember. It was Dave Kinney!"

I had to think quickly. "You said he was a loser, so I figured I shouldn't keep him on my board."

Karina chuckled. "That's true. He's such a loser." She climbed down from my bed. "You can't change your vision mid-quarter, though. Once you do the ceremony, it's baked in."

I wasn't sure where she was getting these rules from, but I promised to be more careful next time. When we'd finished eating, I showed her my piece of 737, which I'd washed thoroughly in anticipation of its unveiling to my guest.

"This object is said to be part of a 737's fuselage," I said, placing the chunk on the floor between us. "I bought it on eBay a few years back. I carry it with me everywhere. Sort of like a good luck charm."

Karina held the chunk in her palm. She ran her thumb along its edges, which I'd worn down over years of rubbing. "It's so smooth," she said. I felt a twinge of pleasure, as though the shard were an extension of my body.

"Do you mind if I lie down for a minute?" she said, setting the chunk back on the floor. "I'm bloated from all that sodium."

"Of course."

I cleaned up our dinner, pouring the remnants of broth down the sink drain. When I returned to the room, Karina's eyes were closed. I nudged her shoulder gently.

"Just a few more minutes," she murmured.

I'd promised Mrs. Chen I wouldn't have an overnight guest, but I reasoned that, if my transgression were discovered, I could say we'd accidentally fallen asleep while working on a project, which was true enough. I turned off the SAD lamp and groped my way into bed. I wouldn't dare to dislodge Karina's head from the only pillow I owned, so I balled up my jacket and propped it under my head, stretching my body alongside hers. At one point in the night, I woke to find Karina's arm thrown across my torso, as though I were her stuffed animal.

16 When my alarm went off the next morning, Karina was gone. I had a hazy memory of her getting up and collecting her things. At Acuity, I found her in good spirits. "Sorry I crashed out like that," she said at lunch. "Your room is perfect for sleeping. Like a cave."

I asked when she'd left, and she said around 3:00 A.M. Anthony had been worried, but luckily, he'd still been up playing video games when she got home. I'd assumed Karina would need a break after our first lesson, and indeed when I asked what she was doing that evening, she said she had some things to take care of, with a caginess that reminded me of my former reticence when asked about my plans after work. I wouldn't pressure her. In fact, I hoped her fear would persist, delaying our practice flight to an unspecified future moment that would never arrive.

But at lunch on Tuesday, she jabbed my shoulder playfully and said, "So what's our next lesson, coach?"

I suggested we visit the airport. We rode BART there, on my insistence, so Karina wouldn't have to park her car in the expensive short-term lot, and because I felt that taking public transportation was essential to the magic of the experience. In the final leg, after departing the San Bruno station, we traveled through a tunnel, the train's wheels making a slicing sound like blades on ice. The train emerged into sunlight, and we were plunged into the airport's domain, with a view of the runways through the window. Planes emblazoned with the United logo idled at the gates of International Terminal G. One girthy fellow, likely an A350, pulled back from his gate.

I led Karina beyond the BART turnstiles and onto the AirTrain platform. Through the station window, I gestured to the A350 as he ambled around the bend to take his place in the lineup. I was able to glimpse his tail number, N15969, which I inputted into my flight-tracking app.

"That plane is currently bound for Singapore," I said.

"How long is that flight?"

"Sixteen and a half hours."

Karina winced. "That's brutal."

I showed her N15969's recent flight schedule. "Looks like he landed from Singapore two hours ago, and now he's heading back." I realized I'd slipped up, referring to planes with male pronouns. Though it was correct to do so, given their obvious gender, I feared Karina would find it strange.

But instead, she smiled. "He's a busy boy," she said.

The Red Line train pulled up, and we boarded an already crowded car. We stood facing the window, our hands gripping the greasy pole, while I narrated the sights out the window. I could have ridden the Red Line for hours, but after we'd completed only one revolution, Karina said she felt sick from the fumes, and we made our way back to the city.

On Thursday, I brought Karina to the Elephant Bar, in lieu of our usual sushi. I felt apprehensive as we approached the host stand; it was the first time I'd returned since the night Jose had spurned me. He looked up from his screen and smiled when he saw me with Karina. I was no longer waiting for my friend. My friend was here, in the flesh, having existed all along.

"Two?" Jose said.

"Yes," I said. "A booth by the window, if possible."

I felt a sense of triumph as Jose led us across the bustling restaurant floor, showing us to a booth with superior runway views. He handed us menus and winked at me before returning to his podium. Through the window, we watched a large plane, perhaps a Triple Seven, descend from the east. The plane was wrapped in the insignia of Eva Air, a Taiwanese airline, his tail painted green. Karina's eyes widened as he drew close to the water.

"Oh, god," Karina said. "They're gonna miss the runway."

But just when it seemed the plane would skid into the bay, his wheels touched down on the finger of land, throwing up a little puff of dust. Karina exhaled. Another plane, marked with the Air France logo, was already making his descent, in the constant procession of landings into Runway 28R.

"See, Karina?" I said. "Planes take off and land here all day, every day, without incident." She nodded, her gaze still trained on the runway. As she continued to watch planes touch down, Karina's posture relaxed, and I observed in her face an expression of awe rather than fear. I was pleased that our coaching sessions seemed to have sanded down the edges of her phobia.

When the server approached, Karina ordered a salad, while I stuck to my usual fries and a Diet Coke. I checked my phone and found a missed call from Dave, along with a text: *Hey Linda. Can we talk?* He'd messaged me a few times since his return from LA, asking when we could have dinner, but I'd barely noticed, as I'd been focused on coaching Karina. The phone call seemed like a disturbing escalation.

"Everything okay?" Karina said. I looked up to find her watching me.

"Stewart wants to talk."

She groaned. "Just block him and be done with it."

"I feel bad for him. He seems desperate."

"It's his own fault, for being a freak."

I longed to tell Karina that Stewart was actually Dave. His behavior was growing increasingly erratic, and I figured she'd know how to defuse the situation. But I'd promised Dave I wouldn't reveal our secret, and I prided myself on being a person of my word. I returned my phone to my bag, leaving his text unanswered.

When our check came, Karina insisted on paying. "I'm feeling good about this," she said, as she entered the tip. "Should we take a flight this weekend?"

"If you want to," I said, with a rush of excitement and foreboding. "Are you sure you're ready?"

"Let's do it before I think about it too much. How's Saturday?"

I told her Saturday was great, attempting to conceal my

inner turmoil. It had been easy to coach Karina when our practice flight remained an abstraction, but now I had to contend with what I might be drawing her into without her consent. I knew I should tell her everything, so she could decide if she wanted to risk flying with me, but I didn't want to introduce a new element of fear that might spoil the progress she'd made. I also worried that if I revealed myself now, she'd deem me a freak, placing me in the same depraved bucket as "Stewart," and want nothing more to do with me.

Karina drove me back to my cube. Fog had gathered over the west side of the city. As we proceeded down Taraval, we moved in and out of denser patches, so that at some points, we could see only a few feet ahead. My phone buzzed with another text from Dave: *I'm outside your place. Five minutes. That's all I ask.*

My chest seized with panic. "Maybe we should go to the beach," I said.

"Now?" Karina said. "It's freezing."

It was too late. As we neared my corner, the fog parted, revealing a white Prius parked at the curb. Dave stood at the side door of the garage, into which he'd once seen me flee.

Karina squinted over the wheel. "Is that . . . Dave Kinney?"

"I wonder what he's doing here," I said, with a drowning feeling.

"Let's find out."

We emerged from the Honda. Dave's face lit up when he saw me. Then he noticed Karina, and his expression shifted into uncertainty.

"Oh hey," he said. "I was looking for a dumpling spot. Do you know of any around here?"

"You could use Yelp," Karina said, in the cool way one might address a stranger who was in the midst of a mental health crisis.

"There's one down that way," I said, gesturing toward the place we had gone to before our flight to Denver, though it was surely closed at this hour.

"Thanks." He walked to the driver's side of his car, where he lingered a moment. I feared he was about to say something that would expose us. "Good night, then" was all he said in the end.

We watched his Prius take a left at the next intersection, rather than continuing to the dumpling place he'd claimed to be seeking. "Okay, Linda," Karina said. "What's going on?"

"What do you mean?" I said, though I knew it was hopeless.

"You're telling me it's a coincidence that Dave was standing in front of your door? He was obviously waiting for you."

I led Karina into my cube, where I sat on my bed and took a deep breath. "I might have gotten myself into something," I said.

Karina's eyes scanned my vision board, with its blank patch where Dave's picture had been. I watched the pieces click into place in her mind. "Oh my god. There's no 'Stewart,' is there? It was Dave all along! That's why you took him off your board."

At last, I told her everything: How we'd run into each

other at the club, and in his intoxicated state, Dave agreed to fly to Houston with me. How we'd fooled around on the plane—this part, I took care to phrase with delicacy—and after, he'd said the experience was an erotic high point of his life and invited me to fly with him again. How I'd tried to break it off but was afraid to reject him outright, as I didn't know how he would react.

"This is crazy," Karina said, pacing the room. "Why didn't you tell me before?"

"We agreed to keep it between us."

"So he groped you on a plane, then pressured you to keep it secret after. That's so messed up. I bet you could sue Acuity."

"I don't want to do that," I said, horrified by the prospect of my secrets exposed in the civil court system. "He only came to the club that night because I put him on my vision board."

"That's a stretch, Linda." She paused at the corner of my room. "God, I'm so sick of men like him. They think the world's their playground. They do whatever they want, no matter who it hurts. Worst of all, they turn it around to make us think it's *our* fault. And now he's harassing you. Stalking you."

"You're right," I said, my own anger rising.

"You want me to call him? I'll set him straight."

"No, I just want to move on," I said. "I'm afraid I'll lose my job."

Karina put her hand on my shoulder. "That wouldn't happen. You're the victim here."

"Promise you won't tell anyone."

"I won't. Not if you don't want me to."

"Not even Anthony."

She looked disappointed. "Okay. Although he'd really get a kick out of this."

It was 11:00 P.M. when Karina went home. I felt keyed up, high off her outrage. I left the garage and walked toward the ocean, salty air filming my arms. I'd forgotten a jacket, but I barely noticed the cold. I called Dave, and he apologized for showing up at my place.

"I was worried about you, since I hadn't heard back from you all week," he said.

"You weren't worried," I said. "You couldn't stand being ignored, so you resorted to stalking me." I passed an elderly man walking a dog, and felt self-conscious about what I'd said while in his earshot.

"That's a little dramatic, isn't it?" Dave said. "I needed to talk to you, Linda, and you weren't answering my texts. I wondered if you were feeling weird about our trip to Denver."

"You wanted to make sure I kept my mouth shut," I said.

"That's not what I meant."

"Well, I hope you're happy, because now Karina knows everything."

Dave was quiet for a moment. "You told her?"

"I had to. It was obvious something was going on."

"Oh well. I suppose it was bound to happen."

I climbed the crest of vegetation that rose up to the Great Highway. "I should never have put you on my vision board," I said.

Dave groaned. "I don't want to hear any more about the fucking vision boards. They're total nonsense, like astrology or tarot cards. It's always amazed me how many otherwise intelligent women buy into that crap."

Not only was he insulting me; he was disparaging the fine women of the VBB. I felt an urge to wound him in return. "I don't want to be your girlfriend," I said.

He laughed. "Who said anything about that? I thought we were friends. It's been nice to have someone to talk to."

"We're not friends," I said. "I was using you for free flights, but it was more trouble than it was worth. Leave me alone or I'll tell Christa everything." I couldn't believe I'd threatened him. I hung up, ashamed, before he could respond.

I mounted the same dune Karina and I had sat on last Sunday. The moon shimmered over the ocean, silvering the black waves. The sky was patched with clouds, and in the clear spots I saw stars and the signal lights of a plane, as though placed there just for me, a message of fortitude. I breathed deeply, reminding myself that better days lay ahead. I was about to take a flight with my best friend, the most intimate act two people could engage in. I watched the red and green lights blink through a clear patch before disappearing behind the clouds. I lay on my back in the scrub, waiting for another plane to appear, but minutes passed, and only the fixed stars remained.

# 17

On my wellness break the next day, I checked my phone and saw Anthony had forwarded a flight confirmation email. Karina and I would depart for Salt Lake City at 10:35 A.M. Saturday. We'd enjoy a leisurely lunch at SLC, then fly back to SFO three hours later. I offered to reimburse him for my ticket, but Anthony replied: *Naw. My treat* ☺. Guilt cycled through me as I bobbed gently on the yoga ball. His gratitude, and Karina's, was misplaced. I was getting more from the arrangement than they knew, though I planned to refrain from my usual in-flight activities when Karina and I were together. I would fly in a strictly professional capacity, ignoring any romantic overtures from the planes, with a focus on delivering her safely back to SFO.

At lunch, Karina asked if she could spend the night in my cube, so we could wake up and set off together for the airport. She said it would be fun, like a sleepover, "like when we were kids," and I agreed it sounded fun, without admitting I'd enjoyed few such experiences in my youth. She'd mentioned Anthony would be out late, selling T-shirts at a show in Oakland. Though she proposed the sleepover in a light-hearted manner, I knew she was afraid to spend the night alone, obsessing over everything that could go wrong with our flight. When we returned to our terminals, I saw she'd brought a backpack, presumably filled with items she'd need for an overnight stay. She'd clearly assumed I would say yes to the sleepover, and I was pleased by how comfortable we'd grown with each other, to the point where Karina saw my home as an extension of her own.

After work we took the bus to my neighborhood, as Anthony was using the Honda to transport shirts to the concert. Karina proposed we get our nails done, wanting a fresh look to celebrate her return to flying. We went to a salon a few blocks down Taraval and requested matching hot-pink gel manicures. As we sat in the spa chairs, I recounted my phone conversation with Dave the night before, concluding with my threat to tell Christa about our affair.

"Good," Karina said, holding her hand steady while the nail tech chipped off her old gel polish. "I hope you made him sweat."

"I wouldn't go through with it," I said. I winced as my nail tech pushed back my overgrown cuticles. I hadn't gotten a professional manicure in twelve years, not since my mom and I had our nails done prior to my flight attendant interview.

"Well, hopefully it scares him enough that he won't try that shit with anyone else," Karina said.

This seemed unlikely, though I'd been surprised by Dave's actions before.

Back in my cube, Karina eyed me in the overhead light and offered to trim the bleached ends from my hair. I conceded it was time, as my grown-out dye job was starting to look ridiculous. I sat on the closed toilet while Karina gave me a haircut using the scissors with which I'd cut out images for my vision board. We then took turns showering. Karina emerged from the bathroom wearing a silk pajama set. She'd brought her own pillow, too, cloaked in a silk pillowcase, which I was glad for, as it meant I wouldn't have to rest my head on a balled-up jacket again.

We lay beside each other in the glow of the SAD lamp. "How are you feeling about tomorrow?" I asked.

Karina gazed up at my flight map. "There's something I haven't told you," she said, "because I know it'll sound crazy."

I was intrigued. "Anything you say will remain in the cube."

"I've done some bad things in the past," she said. "Sometimes I think a plane crash is how God will punish me, since it's my greatest fear."

She'd said cryptic things before about deserving punishment, but I hadn't realized her guilt was directly connected to her fear of flying. "What kinds of things have you done?" I dared to ask.

"So much shit. I used to steal from my mom. I cheated on every boyfriend I had before Anthony. I'm vain, and selfish, and a gossip."

"Everyone does stuff like that."

She paused. "Worse things, too," she said softly. "Things I don't even want to talk about."

I was curious but feared that if I probed too forcefully, Karina might respond by probing me. I wasn't prepared to reveal my own secrets, especially the night before we were set to fly. "Whatever you did, it doesn't mean you're going to be in a plane crash," I said, though I wasn't sure I believed this. "The two things aren't related."

"Yeah, but what if they are?" Karina said, rolling over to face me, her minty breath warm on my cheek. "I've had this nightmare, ever since I was a kid, that I was on a plane that was going down. I always wake up right before we hit the ground."

"I've had that dream, too," I said. I didn't add that for me, the dream had an erotic component. I always woke up slick with arousal.

"What do you think it means?"

I had my own theories, ones it would be unwise to share with her. "I'm sure it's a common dream," I said. "Our minds fixate on things that scare us."

"I suppose." She didn't sound convinced, and indeed, neither was I.

Karina lapsed into silence, her legs twitching as she fell asleep. She threw an arm across my torso, as she'd done the last time she slept over. I lay awake, haunted by what she had told me. Eventually, I extricated myself from her arm and ventured into the outer garage, where I sat among the Chens' dusty boxes. On my phone, I looked up the first plane we'd fly on tomorrow. His name was N549UW, an A319 I'd never been with before, according to my flight notes. He was currently flying from SLC to Austin, where he'd spend the night, then fly to SFO in the morning. I grew aroused, in spite of myself, as I watched the icon representing N549UW creep southeast on my flight-tracking app. Karina feared it was her fate to die in a plane crash, and selfishly, this made the prospect of flying with her more enticing. Perhaps our fates were linked. Perhaps, all my life, I'd been waiting for this final piece to click into place.

I paced the garage until sunrise, debating whether I should tell Karina the truth. I went out to buy coffee and muffins and brought our breakfast back to the cube, where she was stirring in bed. I turned on the SAD lamp, flooding the cube with false sunlight.

"Today's the big day," I said, affecting optimism, though my conscience weighed heavy upon me.

"Yep," she said, sitting up and accepting one of the cups of coffee.

I asked how she'd slept, vowing that if she said she'd had the dream again, I would call off our flight. But Karina reported that she'd slept soundly, seeming unaware of my absence from the bed. "It was nice not to fight with Anthony for the covers," she said.

Karina dressed herself in clothes from her backpack: jeans and a pink hooded sweatshirt with a design on the front of two dogs riding skateboards. She explained that she wanted to wear one of Anthony's designs for good luck. We emerged from the garage to find the Honda idling at the corner. Anthony was punctual for once.

"Hey, girls," he said as we piled in. "Did you have a nice sleepover?"

"Linda's room is so nice," Karina said. "It's like a sensory deprivation tank."

On the drive, Karina and Anthony chatted about the show he'd gone to, while I brooded in the back seat. There was still time to call off our flight. Short of disaster, I would consider any minor incident, any brief stint of turbulence, to be my fault, the result of years of stewing on my destiny. I'd resolved not to touch myself on board the planes, but I feared I'd be unable to conceal my arousal in the event of turbulence. I would humiliate myself, as I'd done during my flight attendant training. My behavior would disturb Karina, further entrenching her fear and ruining our friendship. Still, I could think of no reasonable excuse not to fly at this late juncture. To refuse to fly with her now, after so much buildup, would constitute another form of betrayal.

We arrived at the departures level of Terminal 3. Anthony stepped out of the car, saying he'd return in the evening to pick us up. He kissed Karina on the lips, then brought me in for a hug.

"Thanks again for doing this, Lindy," he said, his mouth close to my ear. "You're a good friend."

I mumbled that it was no problem, feeling like a criminal. I was aware my guilt was hypocritical, as I'd long been in the habit of placing all manner of strangers, as well as Dave, in mortal peril by flying with them. I'd reasoned that, when the time came, it would be all of our fates to die together. But it was different with Karina, whom I'd persuaded to fly against her better judgment, insisting there was nothing to fear.

Karina and I proceeded into the terminal and printed our boarding passes at a kiosk. As we waited in the security line,

I asked her, one more time, if she was sure she was ready. I hoped she'd express some lingering doubt, which would provide me an opening to postpone our flight.

But Karina smiled and said she was. "Your coaching really helped. I mean, obviously getting on the plane will be the real test, but I'm feeling okay about it. I'm excited, actually."

At every juncture, I prayed an external force would intervene, stopping us from boarding the plane. But for once, the process was maddeningly smooth. The TSA agent inspected our IDs and waved us on to the X-ray queue. Karina grumbled as she slipped off her sneakers.

"I forgot about the shoe thing," she said.

We waited for the machine to ingest our belongings—my backpack containing my wallet, phone, chunk of 737, empty water bottle; Karina's Louis Vuitton tote containing, I assumed, her cosmetic items, tissues, perhaps some high-protein snacks, among untold additional treasures. I went into the body scanner first, holding my arms above my head like a whimsical stick figure. Soon, we'd both emerged from the other side of the scanner and were disgorged into the secure sector.

"I can't believe I had to step on that filthy floor with only my socks on," Karina said, as we pushed deeper into the F gates.

"I'm sure they mop it a lot."

"I'll have to burn these socks when I get home." She said it cheerfully, though.

As we neared our gate, my dread deepened. I avoided eye contact with N549UW through the window, fearful of witnessing a spark of recognition in his windscreen. I felt I was leading Karina to the gallows. No amount of coaching could persuade her to embrace a crash, if fate willed it. I'd spent the week telling her such an event was basically impossible, while the most essential fact of my being was my belief that one day, it would happen to me. As we sat in the gate area, Karina noticed my distraction and asked if I was okay.

"I'm fine," I said. "It's almost time!" I tried to embody the persona of a flight coach, which I envisioned as a cross between a camp counselor and an AA sponsor.

On the jet bridge, I told myself the vision boards were probably nonsense, just as Dave had said. Planes were not sentient beings, but machines devoid of agency, emotions, and sexuality. Anyone would have told me this, had I dared to discuss my beliefs with them. But in my heart, I knew planes had souls, just as people did, and as I stepped across N549UW's threshold, an electric sensation coursed through my body. I felt the plane greet me, as if he'd known I was coming. It was the same feeling I'd had on board N92823, all those years ago. This plane wanted to marry me today. All he needed was a nudge, and that nudge was Karina.

We found our seats, 23D and E. Karina took the aisle, as we'd discussed in advance. The boarding process continued, passengers making their way to their seats and stowing their bags overhead. I willed myself to allow the moment to pass, for the safety instruction to commence and the plane to push back from the gate, at which point no further action would be possible. But then Karina laid her hand on mine.

"It's going to be okay, right?" she said. I looked into her

soft brown eyes and was flooded with love for the best friend I'd ever had.

"I should have told you before," I whispered. "Last night, when you said you've always thought it was your fate to die in a plane crash? I've always known it was my fate, too. And I think it will happen today."

She pulled her hand away. "What are you talking about?"

"This plane wants to marry me. I felt it the moment we boarded." As I said this, N549UW's hum intensified, as if confirming what I'd said.

"Linda. You're scaring me." She looked up the aisle. The procession of passengers had thinned, the boarding process almost complete.

"In another minute, they'll close the door, and it will be too late," I said. "If you want to live, you should go now, before it's too late."

She turned back to me with a frantic look. "I thought you said flying was safe."

"In most circumstances, it is. But I believe our fates are somehow interwoven." For a moment, I savored the possibility that she'd consent to dying on behalf of my eternal union with N549UW. "I can't imagine a better way to be married than on this flight with you," I said, my eyes tearing up. "You asked me to be your bridesmaid. Now I'm asking you to be mine." It felt so freeing, to finally tell the truth.

"You're fucked up, Linda," Karina said. She was already in the aisle, pushing her way to the front of the plane. She said something to the flight attendant, who nodded and guided her out the door. I feared she'd reported me—that she'd heard me say something suggesting I was a risk to the plane—but she must not have, as no one came to speak with me. Even after I'd betrayed her, Karina had remained loyal.

THE CHARGE I'D FELT UPON BOARDING N549UW VANISHED THE moment Karina stepped off the plane. My body flushed with the usual heat as we raced down the runway, but for once, I wasn't in the mood. I knew I'd done the right thing, though I had taken too long to do it. I'd saved Karina's life, but in the process, I'd destroyed our friendship, and probably scared her off flying for good. I was overcome with self-loathing and took no pleasure from the flight. When we landed, I hurried off N549UW. In the terminal, I toggled my phone off airplane mode and found no message from Karina, or anyone else.

Numbly, I located the gate for my return flight to SFO and lowered myself into a chair. The magical filter that had always overlaid airport terminals was stripped away, revealing my surroundings as ugly. The people around me were crude, coughing and blowing their noses and quarreling with each other. I snuck glances at their crotches, compressed into jeans or leggings, and imagined unwrapping them, the stink of their genitals rising into the confined air of the terminal. I despised their fleshy bodies, and my own. How superior planes were, sleek and elegant, strong yet supple, graceful in the sky. Planes emitted no objectionable odors, aside from gas fumes, which I huffed with pleasure. I'd been a fool to think a plane would ever want me.

I resolved to be good. If I believed flying with Karina brought danger to her, the same threat applied to anyone who flew on the same plane as me. I did not want to bring harm to others. I would live out my remaining days without flying. I'd live a celibate life, and maybe, one day, my friend would forgive me.

# PART III

18 Upon returning to my cube, I peeled my vision board and flight map from the wall and shoved them under my bed. I placed my chunk of 737 in the shoebox that housed my collection of flight safety cards. I knew I should destroy all the artifacts of my iniquity, but I couldn't bring myself to do this yet, and tucking them out of sight seemed a worthy first step on my road to redemption. I deleted my flight-tracking app, cleared my browser history, and deleted the images of planes I'd archived on my computer and phone. At 7-Eleven, I purchased a 49ers hat, which I planned to wear whenever I was outside, shielding the sky from my view. I'd lost my right to enjoy the sky's offerings. I could not even allow myself to contemplate the sun and the moon, much less the planes themselves and the contrails they etched.

Monday morning, I steeled myself as I entered Acuity. The terminals in the exterior row lay empty, and I saw that Karina had defected to the interior row. She sat next to Simon, who gave me a smug look as I proceeded to my terminal, while Karina's eyes remained fixed on her screen. I'd apologized over text, and asked for a chance to explain, but Karina hadn't replied. I was desperate to know what she was thinking, and whether there was a path to our reconciliation, however long and circuitous it might be. But Karina seemed intent on pretending I didn't exist. She arrived early and stayed late, so our paths never crossed in the stairwell. She remained at her terminal until I returned from lunch.

On Wednesday, I stayed seated at my usual lunchtime, waiting her out. Finally, at one-thirty, she went to the break room, and I followed her.

"Hey," I said. "Can we talk?"

"Not right now, Linda," she said, stooping to pull a container of yogurt from the back of the fridge.

"I just want to explain," I said, drawing near her. "I wasn't completely honest with you before, about my interest in planes. It goes a bit deeper than I let on."

"I'm sure it does."

"I want you to know that everything I told you about flying is true," I said. "It's perfectly safe, as long as you're not with me. I hope I didn't sabotage your progress."

"That's exactly what you did, Linda," she said, shutting the fridge door forcefully, though it was designed to prevent slamming and eased shut with a sigh. "Do you know how embarrassing it was to force my way off the plane? It was just what I was afraid would happen, and for what? Some sick joke?"

"It wasn't a joke," I said, appalled she would think this. "I was trying to protect you."

"Whatever. I don't want to hear any more about your obsession with planes, and your weird thing with . . ." She stopped herself before saying Dave's name. "You know."

"I understand," I said. "I'm sorry, Karina."

She leaned against the sink, facing me for the first time. For a moment, I hoped my apology had landed. "Anthony thinks you did it because you're jealous," she said.

"Jealous? Of what?"

"You can't stand that we're getting married, is that it? Because no one wants to marry a freak like you. So you figured you could at least stop me from going to Hawaii, because if you're miserable, everyone else should be, too."

"That's not true," I said. "I don't want to get married. Not to another person, at least."

"See? What the hell is that supposed to mean? You're fucking weird, Linda." She left, taking her yogurt with her.

I was hurt by what she'd said, and in the days after, I avoided her just as she avoided me. I tried to focus on moderating, but my attention was fragmented. Without Karina, and without flying, I had nothing to look forward to. I rode the bus to Acuity, the brim of the 49ers cap pulled low over my brow. I put in eight hours of work, then rode home, hatted again, to eat a dinner of ramen and string cheese in my cube. The first weekend, I left the garage only to do laundry. When I returned home from the laundromat, I peeled the gel polish from my nails, leaving the nail beds dull and flaky. The sight of the hot-pink shards on my bedspread filled me with sadness, as they belonged to an era in which Karina and I were still friends.

I was bored, but I didn't trust myself to go outside, beneath the sky's canopy, in which commercial jets cavorted, beckoning to me. I needed a hobby. I watched nature documentaries and live streams of zoo animals. My favorite was the koala cam, the koala a gray blur between leaves. I felt solidarity with the little marsupial, who was alone and mostly sedentary, like me.

Sunday night, I was watching the koala cam when Simon texted. This was unusual. My messages app showed we hadn't texted since a few days after our date at Peet's, when I'd sent him a link to Acuity's job site. Back then, I'd had everything, though I didn't appreciate my good fortune. Karina was my friend, and the power of my first vision board coursed at my back. Flying was a fun, sexy ritual, safely cordoned from my work life and relationships. I used to think Simon was a fool. Now I seized upon his text, which simply asked how I was doing. It was a sign I hadn't been cast out entirely from the village of humanity, to die in the forest, feasted on by wolves.

I told him I was okay, a little lonely, and Simon said he'd noticed Karina and I were "beefing."

*Did she say that?*

*No,* Simon replied. *But it's obvious. She won't tell me what happened.*

I knew Karina prided herself on her trustworthiness. Simon didn't share this quality, however, so anything I said to him would likely be relayed back to Karina. I sensed he was always looking for ways to ingratiate himself to her, though I could have told him his efforts were pointless. Even if she broke up with Anthony, she'd never stoop so low as to sleep with Simon.

*I miss her,* I wrote. *I hope one day, she'll forgive me.*

*Damn must have been pretty bad. Did you fuck Anthony?*

I laughed. *No,* I wrote. *Nothing like that.*

Simon asked if I wanted to see a lady getting railed by a horse. I said sure. He sent the video, which was about what I'd expected. It appeared he'd bootlegged the footage on a secret cellphone when it came across his Porn queue. This was a violation of our work contract, one of the only offenses our bosses seemed to care about, as I knew of at least two mods who'd been fired for this during my time at Acuity. I considered telling Simon to be careful but decided it was none of my business. I thanked him for the edifying content and returned to the koala cam. The blotch of gray I'd thought was the koala turned out to be part of the tree.

THE MONTH OF MAY PROCEEDED, DAYS BLENDING TOGETHER IN A slurry of consciousness. I was sluggish and barely ate. Whole days elapsed without my speaking to anyone. A nod to the driver as I boarded the bus was often my only human inter-action. My loneliness deepened, and I realized I'd have to find other reasons to live, now that planes were off-limits. I messaged Dave one night, apologizing for what I'd said the last time we talked. *No worries, Linda,* he replied. *I'm sorry, too.*

The next day, Dave asked if I'd have dinner with him, and in my fragile, friendless state, I agreed. He picked me up, and we drove south. Through the window, the setting sun warmed the right side of my face. The sky was probably beautiful, but I couldn't allow myself to look at it. I stared straight ahead, through the windshield, my view confined to a strip of interstate beneath the brim of my hat.

Dave patted my thigh. "Good to see you, Linda."

"How've you been?" I asked.

"A lot better, actually," he said. "I've been working through some things in therapy. I don't want to be angry at Michelle anymore. I feel like I'm getting some closure around it all, finally."

"That's great," I said. "How's Gabi?"

"She's a moody teenager, but I'm trying not to take that personally. I let her get her nose pierced in Venice. Michelle was pissed, but it was worth it." He paused. "I know I haven't been the best dad. I've been stuck in this victim mentality that prevented me from showing up for her. I'm trying to make up for it now."

I was impressed by the progress Dave had made in the weeks since I'd seen him. "Have you been flying to LA?" I asked, unable to help myself.

"Yep," he said. "I missed you on those flights."

I refrained from asking additional questions, such as which models of plane he had flown in and whether there'd been any turbulence.

Dave chuckled, no doubt thinking about the times we'd flown together. "It seems pretty crazy now, doesn't it?"

I agreed, it did seem crazy. Dave handled his Prius competently, changing lanes in a safe yet assertive manner. He seemed respectable again, like when I'd first met him at Acuity. I now appreciated his positive qualities, while I'd once focused on his flaws. I found myself wanting to confide in him.

"I'm taking a break from flying," I said.

"Why's that?"

"It's not good for me," I said. "It brings out a darkness I can't control."

"I see. Well, you don't want that."

For once, I was grateful for Dave's glibness. I couldn't have handled talking to someone who perceived my suffering and probed it like a tongue in a dry socket.

We exited the interstate, and soon arrived at Dave's house, a two-story, cream-colored structure with a gray roof. It was nice, but not the mansion I'd imagined Dave living in. His lawn, like others around it, was composed of wood chips with little shrubs placed at intervals. Green lawns were out of fashion, he explained, due to the drought.

"It's modern farmhouse style," he said, as we approached the front door. "That's what the realtors call it, anyway. Three beds, two baths. Way too big for a bachelor."

"It's very nice," I said.

"It's all right," he said, turning his key in the lock. "I bought it ten years ago, for eight hundred grand. My realtor says I could sell it now for two mil, easy."

I was stunned by this figure. Two million dollars would buy roughly ten thousand round-trip flights to a regional hub. I dismissed the calculation, which had popped into my head unbidden; I had to break my habit of perceiving the world in plane terms. We passed through the foyer. To the right, through an arched doorway, lay a living room, white couches outlined in dusky light through the front window. Dave led us to the kitchen, gesturing for me to sit on a stool at the butcher-block island. He brought out a knife and began cutting a lime into wedges. The house felt sterile, like it had been staged for prospective buyers. A few items were arrayed on the counter: a wooden bowl of produce, mason jars filled with powders and seeds, a cookbook from a trendy San Francisco restaurant.

"You're thinking of selling, then?" I said.

He opened the fridge and extracted a bottle of sparkling water. "I'm always thinking of selling," he said. "But more seriously, lately."

"So you can move to LA?" I was surprised that the prospect of his departure made me sad.

"Yeah, that's always been the general plan." He poured the water into two glasses, then squeezed a lime wedge into each glass. "I need to get out of here, one way or another. This place is haunted."

"It is?" I said, feeling apprehensive. The last thing I needed was for a ghost to affix itself to me.

He laughed. "Not literally. Haunted by the past, you know." He handed me a glass. "Michelle designed the whole place. It's not really my style."

We sipped our sparkling water. He explained that Michelle had taken most of their possessions when she left, claiming the artwork and furniture belonged to her. "Even though it was all paid for by my money," he said.

"That doesn't seem fair," I said.

"I came home one day to a U-Haul out front. She'd hired some day laborers to pack everything up while I was at work. I was so shocked she'd planned it all out like that, I just let them do it."

"Was Peter there that day?"

"God, no. She knew better than to bring him here. I'd like to think I'd have punched him in the face. But I probably wouldn't have." He set his glass down. "I'm a coward."

"No, you're not," I said. I was trying to be kind to Dave, though I sensed there was more to the story, a version he wasn't capable of telling.

Dave cooked us a meal—chicken for him, sauteed tofu and kale for me. I was touched that he'd finally remembered I didn't eat meat. The food was bland, but I ate it gladly, not having realized how hungry I was.

When I'd finished everything on my plate, Dave crossed behind me and began rubbing my shoulders. "What's on your mind?" he said. I tensed at his touch, then made an effort to relax. As he loosened my muscles, I felt the hold of the last month loosen, too. Emotion swelled within me.

"I've made a mess of everything," I said. "Karina and I aren't friends anymore."

"What happened?" he said, pressing his thumbs into my back.

"It's a long story."

"I've got time."

I told him about our practice flight. How I'd been helping Karina overcome her fear of flying, but then, when we'd boarded, I had a premonition that the plane would crash.

"So I told her she should get off the plane, and she did, because she was terrified, and now she thinks I did it all on purpose, as a mean joke, or that I'm crazy, or both."

"Why did you think the plane would crash?" Dave asked. His hands were back on my shoulders, though I imagined they couldn't be further loosened without breaking my bones.

"I just had a feeling. Maybe because she was so afraid of it happening." I chose my words carefully. I'd resolved to be normal, and I didn't want to divulge my past transgressions to Dave. Besides, it was still too painful to remember that day. "It's like the vision boards, though I know you don't believe in them," I continued. "The law of attraction. The things we focus on manifest in our lives."

Dave sat on the stool next to mine. "That doesn't seem rational," he said. "Maybe you have a fear of flying, too."

"In a way, I guess I do."

"I never got that impression when we flew together." He winked, which discomfited me. "But you took the flight anyway, even though you thought the plane would crash?"

I wasn't sure how to explain that part. "Yes, and obviously, it was fine," I said.

"Did you come on the plane without me?" he said softly, though there was no need for discretion in the empty house.

"No," I said, which was true for the first flight. I didn't mention that I had climaxed many times on the return flight, on board a sporty Embraer 175. I knew it would be my last flight for a long time, if not for the rest of my life, and I wanted to make the most of it.

"You needed me," he said.

I allowed Dave to believe this, when in fact, he'd been a tool I had used that, over time, had become more trouble than it was worth. Perhaps this was what it meant to care for people: to distort reality in a way that flattered them.

"I've missed making you come," he whispered, his lips close to my ear.

I gulped my water, letting the bubbles burn in my throat. It had been three weeks since I'd flown, and though I still longed for planes, their absence in my life was becoming easier to bear, through a simple repetition of days. I felt a tenderness for Dave, after he'd been so kind to me, with the sparkling water and the tofu. I wanted to see how far I could ride this wave of tepid affection. What better way to prove I was reformed than to have sex with a man?

"I've missed it, too," I said. "I'd love to return the favor."

Dave's face stiffened. "Oh yeah?"

"I always wondered why you didn't try to make love to me in Denver."

"We work together," Dave said. "It wouldn't have been appropriate."

I was confused by this. "What about what we did on the planes? Wasn't that inappropriate?"

"It was. Very." He sighed. "The truth is, the antidepressants I'm on have totally killed my libido. Don't get me wrong, it's worth the trade-off. The meds pulled me out of a dark place. But when it comes to sex, I can't be bothered."

I recalled my hand grazing his erection on our flight to Denver. "You were aroused on the plane," I said.

"I know. It was like a miracle. I felt like a sexual being again for the first time in months."

I understood now why Dave had wanted to fly with me so badly. It must have felt like a matter of life and death, to get his dick hard. I saw that sex could be therapeutic for both of us. Perhaps we could both transfer our arousal from the flights. Dave could reclaim his sexuality, while I could forge a new path of enjoying sex with fellow humans.

"Maybe we could lie down together, and see what happens," I said.

Dave's eyebrows rose. "Is that what you want?"

"If you do."

He said we could try it, though he didn't seem excited. We went to his bedroom and lay on the king-sized bed. A streetlight shone through the venetian blinds, casting blades of light on the linen bedspread. I rested my head on Dave's chest. He lifted my chin and kissed me.

"Is this okay?" he asked, and I nodded. He continued kissing me, and I did my best to reciprocate, accepting his tongue into my mouth and running my hands over his chest. I tried to recall the feeling when we'd kissed on the flight to Denver, and felt a flicker of arousal at the memory of the plane lurching in response. I caressed the side of his face. I ran my fingers through his sandy hair. I reached into his sweatpants and gripped his penis, feeling it firm in my hand.

Dave kissed me more urgently and lowered me onto my back. As he hovered over me, I imagined a 737's face, his friendly white nose and intelligent windscreen. I closed my eyes and pretended the plane was penetrating me. With this mental work, I almost enjoyed the sensation of Dave inside me. After a few thrusts, though, I felt him shrivel inside the condom. He rolled off me again.

"I'm sorry," he said.

"It's okay," I said quickly.

"I'm, shall we say, a bit out of practice. And something's not quite clicking."

"It's my fault."

"No, it's not," he said. "But you did seem kind of checked out. Not that I would have minded, in my more virile days." He laughed. "I noticed you had your eyes closed, like you didn't want to look at me. I know it sounds silly, but I thought maybe you were imagining I was someone else."

"We can try again," I said, pawing lightly at his genitals. But Dave stilled my hand.

"It's okay, Linda. I'd rather just lie here with you."

I remained aroused, thanks to my plane fantasy, coupled with Dave's brief infiltration of my body. I wanted to go to the bathroom with my phone and get myself off with images of planes from the internet, but I couldn't allow this. Dave slung his arm across my chest, and I remembered, with a stab of grief, how Karina had done the same, the night before I betrayed her.

19 In June, my mom invited me to her sixtieth birthday party. The event would be held in the backyard of my childhood home in Irvine, a week from Saturday.

I was on the bus when she called, commuting home on a Wednesday. I told my mom I wasn't sure if I could make it, as things were busy at work. This was a lie, of course. The real conflict was that I couldn't fly to Irvine given my vow of abstinence, and driving that distance alone seemed unfeasible. Aside from the expense of renting a car, I'd never driven more than ten miles at a time.

"I'd really love it if you could come, honey," she said. "Al and Denise will be there, with Claudette. And a few of my girlfriends." I knew she meant her friends from the leggings scheme.

I was touched that my attendance seemed so important to her, and wondered if I could persuade Dave to drive me. "Can I bring a date?" I asked.

"Oh, of course, sweetie!" she said. "Are you seeing someone?"

"Sort of." In the month since we'd reconnected, Dave and

I had fallen into a pattern of having dinner a few nights a week. We hadn't tried to have sex again, and with that pressure removed, we'd settled into a friendship tinged, at moments, with romantic overtures that didn't bother me as much as I'd thought they would. He'd gone to LA one weekend and brought me back a present—a hand-poured candle I was too afraid to light in my firetrap of a room. We sometimes cuddled in his bed after dinner, though we didn't bother with kissing. I was grateful for Dave's company, which I'd used like methadone to wean off the heroin of Karina's friendship. We weren't really dating. We were two lonely people passing time together, though perhaps that was all a relationship was.

But my family didn't need to know the details. I'd never introduced them to a romantic partner, or even mentioned the existence of one, and they must have found this lack unsettling. I could use Dave as proof I'd reached the shore of normal adulthood, exempt from speculation. My mom would go to her grave confident in my ability to survive in the world. Al and Denise would amend their judgments of me from when I'd lived with them in Bakersfield. I considered criticisms my mom might have of Dave. He was seventeen years older than me, and divorced, but he was also tall and owned a house. I figured the second set of characteristics more than canceled out the first. She'd be impressed, maybe even envious, that I'd persuaded such a fellow to date me.

I explained the situation to Dave the next night, while we

were having dinner at a ramen place near my cube. He chewed his noodles thoughtfully.

"Doesn't that seem like a big step?" he said.

"Meeting my mom?" He nodded. "Not at all. I thought it might be fun to take a little road trip."

"Would we be staying at her house?"

"No, we'll have to stay in a hotel," I said. We couldn't stay at the house, as my mom was using my old room as an office. It was currently occupied by pants and materials used to ship the pants when people bought them, which seemed to happen infrequently. When I'd visited over Christmas, I slept on the couch in the living room, but I doubted the couch would fit two people. "I can pay for the room," I added.

"It's not about the money, Linda," he said, hanging his spoon off the edge of his bowl. "What does she know about me?"

"Nothing yet. I asked if I could bring a date."

Dave's face took on an earnest expression. "We've been spending a fair amount of time together," he said.

"We don't have to put a label on it," I said.

"Of course. Not a fan of labels myself."

"Except, for my mom, it might be easier if we say we're dating."

"Totally. I mean, I'm great at impressing parents. And I already made you pretend to be my girlfriend, so I owe you one." He laughed at the memory of our visit to Barley Bros.

He asked how old my mom was turning, and when I told him, he frowned.

"Will she think I'm too old for you?"

"I think she'd be grateful that I had a human partner, regardless of the form they took."

"Fair enough." He resumed eating his soup, as if this settled things.

"So you'll go with me?" I said. "I thought we could drive down next Friday, after work."

"Drive? Are you kidding? It's way too far for a weekend trip. We'll have to fly."

My cheeks burned. "I can't do that anymore," I reminded him.

"Right. The dark path and all. Well, let me think about it."

Over the next few days, we finalized our plan. I suggested we stay at the Hyatt Regency near John Wayne Airport, and Dave said he'd book us a room. I asked him to request one that faced away from the runways, so I wouldn't be tempted. I ordered a present for my mom, a pair of socks with her dogs' faces printed on them.

Dave called the night before our departure, while I was in my cube debating which clothes to bring. "Don't be mad at me, Linda, but I went ahead and booked us a flight," he said.

I lowered myself onto my bed, which was strewn with the garments I'd been trying on. I was angry he'd booked a flight after I'd explained to him that I could no longer fly. The main reason I'd invited him was so he could drive me. "I told you, I can't do that anymore," I said.

"My back can't handle two eight-hour drives in a single weekend. Anyway, I thought this would be good for you. I know you've developed some kind of phobia around flying, but there's really no need to be afraid. Statistically, it's very safe."

"I'm not afraid to fly," I said, annoyed that this was how he'd interpreted what I'd told him.

"Then what's the problem?"

I knew it was pointless to try to explain. No matter what I said, he'd dismiss my thoughts as irrational, using terms borrowed from therapy. "I'm trying to be a good person," I said.

Dave laughed. "What does that have to do with flying to Irvine? I booked us in first class. Let's live a little."

I acquiesced to his plan, seeing no other option. After we hung up, I wondered if Dave was right that flying would be good for me. Perhaps taking a practice flight of my own was the final step in my process of rehabilitation. If I could fly without succumbing to temptation, I would know I had truly changed and was worthy of Karina again. I could not white-knuckle my way through my life's remaining decades, wearing a sky-obscuring hat and pretending commercial flight did not exist.

Friday, as we pulled into the airport garage, I felt the old tendrils of desire wrap around me, and I did my best to slough them off. I endeavored to see the airport as a normal person would. A place of tedium, of timetables, possessing no more glory than a bus station. I held myself stiffly in the security line. As we walked through the terminal, I kept my gaze trained on the floor, forbidding myself to look out the windows.

We reached our gate, where I caught a glimpse of our plane, a gorgeous 737. My breath caught, a wave of longing crashing upon me. I averted my gaze, conjuring the image of Karina's horrified face when I'd asked her to be my bridesmaid. The memory of that day helped to dull my desire. I reminded myself I was flying home for my mother's birthday party. Nothing more.

We were seated in 4E and F. As it was first class, we were the only two on our side of the aisle, which afforded us more privacy than we'd had on previous flights. I sat in the window seat and lowered the shade. My identity as a coach passenger was so ingrained, I felt disturbed by the flight attendant's solicitousness, proffering blankets and pillows and beverages prior to takeoff. Suddenly, now that I possessed a first-class ticket, I was a person whose ass demanded kissing. We settled in, unwrapping the blankets and draping them over our laps. Dave took two cups of champagne from the flight attendant's tray, and we tapped the flimsy plastic together in a toast to the weekend.

"To Deborah," Dave said.

"Deb," I corrected him.

Soon it was time to take off, the wretched coach passengers having found their seats and stuffed their bloated parcels in the overhead bins. As the plane pulled back from the gate, I felt my nipples harden, my crotch tingling. Sweat gathered under my arms and at the small of my back. The plane's engines fired. We rushed down the runway, and as his nose lifted, the dam I'd built within myself breached, flooding my body with six weeks of suppressed lust. I shuddered, my vision blurring, my commitment to abstinence diminishing to a speck in the distance, like the houses below us. I felt Dave's hand worm beneath my thin airline blanket. He unbuttoned my jeans, and I raised my hips to allow his fingers access. I opened my eyes and found his face close to mine. His expression was focused but dispassionate, as though I were a complicated machine he was determined to fix.

As the plane continued to climb, Dave leaned forward as if to look for something on the floor, then plunged his fingers deeper into me, at the same moment the plane banked hard to the right. I gasped with pleasure. Dave guided my left hand under his blanket until it found his erection. Unthinkingly, as if heeding a primordial instinct, I pumped my hand up and down his shaft. As my stroking grew more frenzied, the blanket fell away, exposing him to the cabin air. He shuddered, and I felt his fluid, warm and sticky on my hand. It was an unpleasant sensation, like when coffee from an improperly sealed Starbucks cup dripped onto my hand while I climbed the stairs to the office.

Dave rushed to cover himself. I wiped my hand on my blanket, repulsed. As I regained my bearings, I saw that the woman across the aisle was staring at us, her phone held aloft, the camera's lens pointed at us. She was around my age, polished-looking, with a high blond ponytail. Our eyes met. She shook her head in disgust and returned to her magazine.

I was filled with shame, both that another person had witnessed our indecent act and that I'd failed to resist the plane's advances. I kept my face turned away from Dave for the rest of the flight, resenting him for leading me back down the path I'd worked hard to renounce. I wondered if he had planned the whole thing, anticipating a flight would knock me back to my old ways. Why else would he have sprung for first-class seats? Perhaps he'd viewed our dinner dates as the laying of groundwork for a transcendent in-flight hand job.

In the terminal, I told Dave about the woman across the aisle, hoping to off-load some of my shame onto him.

"Oh well," he said. "She got a free show."

"I think she might have recorded us."

"What a pervert," he said, sounding pleased.

We proceeded toward the exit, past the Subway stall where I'd once toiled. I considered telling Dave about losing my virginity in the walk-in fridge, but I knew he'd find it merely titillating, which would show how little he understood me.

Across from Subway, at Gate B16, a 737 was boarding for Newark. I approached the window, drawn by the uncanny intelligence I perceived in his windscreen. I moved to the left, seeking his tail number, and when I found it I felt the ground shift beneath me. Inscribed on the plane's flank were the digits I'd sought since I was thirteen: N92823. I'd thought he was condemned to a boneyard in the desert, but here he was, back in service, about to traverse the continent. It had taken seventeen years, but at last, we'd made our way back to each other.

"What's the matter?" Dave said. I flinched, having forgotten he was standing next to me.

I watched N92823 pull back from the gate. "That's a plane I flew in once," I said softly. N92823 turned right on the taxiway, disappearing around a bend. He reappeared a few moments later, on a more distant runway, awaiting his turn in the lineup.

Dave yawned, stretching his arms above his head. He couldn't have understood the significance of my encounter with N92823, and yet, his indifference filled me with rage. "Come on, let's get out of here," he said.

I ignored him, remaining at the window until N92823's nose lifted and his form was swallowed by the sky. I was flooded with a sense of cosmic rightness. I saw that even during my period of abstinence, I'd remained woven into the tapestry of fate. I would no longer deny who I was. On our way out of the secure sector, I removed my 49ers hat and threw it in a trash can.

AS WE PROCEEDED THROUGH THE STEPS OF RENTING A CAR AND driving to our hotel, I thought of nothing but N92823. My anger at Dave had been displaced by awe at how he'd engineered my reunion with my lost love. I now wondered if the vision board had prompted Dave to book our flight to Irvine, though I'd long ago removed his photo and burned it in the sink. When we reached the check-in desk of the Hyatt Regency, I asked if we could have a room facing the runway, after all. The woman checking us in said there was a room available on the eighth floor, but there was only one bed rather than two.

"That sounds fine," I said. Dave and I had lain together, sexlessly, several times now, and I didn't mind him spooning me if it meant I could watch planes take off and land.

We waited for the elevator. "Why'd you ask for a runway view?" Dave said. "We'll hear planes taking off all night."

"I hope so," I said.

Dave grumbled about needing to buy earplugs. We found our room, and I locked myself in the bathroom, where I looked up N92823 and found that he'd been back in service for six months. All that time, I'd flown on inferior planes. I might have been close to my love without knowing it, at an airport or while airborne. I reviewed his flight schedule. Tomorrow morning, he'd depart Newark for Charleston, then return to Newark, then fly to Houston, landing in the late afternoon. For a moment, I seized on the prospect of meeting him in Houston and flying on with him to O'Hare. I found a morning flight from John Wayne to Houston, but the fare was $339, which would leave me with insufficient funds for a ticket on board my love, much less for a ticket back to San Francisco, on the off chance N92823 declined to marry me.

Dave knocked on the door. "Linda? You okay in there?"

I put my plans on hold. We journeyed down the road for dinner at the same Mexican restaurant my family had taken me to as a celebration for what had seemed, for a brief interval, to be my successful initiation as a flight attendant. The interior was festive, with chains of paper garlands strung from the exposed beams of the ceiling. I ordered my usual cheese enchiladas without looking at the menu. Dave gazed at me across the table, and I knew he was thinking that I looked pretty, or something equally degrading. He was enjoying the idea of himself on a sexy sojourn with a younger woman. I resented him for casting me in this role, though I'd invited him to do so by asking him to accompany me, and letting him pay for everything.

Dave dug into the chips and salsa, and through a mouthful of corn he said, "What's going on with you, Linda?"

"Nothing," I said, surprised he'd noticed my agitation. I needed to calm myself. I ate a chip.

"Are you still mad I made you fly here? Did you not enjoy first class?"

I had to give him something, or he'd persist in thinking my distraction related to him, as he seemed to believe everything in the world did. "It's that plane I saw at the airport," I said. "I recognized his tail number from a flight I took with my family when I was thirteen."

"Oh?" Dave said with an indulgent smile. "An old nemesis?"

I maintained a neutral expression. "The opposite," I said. "The best plane I've ever known."

Our entrees arrived. Dave had ordered fajitas, and the sizzling skillet of meat and peppers was unveiled with a degree of fanfare that annoyed me. It had always been Al's favorite dish, and I'd suspected this was only because he liked the attention. I dug into my enchiladas, hoping my zeal would deflect further questioning, but for once, Dave pressed. What did I mean about the plane? Why was it so great? I wasn't used to him interrogating my moods, as he was usually too mired in his own grievances to notice me. The hand job seemed to have revived something in him, a strain of assertiveness that could only bring me trouble. I preferred the downtrodden, impotent Dave I'd always known.

I put my fork down. "We were flying to Chicago," I said. "Midway through, we hit a patch of clear-air turbulence. For two minutes and thirty seconds, we all thought we would die."

"And that was a good experience?" he said, raising a chunk of chicken with his fork and blowing on it. "It sounds terrible."

A new plan hatched in my mind. "Would you want to fly to Houston tomorrow, for old times' sake?"

Dave laughed. "What are you talking about? Tomorrow is your mom's party."

I no longer cared about the party, though I did want to give my mother the dog socks.

"Are you nervous about introducing me to your family?" Dave asked.

"It's not that," I said. I searched for an excuse that would satisfy him. "I'm nervous about seeing my brother's wife. She never liked me."

"Well, screw her," Dave said. "Don't worry. I'll charm her pants off."

After dinner, we returned to the hotel. I'd been waiting for a chance to be alone with my research on N92823. I drew a bath and lay in it as I investigated. So far, it seemed he'd flown without incident. He'd been a good boy, but perhaps he was waiting for me to turn him bad again. I wondered if he'd been thinking of me all this time, just as I'd thought of him. It was possible that, after years of maintenance and parts-swapping, he was not the plane he'd once been. Perhaps he was N92823 in name only. I hoped not. I hoped the universe had led me to the city of my youth to reunite with my first love. I would have to fly in him to find out.

I wrapped a robe around my body and emerged into the room. Dave lay on the bed, flipping through channels on the muted TV.

"So how did she look?" he said. "Was she scandalized? Turned on?"

"Who?" I said, startled.

"The woman on the plane."

I'd accidentally played into Dave's exhibitionist fantasy. "I don't think she was turned on." I sat on the edge of the bed, facing the window, and was met by a FedEx cargo plane touching down.

"That was wild. I can't believe you grabbed me like that. It was so fucking hot." He inched his hand under the robe, along my inner thigh. I dislodged his hand gently and moved to a chair by the window. Dave seemed unfazed by my rejection. He unmuted the TV.

"So what's our story for tomorrow?" he asked, over the murmur of other people's voices. "How did we meet, what's our status, that kind of thing."

I was glad Dave had the foresight to iron out these details. "We can say we met at work, and that we're dating, I guess."

"Okay, Linda. I'm your boyfriend, then." He'd landed on a cooking show, a woman beating eggs into flour. I felt queasy as I watched the yolks churn.

20　The next day, we rounded the streets of my old neighborhood in the rental car, a gray Nissan Versa. We headed down Woodspring, past the public pool where I'd learned to swim. We continued through the intersection where I'd crashed my bike in a pothole when I was eight; I'd landed chin first, acquiring a gash that needed stitches. On Winterbranch sat the duplex where my friend Abigail had lived. I'd gone there after school most days, to play computer games in her dad's study, until her family moved to Toronto when we were in fifth grade.

My mom's house was located on Beechwood, across the street from a field where Al and his friends played soccer, and where my dad liked to set off fireworks on the Fourth of July. The façade had a triangular roof, under which lay the garage. I told Dave to park around the corner, where a stone path led to the front door. I was surprised, as always, to find the house painted beige, as in my mind's eye it remained the mint green it had been in my youth.

"Nice house," Dave said, as we got out of the car. "What do you think it's worth these days?"

"I don't know," I said. I was increasingly annoyed by Dave's presence. I no longer cared about using him to impress my family, but it seemed easier to go through with the performance, since we were already here.

"A house like this would sell for two point five, easy, in the South Bay."

"We're not in the South Bay, though, are we?" I said.

We rang the bell, and a moment later, my mom opened the door. Her dogs, a Pomeranian named Stella and a corgi mix named Arnold, slipped around her to greet us. My mother was a thin woman with watery eyes and a head of wavy hair dyed a shade of red too vibrant for nature. She wore a knit tunic over a pair of the accursed leggings, black with a pattern of white fish. In one hand, she held a tumbler of white wine. She'd started early today.

"Hi there, sweetie!" she said, wrapping her arms around me. "So glad you could make it. And you must be Dave."

"Happy birthday, Deb!" Dave said.

"You're so tall!" she said, as I'd known she would.

I handed her the dog socks, which I'd forgotten to wrap.

"Oh, they're adorable," she said. "Thank you, honey." Her gratitude seemed perfunctory, and I wondered if I should have brought a bottle of wine instead.

The living room looked the same as it had over Christmas, when I'd spent two nights on the overstuffed leather couch, its cushions perforated by the dogs' claws. The walls retained their wood paneling from the seventies, though some updates had been attempted—new carpet, photos of Ron's sons on the wall alongside photos of me and Al as kids, and some macramé wall hangings from that phase of my mom's life. From the kitchen there wafted a meaty smell that turned my stomach. I made an effort to breathe through my mouth.

"They're all in the back," my mom said, crouching to pick up Stella.

A card table set with drinks had been installed in the yard, and the party's attendees milled around it: Ron and his adult sons, and two women I assumed were involved with the leggings scheme. One of them introduced herself as Trish, the other, Suzanne. They were petite women in their sixties. Suzanne was prettier, while Trish had had more cosmetic work, her cheeks and lips plump and shiny, like hamburger buns.

"We're so happy you could make it down to celebrate Deb!" Trish said. "I hear you're living in San Fran?"

I nodded. "This is Dave. My boyfriend." It was difficult to force these words from my mouth. A plane roared overhead, as if objecting to my betrayal, and I looked up to watch him pass, his fine shape etched against the cloudless sky.

"Love your necklace," Dave said, referencing a gaudy geometric thing Trish was wearing. She explained the provenance of the necklace, something about a friend who'd just launched a jewelry line, and soon she was pushing her phone in his face to show him the friend's Instagram store, insisting he buy something for me. I wandered over to Ron, a stepdad of sorts, though he and my mom weren't married. He was a tall, broad man around seventy years old. His lumpy chin brought to mind the classic Douglas DC-8, whose engine inlets carved dimples in the same region.

"Glad you could make it down, Linda," he said, shaking my hand. After five years, we hadn't progressed to hugging.

His two sons, large and interchangeable, resembling two 747s standing abreast, regarded me with shy smiles.

"So what are you two doing these days?" I asked them. They looked at each other before answering, like coconspirators who hadn't gotten their story straight.

"Electricians' union," Teddy or Ron Jr. said.

"I'm working for our dad," the other son said.

"Teddy's great with computers," Ron said, revealing that the second son who'd spoken, the one with a creased forehead and a mole on his neck, was Teddy.

Al and Denise emerged from the house, Al holding a cake box, Denise carrying Claudette on her hip. I drifted over to them, eager to escape further conversation with the eerie sons.

"Say hi to your aunt Linda," Denise told Claudette. I looked into the baby's moist, inquisitive eyes. Claudette had just turned a year old, and though I loved her in an abstract way, I was nervous around her, wary of leaving too deep an impression on her psyche. Since she was born, I'd always thought of her in relation to my fated demise. She would know me, for the rest of her long and happy life, as her aunt Linda who'd died in a plane crash. I'd become a legend in her mind, and in the meantime, I didn't want to give her too much fodder with which to grieve the real me. She was probably still too young to form conscious memories, but I knew babies absorbed all stimuli, and so I took care not to hold her or speak to her excessively.

Al set down the cake box and hugged me. He had a gap between his front teeth that lent his face a mischievous look, at odds with his Lacoste polo shirt and khaki shorts. "We weren't sure you'd make it down," he said.

"Of course I made it," I said. Al gave me a sardonic look, and I felt embarrassed, remembering the day, four years ago, when I'd called him from the Seattle airport and begged for his help. I didn't tell Al about my flight binge, instead alluding to a stint of "partying" that involved drugs and the company of an unscrupulous man who'd made off with the last of my money. Al bought me a ticket to Bakersfield, and on the drive to his house, he'd lectured me about financial responsibility, reluctantly donning the costume of a father figure, now that our father was dead.

"Mom said you were bringing a date?" he said.

I gestured across the yard to Dave, who remained trapped in a conversation with Trish and Suzanne. Al squinted at him. Dave saw us looking and waved. "How old is he?" Al said, waving back.

"Forty-seven."

Al whistled. "Practically Mom's age."

"Oh, stop," Denise said, slapping his arm. "Good for you, Linda. I don't think I've ever heard of you having a boyfriend before."

"I never have until now," I said.

"How did you meet?" Denise asked.

"We work together."

"Is he your boss or something?" Al said.

Dave, no doubt aware we were talking about him, came over and introduced himself. I watched him and Al shake hands as though they were at a business convention. Denise set Claudette down and coaxed her to pet the dogs. I went into the house, hoping to talk to my mom alone.

I found her in the kitchen, slicing an onion for the salad.

"Dave seems like a catch," she said. "Has he been married before?"

"Yeah. He's divorced."

"Well, sometimes those men are the best bets. They've already worked out their quirks with the first wife." I imagined she was thinking of Ron, whose ex-wife lived in Anaheim. They'd been divorced for twenty years but remained close friends, a situation my mom accepted, though she'd sometimes gripe about it after a few drinks.

"I'm not planning on marrying him, or anything like that," I said.

She gave me a familiar weary look. "Why not?"

I wished I could tell her I was already engaged, in my heart, to N92823. "I'm trying not to worry about the future," I said.

"Just be open to the idea, sweetie. None of us are getting any younger."

I knew this was true, and it urged me to proceed with my agenda. "Do you remember that trip we took to Chicago when I was thirteen?" I said.

"Chicago? I can't imagine why we'd go there."

"Dad had a conference."

She nodded, drying her hands on a dish towel. "That must have been right before he left us."

"He didn't leave," I said. "Well, he did for two weeks, but he tried to come back, and you wouldn't let him."

"I think I remember that trip," she said. "It must have been the weekend you got food poisoning. I stayed with you in the hotel room while Al and your dad went to a museum."

I hadn't had food poisoning, of course. I'd needed an excuse to lock myself in the bathroom, where I'd navigated the contours of my sexual awakening. "Do you remember the plane we flew on? It was a 737-800 with a tail number of N92823."

"You always were interested in those details, weren't you?" My mom poured more wine into her glass. She offered me some, but I shook my head, refusing to be diverted.

"There was severe turbulence midway through," I said. "A flight attendant broke her nose on the edge of the beverage cart. Coffee and wine were splattered on the walls. Everyone was screaming and praying. We all thought we were going to die."

"That sounds unpleasant." My mom took the macaroni out of the oven. "Can you help me bring this stuff out, hon? It's time to eat."

Though I assumed she was evading the subject so as not to encourage me, I was disturbed by the possibility that she truly didn't remember our flight on N92823. Had I exaggerated its drama in my memory? I felt troubled as I carried out the macaroni, gripping the dish's handles with potholders. While I'd been inside, the other guests had assembled a long folding table in the yard and covered it with a plastic tablecloth. Ron brought burgers over from the grill. Claudette sat in a high chair, squeezing a chunk of beef in her fist. I was quiet, biding my time while I ate my macaroni and a salad of romaine lettuce, shredded carrot, onion, and overly sweet dressing. Dave was telling the story of starting his company ten years ago.

"It was a good idea, but we were too early," he said. "Clean tech was a bubble, and it burst."

"I remember reading about that," Al said. "Sounds like you hung in there longer than most of those startups."

Dave shrugged. "To be honest, I wasn't cut out to run a company. I'd rather collect a paycheck and let someone else deal with the headaches."

"You've got to have a healthy work-life balance," Denise said. "Otherwise, what's it all for?"

"Totally," Dave said. I was bored by this conversation and looked at my phone under the table. I'd re-downloaded my flight-tracking app. N92823 had just landed in Houston.

"So you and Linda work together now?" Denise said. "At a content moderation center, right?"

"Not exactly," Dave said. "Linda works for a contractor, and I work for the parent company." I gathered he didn't want them to think he was a lowly moderator like me.

"What do you do for them?" Al asked Dave.

"He's a site inspector," I said.

"That's one of my roles," Dave said, a bit testily.

"He came to inspect our site after a disgruntled employee vandalized it," I said.

"Oh my," my mom said, sipping her wine.

"Linda's the best mod in her vertical," Dave said. "I'm sure she didn't tell you, since she's so modest."

"That's wonderful," my mom said. "We always knew

Linda was special. She knew so many facts about historical events—"

"Plane crashes, you mean," Al said. He'd always teased me about what he viewed as a quirky interest in aviation, the way some girls loved horses or boy bands.

"What's a vertical?" Teddy asked.

"Sort of a subcategory of moderating," Dave said. "Linda's in H&H."

"Hate & Harassment," I said.

"Remember when you wanted to be a flight attendant?" Al said.

"You never told me that," Dave said. I glanced at him, and he winked. Across the table, my mom was watching us, her eyes misty.

"We're so glad you two found each other," she said, her voice sodden from the wine. My cheeks flushed.

"So am I, Deb," Dave said. He cleared his throat, and I realized he was uncomfortable, too.

"I've always worried about Linda making her way in the world," my mom continued. "I feel better knowing she has you. We're so happy to welcome you to our family."

I wanted to melt into my plastic chair. Al stood and proposed a toast, intervening, as usual, to smooth over an awkward moment. "To the best mom in the world," he said. "Here's to sixty more years, Ma." We clinked glasses, and then other people chimed in with their own toasts. I cast Al a grateful look, and he nodded over his glass. In spite of his teasing, I knew that Al loved me and wanted to protect me, though he was baffled by my life choices. For years, I'd allowed him to think I was simply irresponsible, perhaps addicted to drugs.

Denise brought out the cake, lit with a candle in the shape of the number 60, and we sang "Happy Birthday." As the cake was being cut, I asked Al if he remembered our trip to Chicago. My mom's denial still gnawed at me, and I wanted someone to at least acknowledge it had happened.

"I think so," Al said. He had a toothpick in his mouth, probably one of those cinnamon-flavored ones he always carried in his shirt pocket. "Dad had a conference, right?"

"Yes," I said with a rush of excitement. "Do you remember the flight there? We hit a patch of clear-air turbulence."

"Oh yeah," he said, jiggling the toothpick. "That was terrifying. The worst flight I've ever been on, by a long shot."

I felt vindicated. Finally, someone else admitted to remembering. "I saw the plane last night, at the airport," I said. "N92823. He'd been in storage for years, and now he's back."

"'He'?" Suzanne said.

"Yes, planes are male," I said irritably.

"How do they reproduce, then?" Suzanne said, smiling. "Where do plane babies come from?"

I ignored her disrespect. "I just want you all to know that this year, I started making vision boards, and they've been helping me manifest my goals. That's how Dave and I got together."

Dave put his hand on my thigh. "Linda," he said, warning me to stop.

"I placed Dave's image on my vision board, along with

images of planes, and the universe found a way to unite us," I said.

An awkward silence fell over the table. "Linda, don't be silly," my mom said. "You told us you met at work."

"It's true, those boards are powerful," Trish said. "I've been making one at the start of each year, and so far, I've gotten everything I asked for."

"Yes!" I said, grateful for Trish.

"I've been telling you, Deb," Trish said. "Manifestation is a very powerful tool. My downlines have had record sales this year thanks to my vision board."

"Why would you put planes on your board?" Ron Jr. asked me. He rarely spoke, and his question caught me off guard.

"Because planes are my destiny," I said. "I'm glad to have known you all, and whatever guilt you might feel in relation to me, I absolve you from it. Whatever happens, I want you to know that it was meant to be." I took a breath, adrenaline surging through me. Now that N92823 was back, I felt my fate was drawing near, and I wanted to seed in my family an awareness of my death as a joyful event.

Al and Denise exchanged a worried glance.

"The cake is delicious," Dave said.

"Red velvet. My favorite," my mom said, and from there the conversation moved back into safe territory.

When Dave and I were leaving, my mom grabbed my wrist at the door and pulled me close. "Is everything okay, sweetie?" she said.

"Everything's fine," I told her. "I'm glad I got to see you." I restrained myself from adding, "one last time."

"Maybe you could talk to someone," she said. "I met with a counselor after your dad left, and it helped me a lot."

I squeezed her bony shoulders. "You don't need to worry about me."

Dave stood by the Versa. "Nice meeting you," my mom called to him. "Take care of my daughter, okay?"

I watched a shadow pass over Dave's face. Then he grinned and came over to hug her again, showing off the meet-the-parents charm he'd boasted about.

AS WE DROVE AWAY FROM THE HOUSE, DAVE SEEMED SUBDUED. I asked if he'd had a good time.

"It was a nice party," he said. "Your mom's friends were a trip. And it was fun talking shop with your brother."

We idled at a stoplight.

"Some of the stuff you said was pretty weird," Dave said.

"What stuff?" I said, though I knew. I'd figured I would have to account for my conduct at dinner, but I was reluctant to go to the trouble. I didn't want to be Dave's fake girlfriend anymore. Now that I knew N92823 was back in service, it felt disloyal even to pretend.

"I wish you hadn't told them about the vision board," Dave said. "I thought you just put me on there to symbolize work stuff. But you made it sound like it was because you wanted to date me. Like you want us to get married, or something."

"I didn't say that."

"You made it sound like I'm a zombie you've tricked into

a relationship. And what's with your obsession with that plane? N-whatever. You mentioned it last night, too."

He turned right onto Barranca Parkway, heading back toward the hotel. Our speed increased, and I rolled up my window. "I already told you," I said.

"Tell me again."

He didn't know what he was asking for, and yet, I felt the time had come to tell him the truth. Dave deserved to know my heart belonged to someone else. I suggested we go to the beach to watch the sunset. Dave reversed course, driving through downtown, past the Rusty Pelican, where the waitress my dad had an affair with had worked. We entered the Balboa Peninsula. Two miles south lay the marina where my dad's boat, *Wendy*, once dwelled. I felt a pang of guilt, remembering the grizzled man I'd sold her to, who'd probably scrapped her for parts.

Dave parked in the beach lot, and I led us onto the pier. Throngs of people had gathered to watch the sunset, but we found an empty patch, resting our elbows on the splintered railing. The sun was a scorching white dot above the ocean. I admired its clean outline before I had to look away, its afterimage burned onto my retinas.

I summoned the courage to reveal myself to Dave in my entirety. But before I could speak, Dave said quietly, "I think this was a mistake."

"What do you mean?" I said.

"Coming here with you. I'm sorry, Linda. I don't want to give you the wrong idea."

"What idea is that?"

Dave looked down at the surf. "I guess I didn't think about how it would feel meeting your family. They were so happy you'd found someone. It felt a little too real for me."

I recalled his embarrassment when my mom had gushed over our relationship. "Don't worry about my mom," I said. "She gets emotional when she drinks."

I could tell Dave was working through something in his mind. "When's the last time you had a boyfriend?" he asked.

"I've never had one," I said.

He looked at me incredulously. "Never?"

I shook my head.

"Well, you're still young," Dave said, pushing back from the railing, as if having decided something. "You can have it all. A real partner. A family. I can't offer that. I'm sorry for wasting your time."

"I told you before," I said. "I'm not attracted to people. Only to planes. The truth is—"

"Stop," he said, raising his hand. "You don't have to do that, Linda."

"Do what?" I said, startled.

"I remember you saying that before. When we were about to fly to Houston, and I told you we couldn't date. I get that it must be your way of dealing with rejection, but it's not necessary."

I was amazed, once again, by Dave's obliviousness. He thought he had me figured out, when in fact, he couldn't see the truth even when it was presented to him. He could only project aspects of his own personality onto me. His self-centeredness irritated me, but I also saw he'd given me the exit ramp I needed. I only had to swallow my pride and pretend I was hurt that he was ending our phony relationship.

"Maybe you're right," I said.

He put his arm around me, and we stood together in silence, watching the sun melt into the waves. Behind us, I heard the faint cry of a plane and thought of N92823, who was set to land at O'Hare in an hour. From now on, I'd live with a constant awareness of his position in the world, my heart tethered to him until the day he'd take me as his bride. I hoped I wouldn't have to wait much longer.

21 In the hotel room that night, Dave treated me with a new cordiality. He didn't touch me and slept stiffly on his half of the bed. When he showered in the morning, he brought a change of clothes into the bathroom with him, so that he could emerge fully dressed. He was all business, asking if I'd like a coffee from downstairs and reminding me of our departure time.

I was vaguely offended that meeting my family had turned Dave off so intensely he'd ended our affair the same night. More important, though, I was relieved the universe seemed to have finally loosened its grip on his psyche. As we entered the airport, I toyed with the idea of asking Dave for a loan so I could fly to Denver, where N92823 would land in a few hours. I figured his guilt, however misguided, might make him amenable to giving me money. But it seemed too complicated to explain why I wanted to fly on to another destination, and I didn't want my reunion with N92823 to be sullied by any association with Dave. I would have to earn the money myself. It might take me a few months to accrue enough for a proper string of dates, but that was fine—I'd already waited seventeen years.

We flew back on a homely but spirited Bombardier CRJ700. I maintained my composure, resisting the little plane's overtures, as I was now betrothed to N92823, in my heart, if not yet in his. After we landed, Dave and I proceeded to the public sector of the airport, pausing at the foot of the escalator that led to the AirTrain. Dave offered to drive me home, but I said I preferred to take BART. He nodded, a stricken look on his face.

"I understand, Linda. I know it's hard."

I stared at the ground, pretending to be wounded by his rejection. Dave put his arms around me lightly, treating me to one last unsatisfying hug. "I'll always appreciate our time together," he said. "I'll think of you whenever I board a plane."

ON MONDAY, I WORKED WITH A NEW SENSE OF PURPOSE, MODER-ating harder than I ever had before. As each hour ticked past, I knew I'd earned another twenty dollars toward my reunion with N92823. Though it was more like fifteen after taxes.

When I left that evening, Simon cornered me in the stairwell and said we needed to talk. My chest clutched with an old anxiety whose emergence I resented, now that I was on such an optimistic trajectory. I wondered if he had news about Karina and hoped, absurdly, that she wanted to reconcile but was too shy to initiate a conversation herself.

Simon and I went to the Starbucks downstairs. He paid for my iced tea this time, and led me to a table in a discreet

corner near the restroom. I'd noticed Simon had been putting more effort into his appearance lately. He'd grown a
beard of surprising robustness, and the extra hair made him
look more mature, concealing the tender doughiness of his
chin. He leaned toward me, resting his elbows on the table.

"I saw a crazy video today," he said. "I think you're in it."

My mouth went dry, my mind flashing to the woman
across the aisle. "I doubt that," I said weakly.

Simon showed me the video on his phone. He'd recorded
his monitor screen again, and as such, there was no sound.
The footage was less vivid than the original must have been,
but the gist was clear. A ten-second loop of Dave's penis popping out of the blanket and my hand pumping with un-
seemly gusto, reminiscent of a video I'd once seen of a
monkey masturbating at the zoo. Dave's head was tilted
back, his eyes closed, his face rapt with pleasure. For the first
few seconds, my face was obscured by his shoulder, but at
the end of the clip, I leaned forward, revealing my features to
the camera.

I'd always feared exposure, but I assumed it would be for
my usual activities on planes. It was yet more embarrassing
to be exposed for stroking a man's penis, an activity I did not
normally partake in even behind closed doors.

"You shouldn't be recording at work," I said. It was a
dumb thing to say, but it was all I could manage in the moment.

"Yeah, yeah, I know," Simon said. "Once in a while, though,
there's something too good to resist."

"Like the horse video."

"The horse fucker, and now this." He put his phone away, to my relief. "I flagged it, but it's possible it'll get out on other platforms. I thought you should know."

"Okay," I said. "Thanks for telling me."

He gave me a sly look. "I was thinking some people might pay good money to keep this video under wraps."

I felt tired and wished he'd get to the point. "You want me to pay you?"

"Not you," he said. He looked insulted. "You're my friend, Linda. You got me the job. Besides, I know you're broke."

I hadn't realized Simon had such warm feelings for me. Since he'd come to Acuity, he'd only seemed interested in Karina.

"I thought Dave might be willing to cough up some cash," he said.

"I don't know about that," I said uneasily.

"Why not?"

"What would he be paying you for? If the video will get out no matter what."

"It won't, necessarily. But I can say if he doesn't pay, I'll post it on 4chan. Or even Twitter. It'd go viral. People love outrage bait about rowdy passengers. Especially in first class."

"Really, Simon, I'd rather you didn't," I said, feeling nauseated. "This affects me, too."

Simon nodded. "I know. I won't actually do it. Dave just needs to think I will. I can say I'll tell Christa. He'd get fired for sure." Simon leaned back and regarded me with that same grudging respect he'd shown me on our date at Peet's, back in January. "I couldn't believe it was you. I almost lost my shit."

A man in corporate attire passed us, bound for the bathroom. We were quiet until he was safely inside.

"How much do you think it's worth to him?" Simon said in a low voice. "Five grand? Ten?"

"I don't know," I said. "I don't want to be involved."

"I'll cut you in for half."

I considered the possibilities. If Simon extracted ten thousand dollars from Dave, then I'd get five, money I could put toward flying with N92823 for as long as it took for him to choose me.

"Come on, Linda," Simon said. "You deserve compensation. Your boss made you give him a hand job on a plane. That's, like, next-level sexual harassment."

I had to laugh at this. Simon laughed, too.

"He isn't really our boss, though," I said. "And he didn't make me do anything."

Simon rolled his eyes. "Okay, whatever. The thing is, I'm doing it. So, can you give me Dave's phone number?"

I shook my head, coming back to myself. I wouldn't feel right blackmailing someone, especially for an act I'd willingly participated in. "I can't help you, Simon. And I really don't think you should do this. It could backfire on you."

Simon was unfazed. "No worries," he said. "I'll shoot him an email."

I rode the bus home, feeling sick with dread. I considered

calling Dave to warn him, but he'd said we shouldn't have further contact, to allow me to "heal." Alone in my cube, Simon's words kept rattling in my head, along with Karina's, back when I'd told her about Dave. I wondered if I'd let him get away with things, all along, because I assumed my vision board was to blame.

I paced my room, my affair with Dave appearing in a new light. Each step of the way, he'd considered only his own needs, and then he dropped me the moment he was confronted by my full humanity, my identity as a daughter and a sister, a person with a future he wanted no part in. The fact that my feelings corresponded to his, though from a different angle, was irrelevant. Dave was kind of an asshole.

For too long, I'd been content to sit back and allow the universe to work on my behalf, rather than making a decisive move toward my goal. I had a chance now to go after N92823 with all the funds I could garner. I hadn't wanted our reunion to be funded by Dave, but this seemed different from asking for a loan. I wasn't begging for charity; I was demanding compensation. It seemed like a form of justice. We'd make Dave pay for his recklessness, so that maybe he'd be more careful in the future. I texted his number to Simon, writing that I'd changed my mind, and wanted in on the deal. *Hell yeah,* Simon replied.

WHEN I ARRIVED AT ACUITY THE NEXT DAY, SIMON WASN'T AT HIS usual terminal. A cold sensation crept up the back of my neck. I opened my queue and began moderating comments on a news clip from the latest mass shooting. Around eleven, a Slack message from Christa popped up on my screen: *Good morning, Linda! Please stop by my office for a chat :^)*.

In my time working here, I'd never been summoned to Christa's office. The only occasion on which I'd entered that room was for my interview, which had involved few questions about my qualifications, instead consisting mostly of a list of disclaimers that Christa read from a sheet—things I wasn't allowed to sue them for. I recalled the walls were painted orange, and on them she'd taped photographs of a child and a man of her approximate age, a square-jawed fellow with a goatee and prominent canines, likely the same man whose sperm had impregnated her.

Christa greeted me at the door. "Thanks for coming by," she said. She gestured for me to sit in a straight-backed chair, while she settled into the swivel chair behind her desk.

"Linda, I want you to know that your well-being is very important to us," she said. "We know it can be a stressful job, and we want to support you."

My eyes roamed the space. The photographs I remembered were still on the wall, along with a few new additions. The child had grown.

I realized she was waiting for me to respond, though she hadn't really said anything. "I appreciate that," I said.

Christa clasped her hands on the desk. "I know this is a sensitive issue, and I'm sorry to have to discuss it with you. It's been brought to my attention that you and Dave Kinney were recently engaged in a sexual relationship."

I'd expected something like this, and yet I felt mortified,

and a little bemused. I thought of my dealings with Brett in the Subway walk-in. It was funny that I, a person who had no interest in sex with people, was always getting tied up in workplace sex scandals.

"I want you to know that you aren't in trouble in any way," Christa continued. "We're dealing with the matter swiftly and aggressively. Mr. Kinney has already submitted his resignation."

I remembered her email, back in March, referring to Dave as Dave, but now that he was in trouble, he was Mr. Kinney. "So you saw the video?" I said.

"We were made aware of a video, yes. By Mr. Kinney himself, actually." She leaned forward. "Off the record, Linda, I just want you to know I was appalled when I heard what he did to you."

"What he did to me?"

"How he pressured you to fly with him and threatened to have you fired if you didn't engage in sex acts with him on the plane. If it were up to me, he'd be in jail."

I pieced together what had happened. Rather than responding to Simon's blackmail attempt, Dave had fallen on his sword, submitting his resignation in exchange for the company's discretion, to protect both their reputations. I admired him for sacrificing himself, though I knew he'd hated his job, anyway.

"We want to support you however we can," Christa continued. "We'd like to offer you a raise of one dollar per hour, plus two months of complimentary counseling through the wellness app."

I laughed, and Christa flinched. "That's it?" I said.

"What did you have in mind?"

She was only being nice to me because they wanted to keep the incident under wraps. I was the last loose end they had to tie up. They'd have me sign an NDA and throw me a one-dollar raise and some free therapy on their worthless app. But I knew better than to accept this offer. I had my future to think about.

"I'd like to submit my resignation, too," I said. "And I want five thousand dollars, as compensation for my pain and suffering."

Christa smiled, but I could tell she was nervous. "I'm afraid it doesn't work that way."

I stood, taking charge of the situation. "Five thousand dollars, direct deposited into my account by Friday," I said. "Or I'll take my story to the media."

Christa cowered beneath me. She must have been shocked to witness my transformation. I'd always been subservient, slinking along the edges of the workspace, afraid if my supervisors saw too much of me, they'd tire of the sight and fire me.

"I'll check with corporate," she said. "It shouldn't be a problem."

"Good."

"In the meantime, it would be great if you'd sign this for me," she said, pulling up a contract on her iPad.

"I'll sign after I get the money," I said. "Five grand. By EOD Friday. Plus my paycheck for this week, though I'm leaving now and I won't be back."

She nodded, a grudging respect in her eyes. As I left her office, I wondered if I should have asked for more money.

I returned to my terminal and gathered my few belongings. I sensed Karina watching me with curiosity, and felt a pang of sadness that now there would be no opportunity to rekindle our friendship. Sadness and also bitterness, remembering what Karina had said the last time we spoke, accusing me of being jealous of her relationship and saying I was weird—which I certainly was, but such an insult seemed beneath the person I'd thought she was. I saw Karina differently now. She was blinkered by conventional values, swaddled by her own beauty, the adult version of the popular girls I'd grown up with in Irvine. I looked her square in the eyes. My expression must have betrayed my anger, as she looked shaken. Her lips parted, as if she were about to say something, but before she could, I left.

I thrust myself from Acuity's headquarters, pulled by force of habit to the BART station. I went to the airport, where I rode the infinite loop of the Red Line for an hour. Wave after wave of air travelers boarded my car, rode to their terminal, left, and were replaced by fresh travelers, in the anonymous exchange of the airport monorail. As I sat on an upholstered seat in my favorite terrestrial vehicle, I felt giddy, amazed by what I'd pulled off. I remembered the stacks of cash I'd placed on my last vision board and wondered if this had been the universe's convoluted way of delivering money to me.

Simon texted, telling me what I'd already guessed—he'd been fired for using his phone to record confidential material, and for attempting to blackmail Dave.

*Guess you were right,* he wrote. *Oh well. YOLO, right?*

I'd heard nothing from Dave. I wondered if Simon had told him I was involved with the scheme. From what Christa said, it sounded like Dave had taken the fall to a greater extent than he'd needed to, making himself out to be a villain and me the blameless victim. As I considered this, I felt a grudging affection for Dave. I hoped he'd find his happiness in a new phase of life, just as I was about to find mine.

I was still riding the AirTrain at 2:00 P.M. when my phone buzzed with a notification: a new message in the VBB WhatsApp. Amid recent turmoil, I'd forgotten it would be July in a few days, and time for the third-quarter VBB. I reviewed the messages I'd missed over the last several weeks. Morgan had sent photos from Costa Rica, to which other members had heart-reacted. Judy had attempted to start a "gratitude chain" one morning by sending the group a list of five things she was grateful for—*cold brew, my wonderful wife, SoulCycle, the ability to pause before making a decision, all my amazing friends!*—but no one had replied with their own list, or even heart-reacted to hers, and she hadn't tried again.

More recent messages revealed that planning was under way for a VBB this Sunday. It was Nikki's turn to host, but she'd just texted, saying her in-laws had sprung a last-minute visit upon her. *Sorry, ladies!* she'd written. *Can anyone else swing it this time?*

I texted back quickly, before anyone else had a chance: *Hey, ladies! I can host!*

22 I'd come a long way in six months, evolving from nervous initiate to host of the VBB. I didn't bother asking my landlords' permission to entertain a gathering of six or seven women, give or take Karina, as I didn't know if she'd deign to attend an event on my turf. I hoped she wouldn't come, as I knew my latest board would only add fuel to her disgust. But our friendship was dead, anyway. I no longer cared what the Chens thought of me, either. I didn't mind if they evicted me, as I was about to evict myself from the world.

On Friday, I moved my furniture to the center of the cube and scrubbed the walls with a washcloth dipped in warm water with a dollop of dish soap. I vacuumed with a cordless Dirt Devil I'd found discarded on the sidewalk a few months before. Though its exterior was filthy, the devil able to clean all but its own body, the device functioned as advertised, its canister filling with my skin cells and hair, crumbs of past meals, and a few tiny dead bugs. In the bathroom, I wiped down the sink, toilet, and tile floor, and then—why not?—I extended my cleaning to the shower stall, though I doubted any of my guests would wish to bathe during their brief visit to my quarters.

I took a break, lying on my bed, which remained adrift in the middle of the room. I logged in to my bank account, a compulsive habit since my showdown with Christa. All week, the total had remained stuck around five hundred dollars, decreasing incrementally as I purchased food and sundries. Now, when the screen refreshed, I discovered my wealth had soared to more than six thousand dollars! Payroll had deposited my hush money, plus post-tax earnings for a final week of work I hadn't actually done. I checked my email and saw Christa had sent a contract, which I signed after a cursory skimming. I got the point: they didn't want me to talk about Acuity or my relationship with Dave, and I had no intention to. I'd gotten my money, an amount large enough to enact the next phase of my plan. After a moment's deliberation, I venmo'd Simon five hundred dollars, as I wouldn't have had the confidence to demand payment if it weren't for his scheming.

I'd embark on my reunion with N92823 directly after the VBB. My fate hadn't actualized during my last binge, but this time would be different, as I'd be flying with my soulmate. I would fly with him for as long as it took for him to remember me. In the meantime, I decided to purge my room of its embarrassing relics, as I didn't plan on returning. I loaded my backpack with the items I'd bring on my journey: a few spare T-shirts and underwear, granola bars, and a plastic bag of toiletries in TSA-approved quantities. The rest I put in garbage bags, which I then stuffed in the closet. I removed my old vision boards and flight paraphernalia from under my bed. On Saturday afternoon, I brought it all to Ocean Beach and burned it in a fire ring. I kept only my chunk of 737, which I held in my fist as I watched my secret life reduced to ashes.

I surrendered the fire to a cluster of youths hovering nearby and made my way home, stopping at 7-Eleven for brunch fare. I purchased four six-packs of mini donuts in powdered sugar and chocolate varieties, bottles of sparkling water, two bags of Ruffles potato chips, and a twenty-four-pack of Miller High Life. I lugged it all back to my cube and spent the rest of the night constructing my vision board.

Sunday morning, I laid the only towel I owned, still damp from my shower, across the foot of my mattress, and arrayed upon it the spread of refreshments. I set bottles of High Life on their sides, parallel to each other, like guns displayed by a dealer in a seedy motel room. It looked shitty, but it didn't matter. Any tepid affection my guests had harbored for me would be extinguished once they saw my vision board. I needed them only as witnesses, to amplify my appeal to the universe.

I put on my gold dress and blow-dried my hair. I excavated my makeup bag from the cabinet under the sink and made use of its crusty offerings, applying concealer beneath my eyes, powder across my T-zone, and mascara to my eyelashes. With ten minutes remaining before the appointed start time, I realized my guests would need to find their way to my cube. I scrawled *VBB* on an old envelope and taped it to the garage's side door.

Judy was first to arrive, texting me from outside the garage, in spite of the clear signage I'd posted. Her curly hair was pulled into a bun, highlighting the freakish length of her neck. I led her through the garage, and she stood in my doorway, taking in the lay of my cube with a neutral expression. "It's cozy," she said, echoing Karina's prior sentiment. I offered her a beverage, gesturing to the spread.

"I'll take a sparkling water," she said.

"Are you sure you don't want a Miller High Life?" I said, holding a bottle aloft. I hoped to lubricate my guests with alcohol, so they'd be more receptive to my board.

"'The champagne of beers,'" she said with a laugh. "Okay, why not."

I twisted off the cap and handed her the bottle. "I haven't had one of these since high school," she said. She took a sip and winced.

"The bathroom is right through that door, if you need to use it," I said, remembering my panicked moments at Esme's condo. A good host should never conceal their toilet's location.

I knew the next step of proper hosting was to offer Judy a place to sit, but my bed was occupied by refreshments, aside from a two-foot strip at its head, where I'd anticipated people would stand to present their boards. I dragged out two of the garbage bags full of my possessions and said we could use them as beanbag chairs.

"It's okay. I can stand."

"They're not full of garbage," I said. "It's stuff I'm donating to Goodwill." I realized this sounded the same as garbage.

Judy put her hand on my arm. "I wanted to get here early so we could talk about Karina."

I stiffened. "What about her?"

"She mentioned you two had a falling-out. I was sorry to hear it. I could tell you were a good friend to her."

"It was unfortunate," I said. "I've missed her."

"I'm sure she misses you, too."

I wished this could be true. "I'm pretty sure she hates me," I said.

"Oh, I doubt it," Judy said, pausing to take another swig. This time, she didn't wince, and I hoped she was warming to the beverage. "Karina does this with all her girlfriends. She has trouble trusting people, so when she gets close to someone, she winds up lashing out, and then regrets it, but is too embarrassed to apologize. It's happened a bunch of times with us. I've learned to just let her blow off steam. After a few weeks I'll call her and we'll both pretend nothing happened."

I thanked Judy for providing this context, though it didn't seem relevant to our situation, in which I was far from blameless. "How's she doing these days?" I asked.

"I don't know, honestly," Judy said. "I've tried to hang out with her a few times, but she says she's busy with wedding stuff."

"Do you think she'll come today? She hasn't said anything in the chat."

"She's coming. We texted this morning."

My stomach knotted with anxiety. Still, I was determined to follow through with my plan. I'd have no need for friends, where I was bound.

Esme and Stacy arrived next, having carpooled together. Esme scanned the room critically. "So this is where you live," she said, as if trying to convince herself it could be true.

"I'm into it," Stacy said. "Reminds me of my old dorm room."

I invited them to partake of the brunch spread. Stacy opened the bag of cheddar and sour cream Ruffles, saying it was her favorite flavor. Esme primly selected a bottle of plain sparkling water. Morgan and Nikki appeared in the doorway, and the other women exclaimed over Nikki's presence. We'd assumed she wouldn't be able to come, due to her in-laws' visit.

"It all worked out," she said. "My in-laws are taking Sean to the zoo. I didn't want to miss another VBB!"

Morgan stepped past the other women and peered into my bathroom, like an apartment inspector. "How much is your rent, if you don't mind my asking?" she said.

"Nine hundred a month."

"So cheap!" Stacy said, around a mouthful of Ruffles. "And you have your own bathroom. I pay twelve hundred and I have two roommates."

"Is it legal not to have a window?" Nikki said, her eyes scanning the ceiling.

"Probably not," I said.

"What happens if there's a fire?" Morgan said from the doorway of the bathroom.

"I suppose I would burn to death," I said. "Please, everyone, have some donuts."

The space was tight now, the cube's temperature rising, the air thick with a yeasty smell from the beer, mingled with the women's perfumes and hairstyling products. The garbage bags further reduced the floor space. No one seemed to recognize them as makeshift beanbag chairs, and I feared the women would think I was such a slob, I'd left trash strewn around the room.

"These are chairs, by the way," I said, gesturing to them. Stacy plopped down on a bag, too exuberantly, it turned out, as the plastic burst, exposing a tangle of old leggings and underwear.

"Maybe we should do this at the beach? It's a beautiful day," Esme said, her hand on her stomach, which had swelled slightly with pregnancy. Inwardly, I cursed Esme for making this suggestion. It seemed important for the ceremony to unfold in my cube, as the psychic energy of manifestation would diffuse in the open air.

Before the others could respond, Karina appeared at the door. "Hey, everyone," she said. "Sorry I'm late. Got stuck in traffic." She was dressed casually, in an oversized pink T-shirt and black Lululemon leggings. She greeted the other women before turning to me with a practiced smile.

"Hey, Linda," she said. "Thanks for hosting."

I was flooded with emotion, the weight of how I'd missed Karina crashing against me. I cleared my throat. "Let's get started," I said.

Judy said she'd go first. I gestured to the head of my bed, and she kicked off her flats and climbed up. She bounced a few times, as though my mattress were a trampoline, and everyone laughed. I wished I hadn't pressured her to drink the beer, which had made her excessively irreverent.

Judy's board was a soothing collage of nature-themed images: Baker Beach on a rare warm day, a flower bed, a hiking trail in Marin, a cluster of grazing deer. Judy explained that she wanted to volunteer for a beach cleanup and spend more time gardening.

"I've been really stressed with work lately, launching the STEM camp," she said. "The modules were so buggy, I was staring at a screen for, like, ten hours a day. I want to be intentional about making sure I spend some time outside every day, getting my hands in the dirt."

"It's gorgeous," Nikki said. "Beautiful photos."

"That's the other thing," Judy said. "I took these myself. I want to get back into photography this quarter, too."

"Damn, original photos?" Stacy said. "You're really setting the bar high."

"Oh, thanks," Judy said, blushing.

We clapped, and Judy stepped off the bed with an ironic curtsy. "Okay, who's next?" I said, impressed by my own domineering attitude.

Nikki's board featured images of women talking and laughing, a child crouched over a book, and a plate of linguine with clams. She told us she hoped to mend relations with her sister on the East Coast, with whom she'd recently gotten into an argument about homeschooling, and learn how to cook her Italian grandmother's recipes. Stacy's board contained mostly dogs, with one prominently displayed at the center, a golden retriever named Broccoli who suffered

from a mysterious ailment. She implored the universe to as-
sist in Broccoli's full recovery, so that he could find his forever home. Morgan's board centered on the project of
converting their downstairs unit into an Airbnb, while
Esme's board prioritized rest, self-care, and the consumption of foods rich in prenatal vitamins.

Soon it was down to me and Karina, just as it had been at
the previous VBBs. Our eyes met, and Karina smiled shyly.

"I'll go," she said, mounting the bed. The women were
silent, probably fearing that Karina would show us the same
board for the third straight quarter. They'd have to repri-
mand her, or the affair would descend into farce. Karina
struggled to remove the hair tie she'd secured her board
with, increasing our suspense. When she released the board,
though, it was clear this was an entirely new creation. We
gathered closer. A constellation of wild animals, clouds, the
planet Saturn, a lamb, and an icon of the Virgin Mary, all
swirling around the word "SURRENDER."

"I've been doing a lot of soul-searching lately, and I realized you all were right," Karina said. "I've been trying to control my life in an unhealthy way. I was searching for
fulfillment through external milestones, but even when I
got what I wanted, it didn't make me happy." She closed her
eyes and took a breath. "Wedding planning has been so
stressful, and I've realized that I have to chill out, or I'll drive
myself crazy," she continued. "Let go or get dragged, right?
So, this quarter, I'm not setting any concrete goals. I want to
let the universe guide me. I'm giving up. In a good way."

The other women remained silent for another beat, reflecting on Karina's words. I heard the door from the main house open and footsteps approach the washing machine. Presumably, Mrs. Chen was doing her usual Sunday load. I held my breath, knowing that in another moment, the women would betray their presence in my cube.

As I'd expected, they erupted in cheers. Judy jumped onto the bed and hugged Karina. Two unopened bottles of High Life clattered to the floor, though luckily neither of them shattered. I heard the door to the house slam, as though Mrs. Chen were rebuking me.

Karina climbed down from the bed, wiping tears from her eyes. When the other women had finished hugging her, I approached her timidly. Karina laughed and threw her arms around me. "Oh, Linda," she said. "I've missed you."

My VBB was a success so far. More than half of the mini donuts had been consumed. I'd laid the groundwork. All that remained was to unveil my board. My phone buzzed in my pocket, and I saw Kevin had texted: *Hey Linda. You having a party?* I had to work quickly, before the VBB was broken up.

I stood on the bed and unspooled my board, allowing the women to drink in its horrifying images. Dreamliners and 737s pitched downward, flames rising from their engines. A plane flying inverted. Mangled debris, charred plane parts lying in a field. Headlines of doom, taken from flight disaster simulations: "Falling from the Sky at Over 34,000 Feet Per Minute." "Airbus A320 Takes Off by Itself." "This Plane Tried to MURDER Everyone on Board." The registration numbers of crashed planes, along with brief descriptions of the horrors that had befallen them. At the center of the board, an image of a 737 with N92823 printed on his flank, next to a photo of my face, from the series Karina had taken for my dating profile. Above us stretched a flower-strewn arch that read "Just Married."

The women squinted, confused, except for Karina, who stared at my board with resignation, as though it only confirmed what she'd already known.

"You might recall my first board featured pilots," I began, my voice clear and strong. "The pilots were a stand-in for my true desire. The truth is, I love planes—in particular, a 737 named N92823, who I told you about at the last VBB. I thought N92823 was lost to me, but I saw him last weekend, and now I'm going to find him again." I couldn't bring myself to look at the women's faces. Instead, I stared at the wall opposite me. "I've always known my fate was to marry a plane—that is, for myself and a plane to be united in death, our love sealed for eternity. I pray the universe will look upon me with favor and grant me my only wish." I stopped there.

Morgan was the first to speak. "Wait. What are we talking about here? A plane crash?"

"If you want to phrase it in such vulgar terms," I said.

"You're full of shit," Nikki said. "No one wants to die in a plane crash."

"Is this a joke, Linda?" Esme said quietly, from her position by the closet. "I don't think it's funny."

"Not a joke," I said. "I hinted at these goals on my previous boards. I finally have the courage to ask for what I want directly."

"You're making a mockery of tragedy," Morgan said. Her skin flushed pink, though that might have been due to the room's excessive heat. "What about the people who've actually died in plane crashes? You're making light of their deaths."

"I honor their deaths," I said. "I hope to join them."

"Linda, the vision boards are supposed to be used for *positive* goals," Judy said. "You can't use them to bring about mass death."

"It's not normal to want to die in a plane crash," Esme said. "It's sick."

Karina remained silent in the corner, her arms crossed over her chest.

"I dunno, I think it's kind of romantic," Stacy said. The other women stared at her. "Well, let's be real. It's not like these boards actually do anything. Linda's not going to make a plane crash just by gluing some crap to a board."

"And I would never meddle directly," I said. "But if it's my fate, I can't escape it. I'd prefer to run toward it with an open heart."

A knock came at my door. The women startled, as though I'd summoned a demon. Judy opened the door to reveal Kevin. I turned my board to face the wall before he could glimpse its imagery.

"Hey, everyone," he said. "Sorry to interrupt, but this room happens to have a maximum capacity of one person.

This gathering is actually illegal, so you'll all have to leave now."

The women began shuffling out. "Wait," I said, climbing down from the bed. "We have to recite the manifestation mantra."

Stacy hugged me. "Don't listen to them," she whispered in my ear. "Go after your dreams, you crazy bitch."

Karina lingered at the door. "Simon told me what happened," she said. "Are you okay, Linda?"

"I'm better than okay," I said. "I'm finally free to pursue my dreams. Isn't that what you always told me to do?"

She glanced at Kevin, who held the door open with an air of impatience. "Okay. See you later, then."

"See you later," I said.

Kevin and I stood in the wreckage of the VBB: the empty beer bottles, fallen potato chips, and a dusting of powdered sugar from the donuts. "I assumed you knew you couldn't have a party here," he said. "My parents are pretty upset, and so am I, to be honest. I thought you were going to keep it low-key."

"Sorry, Kevin," I said. I folded my board into a dense square and tucked it into my backpack. "I'm moving out, so you won't have to worry about me anymore."

"You have to give thirty days' notice."

"Fine, I'm giving it now."

Kevin scratched the back of his neck. His anger was gone, replaced by curiosity and, I hoped, a tinge of sadness that I was leaving. "Where are you going?"

"I'm meeting my soulmate in Seattle."

"Well, good luck."

I realized I'd never see Kevin again and was moved to embrace him. His shoulders were stiff, but he endured the hug. I offered him the leftover beer.

"Sure, thanks," he said, and took the case with him.

23 After Kevin left, a shadow of the old shame flickered under my excitement, like a shark passing beneath a canoe. I'd anticipated my guests' horrified reactions, the intensity of which, I hoped, would pique the universe's interest. Still, my act of exposure left me queasy. I reminded myself that my reputation would be amended after I'd married N92823. A chill would run up the women's spines when they heard the news. A plane crash was frightening to begin with, and their horror would be compounded by the memory of my vision board. They'd investigate, and find the plane involved was the same one I'd placed on my board. At first, they might suspect I'd tampered with the plane, though I had insisted this was against my moral code. Once the NTSB cleared my name, they'd repent of their blame-casting. They would miss me and wish they had at least thanked me for the donuts.

I rallied my spirits for the adventure I was about to embark on, shedding the gold dress in favor of hardier apparel—jeans, sweater, and camel coat—and tucking a few last items into my backpack. I bid farewell to my cube, kissing each of its corners, and departed for the bus stop.

It was a foggy summer day. Through the bus window, I

admired the shaggy eucalyptus trees of Stern Grove, and then the gray rectangles of the Stonestown Galleria complex, where Karina and I had enjoyed many shopping excursions. The snack kiosk on the San Francisco State campus was swarming with youths clad in shorts and sundresses, determined to abide by summer's conventions, even at the expense of their comfort. A plane flew north, parallel to the bus, low enough that I could make out the windows dotting his fuselage.

I completed my well-worn circuit for the last time: bus to BART to AirTrain, whose Red Line conveyed me to Terminal 3. I approached the TSA podium nervously, fearing I was marked by scandal, though as far as I knew, the video of me and Dave remained suppressed. Possibly, the nosy woman who'd shot it had filed a complaint that was working its way through the airline's bureaucracy. Simon had promised to monitor the forums and keep me apprised of any developments, though I hadn't asked him to do this. He'd called to thank me for the five hundred dollars I'd sent him, telling me I was a real one, his friend for life.

The stoic TSA agent inspected my face against my ID, fed it into the CAT machine, waved me on. My bag, too, passed through the X-ray unremarked, my vision board folded, obscuring the images from the machine's eye. I pierced the secure sector's membrane for what I hoped would be the last time. One way or another, my journey would end within the post-security zone.

. . .

N92823 WAS CURRENTLY FLYING FROM CHICAGO TO SEATTLE. AS he wasn't scheduled to fly through SFO anytime soon, I planned to meet him at SEA, deadheading there on another plane, as pilots sometimes had to do. We'd spend the night in Seattle, then fly back to O'Hare together in the morning, a flight I hoped would never land, at least in the traditional sense. Universe willing, tomorrow would be our wedding day.

My flight to Seattle was operated by a handsome 737-900 named N18324. I resisted his seductions as we took off, determined to remain faithful to N92823. No longer would I behave like a frivolous youth, driven by lust for any plane I could afford a date with. I shouldn't gorge on hamburger when I had steak waiting at home, or so went the saying, though I ate no form of beef and found the analogy distasteful. As we made our initial climb, N18324 banked gently right, and my window filled with a view of the coastline, down which I'd just traveled in the bus. I glimpsed the Outer Sunset, the dense grid in which the Chens' house nestled, and felt a twinge of nostalgia for the home I'd cast off, like a shell I'd outgrown.

When we landed, I rushed toward Gate A13, where N92823 had arrived twenty minutes ago, according to my flight-tracking app. Down the corridor, at the farthest reaches of the A Concourse, I spotted my love through the window. I slowed, approaching him with reverence. I beheld the soft curve of his nose, and the rectangular panels of his windscreen above it. His joints must have ached after a long day of flying. I wished I could rub oil into his wings. "It's me," I whispered, placing my palm against the glass. "I found you."

I made a nest beneath the window, as close as I could legally draw to N92823, short of boarding him. I laid my head upon my backpack and used my coat as a blanket. At one point in the night, I opened my eyes and found his windscreen gazing back at me, as though we were lying in bed together.

I WAS WOKEN BY THE ROAR OF A VACUUM DRAWING CLOSE TO MY head. I stood and stretched, greeting my fiancé through the window. The tarmac was wet; it must have rained overnight. Now the sun shone upon my love's back, his form bright against the gray runways and, beyond them, a fringe of pine trees.

I was excited and nervous, as brides are known to be on their wedding day. As boarding began, it occurred to me that I should text my family members. I wanted to say goodbye in a coded fashion that wouldn't alarm them. I started with Al: *Great seeing you guys last weekend! I love you all.* To my mom I wrote simply, *Love you!*

My mom replied immediately, asking if everything was okay. *Everything's great,* I wrote. *Just thinking of you!* I hoped one day she'd accept my marriage to N92823, though she wouldn't understand it in those terms.

My group was called. As I shuffled toward the mouth of the jet bridge, I had an urge to text Karina. I assumed my vision board had further alienated her, but I didn't want her to feel any regret after I was gone. *Hi Karina,* I wrote. *I just want you to know that I think you're an amazing person, and I hope you get everything you want from life. No need to respond. Love, your friend Linda.*

The text went through. I toggled my phone to airplane mode.

As I proceeded down the jet bridge, I recalled the day I'd last flown on N92823, seventeen years ago. My family's journey to the airport had been fraught. We were late, due to an errand my dad had put off until the last minute, a run to the marina to hand off a check for *Wendy's* docking fee. My mom made snide comments from the Camry's passenger seat, annoyed he hadn't taken care of it sooner. At the check-in counter, my dad heaved my mom's suitcase onto the scale dramatically; she'd packed too much, in his opinion, for a weekend trip. I'd been excited to fly, a rare treat, and my parents were spoiling it. As we waited to board, Al tried to lighten the mood, reminding us that vacations were supposed to be fun. He was rallying his own spirits, too, as he hadn't wanted to go on the trip. He'd just started dating a girl from his chemistry class and would have preferred to spend the weekend with her.

Back then, I didn't appreciate what I had—my family still intact, all its members alive. I'd taken them for granted, as only the lucky could. I glanced over my shoulder now and imagined our spectral forms shambling down the jet bridge, sunk in our private grievances. We'd been estranged when we entered the plane, but turbulence brought us together.

We clung to each other, and I'd hoped our union would be permanent, but it hadn't lasted through the cab ride to the hotel, by which point my parents had resumed their quarreling.

As I entered N92823, I braced myself for the charge I'd felt when Karina and I boarded the flight to SLC, but I perceived no more than the usual thrill, no indication yet that he'd recognized me. I grazed my fingers along his seatbacks, hoping to awaken him to my presence. I perceived time marked on his body—his wall panels yellowed, his seats dingy. I wondered if he would similarly note my body's aging, and hoped he would still desire me.

I found my seat, 26F, a window on the starboard side. The aisle- and middle-seat passengers, young men who seemed to be strangers to each other, politely shuffled into the aisle to allow my passage, and after that minded their own business. I draped my coat over my lap. I pretended to fiddle with my seatbelt, and in the process, tucked the chunk of 737 into my underwear.

With other lovers, I'd felt uneasy in the midst of my enjoyment, unable to shake the sense that I was cheating on N92823. Now I felt perfectly contented, having arrived exactly where I was meant to be. My pulse quickened as we pushed back from the gate. N92823's engines fired, and I took a deep breath, my body filling with his power. We raced down the runway, the landscape blearing past. I was pinned to my seat, my mouth open, my love's voice screaming in my ears. His nose lifted, and as we rose into the sky, I was overcome by a sense of limitless freedom, as though I were shedding the sticky tendrils that had bound me to the world. At last, we'd finish what we started when I was thirteen. Our love would be infamous, immortalized one day by eerie animations of our doomed flight.

We banked left, and I looked across the aisle to the opposite window, through which I saw gray housing tracts, swaths of forest, a highway slicing north to south. I held my breath, feeling I was suspended on the tightrope of destiny. In a haze of pleasure, I lost equilibrium, and felt the ground rush up to meet me. It was going poorly, this takeoff. N92823's passions could not be constrained by any pilot.

A moment later, N92823 broke through the clouds and leveled, finding his eastward trajectory. The flight attendant came on the PA with the usual scripted spiel. I detected no hint of agitation in her voice. I assured myself this meant nothing. After all, on our first flight together, the trouble hadn't begun until several hours in.

FOUR HOURS LATER, WE LANDED AT O'HARE. I WATCHED THROUGH the window as we taxied to our gate, glaring at the ground crew worker with his stupid lighted batons. The other passengers deplaned, while I remained seated, unwilling to accept that our first date had been a bust. Finally, I had no choice but to make my way up the aisle. The captain, a portly gentleman with bushy eyebrows, stood in the cockpit's doorway with a hopeful expression, as though he wanted me to praise him for his perfect landing. I nodded, resenting his need for validation. He hadn't even needed to wrestle the plane to keep him flying smoothly. N92823 had snubbed me.

In the terminal, I tucked myself into a restroom stall and wept. I'd hoped N92823 had pined for me all these years, just as I'd pined for him, and that he'd claim me the moment I entered him, refusing to let me go a second time. Instead, he'd treated me like a stranger. After a few minutes, I pulled myself together, emerging from the stall and splashing my face with cold water. I reminded myself that I'd known it might take several dates to persuade N92823 to marry me, which was why I'd secured a sizable chunk of money before embarking on our reunion. We'd been apart seventeen years; it made sense he'd want to take it slow. A few awkward dates were nothing relative to the eternal bliss that awaited us.

When I returned to the gate area, N92823's next flight, to Dallas, was already boarding. It wasn't easy to be the fiancée of a plane, as they were always leaving. From my flight-tracking app, I saw he'd return to O'Hare around 6:00 P.M., then fly on to Denver, where he'd spend the night. I purchased a ticket on the Denver flight. I checked my messages and found a reply from Al: *Hey good seeing you too! How's Frisco?*

Karina had also replied: *Do you want to get coffee sometime?*

I stared at Karina's message in amazement. A month ago, I would have leaped at an opportunity to have coffee with her. But it was too late. Ties to my old life would only distract me from my goal. I didn't respond to either message.

Our flight to Denver was delayed an hour due to weather. On my radar app, the storm system resembled a green scab stretching diagonally across the country's midsection. The wait increased my excitement, so that by the time I boarded N92823, I frothed with desire, the sting of his initial rejection having faded. Our ascent was shaky, and with each jolt, I felt N92823's heart thawing. I was grateful for this show of affection, and even after we'd reached cruising altitude, breaking through the stormy nimbostratus into the sunny reaches above, I felt confident that the universe would unite us when the time was right.

We landed in Denver at 10:45 P.M., Mountain Time. I purchased a dinner of fries from McDonald's and brought it back to A16, where N92823 was resting after a long day's work. I ate my fries, gazing at my love's white back, which glowed in the light of a full moon. I felt at peace, having resolved to be patient. I wouldn't pressure N92823 to commit before he was ready. I decided to slow my pace to a single flight per day, giving my love a chance to miss me. I wanted each date to feel special, as opposed to the frenzy of a binge. As I drifted to sleep, I recalled my trip to Denver with Dave, back in April. Fifteen miles southwest of my current position, Dave's old enemy Mike was in his office at Barley Bros, or home with his family. I wondered if the new baby had arrived.

WE FLEW FROM DENVER TO NEWARK. NEWARK TO HOUSTON. Houston to Chicago. Chicago to Dallas. My hopes soared upon each takeoff, and were crushed anew when we landed safely at our destination. I tried not to betray my disappointment. I wondered if N92823 was angry that I'd made love to other planes while he was out of commission. I'd have to prove to him that my love was true, and that those other planes had meant nothing.

After a week of flying, I was beginning to feel the first stirrings of desperation when an event occurred that restored my faith. I'd arrived at O'Hare after deadheading from Dallas on board an A319 who did his best to tempt me with turbulence shortly after takeoff. Around 9:00 P.M., I boarded N92823 for a red-eye to Newark. I noted a peculiar energy in the air as I settled into my seat. The cabin grew hot while the flight attendants performed their safety demonstration. Around me, passengers fanned themselves with safety cards. We pushed back from the gate and circled the taxiway for a protracted interval, N92823's engines revving and sighing. Rather than lining up on the runway, however, we returned to the gate. The captain came on the PA to inform us the heat indicated a problem with the auxiliary power unit, which powered the air-conditioning and also affected pressurization. A maintenance team was on its way.

A problem with pressurization! This was the type of incident I'd always dreamed of. The maintenance crew would apply a cursory fix that would come unraveled in flight, a series of tiny missteps that would later be documented by the postcrash NTSB report. We'd reach cruising altitude, at which point oxygen would leach from the cockpit before the pilots understood what was happening. Oxygen masks would dangle from the ceiling, too late for the already un-conscious passengers. I'd grab a mask, having miraculously remained conscious. N92823 and I would cruise together through the night, until his engines flamed out from fuel exhaustion, and the earth pulled us into its embrace.

After a two-hour delay, we took off. I breathed shallowly to conserve the oxygen in my cells. When the flight atten-dants made their way down the aisle, I observed their move-ments closely, monitoring for erratic behavior that would indicate the onset of hypoxia. A woman in the row ahead of mine was served regular Coke, when she'd asked for Diet. The hairs rose on my forearms. Perhaps N92823's pilots were already unconscious beyond the locked door of the cockpit.

The fix must have held, though, as we ultimately pro-ceeded to a safe landing in Newark. Still, I deplaned in good spirits, having gotten the sign I needed. N92823 was trying to sabotage himself so we could be together, and he might have succeeded, if not for the pilot's last-minute decision to return to the gate. On our next two flights, I perceived addi-tional signs of N92823's growing affection. A shaky landing into O'Hare through high winds, N92823's wings pitching with a passion that rivaled my own. The next day, on a flight to New Orleans, we encountered a patch of moderate turbu-lence, though the sky was clear. After a few minutes, our path smoothed, but the captain kept the fasten seatbelt sign on for the duration of the flight and suspended beverage ser-vice. As we descended, I felt a lust in my teeth. I was so close. Surely our next flight would tip N92823 over the edge.

When we landed, I found a new text from Karina, saying she was coming over to check on me. She'd sent a few texts since the one asking if I wanted to have coffee, and I hadn't replied, which must have alarmed her. I was embarrassed to imagine her talking to the Chens about me, but I didn't try to stop her. What happened back in San Francisco was none of my business.

OUR TWELFTH DATE BROUGHT US TO MIAMI. I SAT IN AN EMPTY GATE area, shivering in the aggressive air-conditioning. N92823 had already departed for Cancun, a flight I couldn't join him on, as I didn't have a passport. He'd return tomorrow morning. In the meantime, I had to grit my way through eighteen grounded hours.

I closed my eyes, images cycling across the screen of my mind. The comb lines in my dad's hair as I sat on his shoulders outside John Wayne Airport. Guillaume Faury. The crucifix on Celia's wall. I thought I heard Karina saying my name, and startled awake to find the gate area had filled with passengers bound for Nashville. In the chairs opposite mine, a teenage boy nudged his dad and whispered something into his ear. They both looked at me and laughed.

In the restroom, I confronted my image in the mirror, and understood why I'd become an object of ridicule. It had been almost two weeks since I'd showered, and my habits of upkeep had grown lax. My eyes were bloodshot. My cheeks and chin had broken out with a smattering of pimples. My shirt had ketchup on it, and when I removed it, I was met with a stench of body odor. I stood at the sink in my bra, scrubbing the ketchup stain with hand soap. I washed my armpits, applied deodorant, and put on one of the two spare shirts I'd brought. I'd already cycled through them in the first days, and they also smelled, though not as badly as the shirt I'd just removed. Nothing could help my hair, which hung heavy with oil. I considered washing it in the sink and drying it using the Dyson, crouching to feed hanks of hair into the gray receptacle. But I'd already noticed women casting sidelong looks of disapproval in my direction as they entered and exited the restroom. I was mortified to have allowed my physical condition to deteriorate to such an extent that it caused offense to strangers. At the same time, I wanted to snap at those women. What did they want? For me to be filthy or wash myself in the sink?

That night, as I assembled my sleeping nest in yet another gate area, I resented N92823 for making me debase myself. What more did I have to do to prove myself to him? Since our flight to New Orleans, he'd reverted to his prior aloofness. Perhaps he regarded me as Anthony had once regarded his coworker Beatrice: as a pesky woman with a crush, a source of ego gratification, to be swatted away like a fly when my presence became tiresome. When he pulled into his gate the next morning, I stared into his haughty windscreen with bitterness. Here he was, back to torture me some more.

. . .

THE END DREW NEAR. I SAT IN A FOOD COURT AT DFW, INSPECT-ing my finances over a limp salad. After sixteen flights with N92823, along with five deadheads on other planes, I was almost out of money. My checking account was down to $280, enough for one last spin of fate's wheel. I booked a seat on N92823's flight to Chicago the next morning, at a cost of $189. I told myself that the universe might be waiting to unite us at the last possible moment, out of its perverse love of suspense. But it had become difficult to muster enthusiasm after so many disappointing dates. I wondered if N92823's soul had been sucked out during his long rehabilitation. Or maybe the truth was simpler. Maybe N92823 had never loved me, and the turbulence I'd enshrined in my memory had been the product of nothing more remarkable than air patterns, as everyone else assumed.

I'd felt similarly defeated at the end of my last binge, four years ago. I'd been trying to outrun my grief, and it worked as long as my money lasted. While I was airborne, I could imagine my dad was still alive. Flight was suspended animation, a period in which a person was exempt from obligation, cut off from the grounded world. I felt secure while locked in the pressurized cabin, 35,000 feet above the earth. But planes always land, one way or another. Back then, I'd retained hope of finding my soulmate plane one day, after my life had stabilized and I'd begun earning a steady income. This time, it was worse, as I clung to no such illusions. I'd found my soulmate, and so far, he'd rejected me. If he didn't choose me on our final flight, I'd have no reason to go on.

That night, I sat at the bar at a Buffalo Wild Wings in Terminal D, getting drunk on rum and Cokes. I no longer cared about conserving my funds, as they weren't sufficient to purchase another flight, anyway. I'd pinned my remaining hopes on our flight to Chicago in the morning, so I might as well enjoy one last send-off. I hadn't spoken to another person in weeks, aside from brief exchanges with flight attendants and cashiers, and as the alcohol loosened my inhibitions, I grew itchy with an unexpected desire for human connection. To my left sat a man in a plaid shirt. He drank a pint of beer, his eyes fixed on the TV above the bar, which was showing a football game.

"Where you headed?" I asked.

He glanced at me, then back at the TV. "Cincinnati," he said.

"I'm headed to Phoenix, allegedly," said the woman to my right. She was in her late forties, wearing red lipstick and cat's-eye glasses. "My flight's been delayed six hours," she continued, sipping her Bloody Mary. "Looks like I might be spending the night here. Next time, I'll rent a car. I'm done with the airlines."

Normally, I had no patience for people who griped about air travel. They failed to appreciate the privilege of being alive in the era of flight. How many humans, throughout history, would have paid a lifetime's salary for the chance to sail through the sky like a god? But my recent experiences had rendered me more cynical than usual toward the endeavor. I clucked my tongue in sympathy and asked why she'd come to Dallas.

"My daughter lives here," she said. "She's getting married next year. I was helping her pick out a dress."

I thought of Karina. Her wedding was a month away. My eyes grew teary, and the woman placed her hand on my arm.

"Everything okay, hon?" she said. She was looking at me with kindness.

"I've been flying all over the country, trying to get close to someone," I said. "I'm afraid he doesn't feel the same way I do."

"Well, that was a mistake," the woman said, rather harshly. "You should never chase a man. If he wants you, you'll know."

I wondered if she was right, though she didn't know my lover was a plane rather than a man. "I was hoping he just needed more time to decide," I said.

"That's BS," she said. "They know right away. Don't let them string you along until they find the girl they really want to marry."

The woman's phone buzzed, and she let out a whoop. Her flight was boarding.

"You'll find someone better," she said, signaling the bartender for her check. "My daughter got dumped by some jerk last year. She didn't get out of bed for a week. Now she's marrying a guy who owns a landscaping company."

She left, and no one took her place. It was just me and the silent man in plaid, until an hour later the bar closed, and I stumbled off to make my bed beneath a bank of defunct pay phones.

## 24

When I came to the next morning, my flight was boarding. I ran to the gate, my head throbbing due to my overindulgence at Buffalo Wild Wings. As we took off, I felt no desire for N92823, whom I now associated only with pain. I was hungover and grumpy, and wanted to get our last date over with. I recalled my conversation with the woman at the bar, and wondered if N92823 was simply a jerk, like her daughter's ex. A furtive part of me hoped my negative attitude would spark his interest, as I'd gotten nowhere with adoration. I remembered how Dave had pursued me when I'd ignored him, and been repulsed when he thought I'd grown attached.

But planes are better than people, and N92823 remained indifferent as we cruised above Oklahoma. I was enraged by the clouds, whose fluffiness was an affront to my dark mood. I flouted my usual rules, requesting a can of Coke and a bag of pretzels from the flight attendant. Soon I needed to use the lavatory. I peed and flushed, exulting in the violence with which my urine was sucked away. For once, I felt no shame in sullying a plane's holding tank with my fluids. It was my spiteful parting gift to him.

By the time we landed, I'd entered a state of grim acceptance. Not only had N92823 rejected me—so had the universe. The vision boards were a fraud. No transcendent fate
awaited me, only a dull procession of days. Upon exiting the
jet bridge, I rushed away from N92823's gate, eager to distance myself, as I could no longer bear to look at him.

I'd decided that O'Hare would be my final destination. I
had no interest in returning to San Francisco, even if I'd had
the money to purchase a ticket. There was nothing left for
me there, or anywhere else in the world. If I remained in the
airport, grounded among an endlessly revolving set of
strangers, I couldn't cause any more trouble. I would quar-
antine myself here until my body expired, whether it took
weeks or decades.

That night, I spent my last twenty dollars on a bag of trail
mix and a Snickers. At an empty gate, C22, I plugged in my
phone and sat against the wall, nibbling the Snickers bar's
shell. I reviewed the stream of texts Karina had sent over the
last two weeks, feeling guilty I hadn't responded to any of
them. I figured there was no harm in writing to her now.

I sent Karina a simple *Hey*.

She replied immediately: *Omg. Where are you, Linda??*

I ignored her question, asking what was new in San Francisco. She told me about going to the Chens' house the week
before and talking to Mrs. Chen, whom she deemed a "nice
lady." Mrs. Chen, of course, had no idea where I'd gone, but
then Kevin returned from his shift at 24 Hour Fitness and
reported I'd said something about finding my soulmate in

Seattle. Karina wrote that she missed me and asked when I was coming home. I told her not to worry and that I'd be in touch soon, though this was a lie.

A new day dawned. I was woken, as usual, by the sound of a vacuum, the airport's rooster. I roused myself from the floor and descended the escalator to the tunnel that connected Concourse C to the rest of the airport. The tunnel was famous for its light display, curving strands of neon that raced across the ceiling, synchronized with a playful electronic score. I stood on the right side of the moving walkway. Travelers streamed around me, jostling me with their bags as they rushed to make connections.

I regretted texting Karina, as now she wouldn't leave me alone. I declined her calls and ignored her texts. That afternoon, as I was strolling through Concourse B, I received a message from Dave: *Hey, Linda. How you holding up?* When I didn't respond, he sent a photo of three chicken tacos on a paper plate. *Got a new place in Santa Monica. Selling the old haunted house. Life is good! I'm here if you ever want to talk.*

I assumed that by contacting me, he was violating the contract he'd signed with Acuity. Karina must have asked him to reach out, on the off chance I'd reply to his message while ignoring hers. I didn't want to talk to Dave, though I was glad he didn't seem angry. He was back to his old self, sending me unsolicited pictures of meat.

By the third day, I'd finished the trail mix. My hunger intensified until I could think about nothing but food. That evening I sat in Concourse C's jazz-themed food court, watching people eat. Behind me rose a sculpture of three eyeless, suited men playing instruments—trumpet, trombone, saxophone. To my left, through the grid of windows, the sun was setting, casting the plane docked at C19 in pink light. A family sat at a nearby table, having a rushed dinner of pizza. The parents cajoled their son to eat more. "Come on, one more bite," the mother said, holding a slice toward the boy, but he turned his little face away. They gave up, dumping their tray in a trash can. After a moment, I went over and casually plucked out the pizza, which was unsullied aside from a small bite at the tip.

I proceeded to feast on trash, feeling like a clever rat. I observed people eating and tracked their progress to the trash receptacles. I reasoned that if I'd seen them throw it out, it wasn't as bad as eating food that had lingered with the other garbage. I ate chow mein, more pizza, and half a salad, preserved in its plastic shell. When I'd had my fill, I sat by the windows, feeling proud of my resourcefulness, my indomitable will to survive. As I watched a Triple Seven pull back from C19, I felt the first stirrings of arousal since I'd moored myself at O'Hare. I could no longer fly, but I could content myself with spectating on planes for the remainder of my hopefully brief life.

I was still tracking the Triple Seven's progress on the taxiway when my phone buzzed. Simon was trying to facetime with me. I was curious about what he wanted, and wondered if he had an update about the video, though it hardly mattered now. I picked up before realizing I'd fallen into a trap Karina had laid.

Simon was outdoors, standing against a gray wall. It was

8:00 P.M. in California, and the sun was setting, the golden light elevating his doughy features.

"Where you at?" he said.

"An airport," I said.

"Which one?"

"It doesn't matter." I wouldn't be tricked into revealing my location.

"Where you flying to?"

"Nowhere," I said.

He snorted. "Okay, whatever. Just come home. Karina's losing her shit."

"I don't have any money."

Simon took a drag off a vaping device. I hadn't realized he consumed nicotine, and wondered if he'd refrained from doing so on our coffee date to make a good impression. "I could buy you a ticket," he said as he exhaled, his head concealed within a cloud of vapor.

I was moved by his generosity, though his offer seemed reluctant. "Thanks, but I'm not coming back," I said. "This is my home now."

"The fuck you talking about, Linda?"

I wished Simon well and ended the call.

AS I WANDERED THE CORRIDORS OF O'HARE, DAY AFTER DAY, MY senses began to warp. The ground seemed to undulate, the floor's checkerboard pattern rising up to greet me. I felt like a fish in an aquarium, safely contained. Beyond the glass, the world moved on without me. I explored other terminals, watching planes take off and land, returning always to Concourse C, an oblong island accessed only via the light tunnel.

Without the thrill of flying, though, I grew bored and lonely. I considered trying to strike up conversations with travelers at various gates, but my already clumsy social skills had become even clumsier through disuse. When I smiled at people, they turned away, seeming unsettled. I knew I looked strange and feral. For years I'd worked hard to blend in with respectable society, but I was too far gone now to pretend. I kept to myself, moving frequently between gates, to avoid the scrutiny of any airport official who might attempt to oust me.

On the fourth night, I lay in my nest at C22 and perused the social media accounts of my loved ones. Denise had posted a video of Claudette taking a few wobbly steps across the plush rug of their living room. Karina had posted a photo of herself and Anthony holding hands on Baker Beach, with the caption: *Can't wait to be this guy's wife!* I wished I could talk to her, but I knew she would only pressure me to fly back to San Francisco. I hoped that, with time, everyone would simply forget about me.

The next day, I was making my rounds through Concourse C when a figure appeared in the distance. A woman, dressed in black leggings and a pink sweatshirt on which dogs rode skateboards. She spotted me, her face lighting up, her form moving toward me. For a moment, I wondered if I was hallucinating.

"Linda!" Karina said. "Thank god." She threw her arms around me, and from the pressure of her bones I knew she was real. Her face was clean of makeup, which made her look younger, her skin firm and dewy.

"You flew here?" I said, amazed.

She nodded, beaming. I was relieved our aborted practice flight hadn't traumatized her permanently. I asked how the flight had been.

"There was a little turbulence, but I closed my eyes and took some deep breaths, and it passed. If anything, it was boring." She gripped my elbows. "I'm so happy I found you. I've been walking around this airport for an hour."

"You came here just for me?" I said, feeling guilty.

Karina rolled her eyes. "Obviously." She explained that Simon had determined my location from our FaceTime. The window beside me was dark, so he knew I was somewhere east of California. Then, when I'd shifted in my seat, he'd glimpsed the jazz-playing statues, which allowed him to trace me to the food court. I should have known better than to accept his call. Simon was too good at the internet.

We settled into seats at the nearest gate. Though I was happy to see her, Karina's presence made me uneasy. I figured she'd want me to return to San Francisco, and I dreaded having to rebuff her after she'd come all this way. She ran a hand through my greasy hair and let it fall against my back.

"Are you okay?" she said. "You look . . . terrible. No offense."

I knew I had to appear stable, so she would leave me alone. "I'm fine," I said. "I feel great, actually."

"How long do you plan on staying here?"

"Just a little while longer, while I plan my next move."

"Aren't you out of money?"

I was irritated by her questions. "I'm happy here. The airport provides for all my needs."

A plane had just arrived at the gate. From his pointy nose and diminutive form, I surmised he was an Embraer 170. Passengers emerged from the jet bridge, looking rumpled and dazed.

"Did you ever find the plane from your vision board?" Karina asked.

I nodded. "I flew on him seventeen times. But it was pointless. He didn't want me."

"I don't think planes can want things," she said gently. "They're just machines, you know?"

"That's what everyone thinks," I said. "But I know the truth."

"I get it, though," she said, surprising me. "It sucks to feel rejected. I've been through breakups where I felt like I was going to literally die. The only thing that helped was time. Focusing on other things. Eventually, it passes. You'll see."

"I didn't just want some guy to be with me," I said, more bitterly than I'd intended. "It was more extreme than that."

Karina smiled, seeming unfazed. "I know. It's okay to have fantasies. Your thoughts aren't powerful enough to make anything happen."

I wished I could buy into this banal interpretation. Self-loathing crashed upon me, and I unwisely launched into a confession. I told her how I'd spent six thousand dollars on flights in the past two weeks. I told her how, after my dad died, I'd sold his boat, the thing he loved most in the world, and used the money to fly for a month straight. My brother had helped me get back on my feet, and I'd wasted his gift, ending up worse off than ever before. "I only bring trouble to the people who love me," I said. "I can't do it anymore. I'm sick of being selfish."

"Don't you see that it's selfish to stay here?" Karina said, with a note of anger that took me aback. "We all want you to come home. Not everyone has that, you know. People who miss them when they're gone."

My face burned with shame. I knew she was right about my selfishness. Yet I also felt she wasn't understanding the full extent of my transgressions. "If you knew about the things I've done, you wouldn't miss me," I said.

"Like what?"

"I touch myself on the planes," I said, keeping my voice low. "That chunk of 737 I showed you, in my room? I put it inside me. I get off on simulations of plane crashes." I waited for her reaction, but her face was blank. "I've been eating out of the trash," I added.

Karina grimaced, and I saw I'd finally managed to offend her. "Ew, Linda," she said. "Don't do that."

The screen above the gate desk indicated the Embraer 170 would board for Detroit in twenty minutes. Travelers had begun gathering around us. Karina turned to me and placed her hand on my arm.

"Look, Linda," she said. "None of that matters to me. The important thing is, you've always been a good friend. Other people, I can tell they're angling to get something. I'm always on my guard around them. Even Judy acts awkward with me, like I'm a mental patient she has to keep her eye on. But with you, I can be myself. I miss hanging out with you. I miss eating ramen in your weird little room."

I couldn't believe it. I'd told Karina everything, and she still wanted to be my friend. This was what I'd wanted for so long, and thought was impossible—to reveal my true self and be accepted as I was.

I suggested we take a stroll through the light tunnel, as the gate area had grown crowded. On the walkway, Karina asked me to take her picture beneath the streams of neon. She posed glamorously, leaning back with her elbows on the handrail, and I was reminded of our photo shoot back in January, when she'd taken pictures for my dating profile. We laughed as travelers pushed past us with indignant looks. By the time we'd traversed the tunnel, and emerged into the bright halls of Concourse B, my perspective had shifted. I'd forsaken humanity on behalf of planes, but humanity, in the form of Karina, had arrived to pull me back into its fold.

I stood beside my friend as she refilled her water bottle.

"When are you flying back?" I asked.

She screwed the top back on the bottle. "Whenever you're ready."

"I'm not going anywhere."

"Then neither am I," Karina said, tucking the bottle into her bag. I couldn't tell if she was bluffing.

She walked toward the escalators to baggage claim, and I followed her. "Karina," I said. "We can't fly together."

"Sure we can."

I was intrigued. We stood on the escalator, Karina on the step below mine. "Why don't we get out of here?" she said. "It's getting late. We can spend the night at a hotel."

We approached the exit door. A sign warned that no re-entry was permitted past this point. I paused a few feet from the threshold, reluctant to eject myself from the secure sector.

"Come on, Linda," Karina said, grasping my wrist. "I've got a room booked. You can take a shower, and then we'll have a nice dinner."

My resolve crumbled at the prospect of a shower. I allowed Karina to lead me through the doorway, back into the world.

OUR ROOM WAS ON THE TWENTIETH FLOOR OF THE HYATT RE-gency, the same chain I'd stayed in with Dave in Irvine. From our window, the downtown skyline appeared at a distance, through a gauze of storm clouds, a weather system that would likely delay flights into and out of O'Hare. I showered, rinsing weeks of grease from my hair and scrubbing every inch of my body with a washcloth. I emerged from the bathroom feeling dizzy, my blood pressure plummeting from the hot water. I collapsed onto the nearest bed, still wrapped in a towel.

"You okay?" Karina said. She sat in the chair by the window. Rain pattered softly against the glass.

"What day is it?" I asked, feeling as though I'd surfaced from a spell.

"Sunday."

"Don't you have to work tomorrow?"

"That's the thing, Linda," Karina said, her eyes bright. "I quit!"

She proposed we go to the lounge, where she'd tell me everything. I put my dirty clothes back on, and we headed downstairs, settling into low-slung red chairs on either side of a small round table. Karina ordered a bottle of rosé, dismissing my concern about the cost.

"I hated how they treated you and Simon," she said, swirling her glass in a sophisticated manner. "They were so eager to cover up for Dave being a pervert. They gave me a one-dollar raise in exchange for keeping quiet. I went along with it for a few days, but it didn't feel right."

I was a little annoyed they'd offered her the same deal they'd offered me, when I was the one who'd endured the supposed harassment. Dave hadn't been the only factor in her decision, however. The center seemed to be going downhill. The terminals were dirtier in the mornings. Christa didn't make her quarterly Costco run; when pressed, she said simply that the snack budget had been cut.

"That place is a sinking ship," she said. "Besides, Anthony signed a deal with a streetwear company, so that gives us more flexibility. We moved into our own place last week. A one-bedroom in the Excelsior."

I was impressed. "Is he still working at the pizza place?"

"No, he's doing shirts full-time now. It's gotten me thinking about what I want to do. I might get my esthetician license. I think it would be cool to have my own eyelash business."

I took a sip of rosé, feeling the wine warm my stomach. "I always wondered why you stayed at Acuity so long."

"I know," Karina said. "I thought it was what I deserved."

"But why would you think that? You've never explained."

Karina regarded me steadily. "Do you really want to know?"

"It can't be worse than what I've done."

She set her glass on the table. "Because of me, a person died," she said.

I was shocked but tried not to show it. "What happened?"

"There was this girl in high school," she said. "Her name was Cammie. Her family had just moved to the city from Ohio. She was awkward. Weird clothes, bad teeth. She was lonely. You could practically smell it on her. She kept trying to be friends with us, and in the hierarchy of the school, that was an insane move on her part. That's what we thought. She should have tried to be friends with people on her own level."

"You were the cool kids."

"You could say that, yeah."

I'd been correct, then, in my assumption that Karina had been a popular girl, someone who would have snubbed me, if not viciously bullied me, had we grown up together. "So you were mean to her," I said. "That's what kids do."

"It was worse than that. We acted like she was the coolest girl ever and invited her to everything. It was obvious that we were making fun of her, but she didn't seem to realize, no matter how far we pushed it."

I was reminded of the early days of my friendship with Karina, when I'd feared it was all an elaborate prank. "Okay," I said. "And then what?"

Karina's eyes had a distant look. "We invited her to come on a camping trip one weekend, at the Russian River. This big group of us. Judy's dad paid for it all, to celebrate our graduation."

Long-Neck Judy, I thought with fondness.

"So that night we were sitting around the campfire, playing truth or dare. And I was a little drunk and it started bugging me that Cammie was there. The joke had gone on so long, it was like everyone had forgotten it was a joke. She was sitting there smiling and saying goofy shit. It pissed me off, I guess, that she'd gotten so comfortable. When it was Cammie's turn, she chose dare and I said . . . Oh, god, it was awful."

"What did you say?"

Karina closed her eyes. "I said, 'I dare you to kill yourself, Cammie. Don't you know we all fucking hate you?'"

We were both quiet for a moment, her words hanging between us.

"So she jumped in the river?" I said.

Karina shook her head. "Nothing happened that night. After the trip, Cammie kept her distance. And then, a few years later, we found out she'd died. The details were kept private, but it sounded like an overdose, or suicide. Judy asked around, and it turned out Cammie had gotten pretty heavy into drugs after high school." Karina dabbed her eyes with a cocktail napkin. "She was such a sweet girl. And all I could think was if I'd kept my mouth shut that night, she'd still be alive."

I waited for her to say more, but as I watched Karina sniffle, I realized this was the extent of her secret. I'd expected something worse, perhaps a body stashed in Celia's crawl space.

"It wasn't your fault," I said. "You don't know what her life was like."

Karina nodded slowly. "All I know is, I made her life harder. I've always believed people get what's coming to them, eventually. I feel like the universe is waiting for the right moment to punish me. By working at Acuity, I was trying to punish myself, to let some of the pressure off, so I'd be spared from a worse punishment in the future."

"Like a plane crash," I said.

"I know it sounds crazy, but I couldn't shake it. Not until you disappeared, and I knew I was the only person who could bring you back."

I understood now why she'd come all this way. She had killed one weird girl, by her telling, but now she had a chance to save another.

"You really aren't afraid to fly with me?" I said.

Karina shrugged. "Whatever happens, happens. I'm done living in fear."

Her mood seemed lighter now that she'd unburdened herself. She poured the rest of the bottle into our glasses and signaled for the waiter, ordering another bottle of wine and some parmesan fries. I asked what Anthony had thought about her coming here.

"He was all for it. He said, 'We gotta get Lindy back in time for the wedding.'" She smiled. "It's in three weeks. You're still down to be a bridesmaid, right?"

I was incredulous. "You really want me to do that?"

"Of course. I need you there, Linda."

We grew drunker, and in the midst of our merriment, Karina facetimed Anthony, and I was treated to a view of his jovial face.

"Sup, Lindy?" he said. "You about ready to come home?"

I was moved by this simple question. All these years, I'd chased planes in pursuit of fulfillment, neglecting the home I'd made in San Francisco, in the windowless room that had probably by now been rented to someone else. I could find another place to live, and a new job, perhaps one well-paying enough that I could rent a room with a window. A path forward revealed itself. I would resign myself to the satisfactions of a normal life, without the highs and lows to which I'd been accustomed. I would content myself with eating and sleeping, watching the sun rise and set, spending time with Karina and Anthony and their inevitable children, until at an advanced age I died an ordinary death no one would deem tragic. Who was I to insist on more?

Besides, I had more than my own future to consider. Karina wouldn't fly back without me, and I refused to let her miss her own wedding on my account. I realized I'd already made my decision when I had allowed her to lead me out of the secure sector, into which I could not enter again without a ticket. When we'd hung up with Anthony, I told her I was ready. "Let's fly back tomorrow," I said.

"Oh, thank god," Karina said, sinking into her chair. "I didn't want to push, but I couldn't afford another night at this hotel."

# 25

Karina booked our tickets to San Francisco, departing at 1:39 P.M. the next day. When we arrived at the airport, I was prepared to be selected for additional screening, assuming my flight binge might have thrown up red flags within the TSA system. One-way flights were considered suspect, and I'd taken twenty-two of them in quick succession—seventeen on board N92823, plus five deadheads. Terrorists, saboteurs, and rowdy passengers were my enemies; I hated being lumped in with those miscreants, but I would submit to extra screening with gratitude that the security apparatus was functioning healthily.

Instead, when we printed our boarding passes, Karina's was the one bearing the symbol *SSSS*.

Her face paled when I explained what the letters meant. "Why me?"

I shrugged. "They don't need a reason. It might be random."

In the TSA line, Karina remained stoic as she was led to a separate table, where her Louis Vuitton bag and backpack were thoroughly probed, her body patted down, her hands swabbed. Meanwhile, I passed through without incident.

Only when I saw my backpack on the belt did I remember my vision board and chunk of 737 were still tucked inside it.

I waited for Karina on a bench. She emerged looking rattled. "That was such bullshit," she muttered.

As we made our way through the K Concourse, I told her I was still carrying the vision board.

"It's okay," Karina said. "Stacy was right. The boards don't do shit."

I could tell she was uneasy, though. She suggested we destroy the board, for good measure. In a corner of an empty gate, we unfolded the posterboard and ripped off its images. Karina then tore apart the board itself, reducing it to fragments the size of playing cards. We took it all to the restroom, where we flushed the clump of images down a toilet. Karina left to refill her water bottle, while I lingered before the mirror, admiring my freshly shampooed and blow-dried hair, along with the tasteful makeup Karina had applied. I withdrew my chunk of 737. I knew I should throw it away, too, but I felt sad to imagine it lumped in with the bathroom trash and taken to a landfill somewhere. In the mirror, I watched my lips kiss the plane shard. I tucked it in my back pocket.

THE DAY BEFORE, KARINA HAD BEEN CALM AND CONFIDENT, TAKing me firmly in hand and leading me out of the terminal in which I'd previously sworn I would die. Now, as we sat at K16 waiting for our plane to arrive, she seemed full of nervous energy, her knee jiggling, her head swiveling to take in our surroundings, which she found deficient in every way.

"It's too hot in here," she said, removing her sweatshirt and fanning herself with her boarding pass. "These people are disgusting," she whispered a moment later, as humanity swarmed around us. I watched her sanitize her hands twice in the span of five minutes, though they hadn't touched anything.

"Are you sure you want to do this?" I said.

"We're doing it," she snapped. "Don't give me an out."

She said she had to use the restroom again, leaving me alone at the gate. A few minutes later, our plane pulled in. My breath caught as I beheld what appeared to be a fine young A320. His windscreen glinted with sunlight, giving him a mischievous look. I resisted the urge to inspect his flank and discover his name. I'd resolved to approach our flight like an ordinary passenger. Most people didn't even know what model of plane they flew in, much less the plane's registration number.

Passengers streamed out of the jet bridge. They must have come from a tropical locale, as many of them wore straw hats and floral-printed shirts, their faces flushed with sunburn. I gazed into the plane's windscreen, my desire to fly resurging. I'd ruined previous dates by being too focused on my goal. On this flight, I'd relax and enjoy myself, getting to know this handsome stranger on his own terms.

Minutes passed. The plane was cleaned and inspected, and soon, the boarding process for our flight began. Karina returned to the gate just when I'd begun to worry. She sat next to me, smiling apologetically. "I had a little freak-out, but I'm good now," she said. "I called Anthony and he talked me down."

"We'll be home soon," I said, patting her thigh. I was excited to see Karina and Anthony's new apartment. Karina had told me I could sleep on their couch for as long as I needed, though I planned to limit my stay to a week. I had faith that something would work out. I embraced the unknown, trusting that the universe's plan was superior to mine.

As we proceeded down the jet bridge, I remained determined to approach our flight like a regular person, without an agenda aside from safe transport from one location to another. But when I crossed the plane's threshold, an electric pulse surged through my body, a liquid sensation pooling at the base of my spine. It was the same feeling I'd had when I boarded my previous flight with Karina, the feeling all my flights with N92823 had lacked. This plane recognized me—or did he recognize both of us? Perhaps I'd been right all along to suspect my fate and Karina's were intertwined.

We reached row 29, a middle and aisle seat on the starboard side. Karina took the middle seat and wiped down her area the way she used to prepare her terminal at Acuity.

"I have to tell you something," I whispered, but Karina cut me off.

"Stop," she said with a firmness that startled me.

I was shocked by what I saw in her eyes: understanding and acceptance. Not of me, but of fate.

"Linda," she said softly, "I know." She took my hand and squeezed it.

The door was sealed. We pulled back from the gate. Sunlight spilled across Karina's lap, highlighting the raised fibers of her leggings. She took a deep breath, then exhaled slowly through her mouth.

"I'm going to close my eyes now, if you don't mind," she said. Her hand still gripped mine.

As we rose into the sky, a powerful vibration began, rattling my teeth in my skull. In my back pocket, the shard of plane gathered heat, until I feared it would burn through my jeans. The fuselage shook with greater intensity as we rose above Chicago. We rolled left, the plane's wing pointing to the earth, a thin trail of smoke visible through the window. All the while, Karina's eyes remained closed, a vague smile on her lips. I held her hand until I could hold it no more.

## ACKNOWLEDGMENTS

I want to thank Clio Seraphim, Leila Tejani, and the whole team at Random House for helping bring the best version of this book into the world. Thanks to my agent, Emma Patterson, for always supporting my creative vision. Thank you to the 2019–21 Stegner fiction cohort, especially Brendan Bowles, Lydi Conklin, Matthew Denton-Edmundson, and Fatima Kola, for your feedback and friendship. I'm grateful for the literary guidance and wisdom I received from Elizabeth Tallent, Chang-Rae Lee, Mat Johnson, and Adam Johnson as I forged my way through early drafts. Special thanks to the Headlands Center for the Arts, where I began the book, and Willapa Bay AiR, where I completed it. Thanks to my parents, for everything. Thank you to David for being my partner in life and going to SFO with me to watch planes.

Many books and sources contributed to the writing of this one. Foremost among them is Herman Melville's *Moby-Dick,* with which *Sky Daddy* is in casual conversation. Melville's brilliance was my companion while writing, a pleasant version of the "supernatural hand" Ishmael recalls holding

ing his one time as a child. Additionally, TheFlightChannel on YouTube was an early source of inspiration. Thanks to Greg for providing special insight into the world of content moderation. In my research I made use of the NTSB database, flight tracking websites including FlightAware and Planespotters.net, and the app Flightradar24. Whenever I hear a plane's engines overhead, I check to see which fine gentleman is flying above me.

## ABOUT THE AUTHOR

KATE FOLK is the author of the short story collection *Out There*. Her work has appeared in *The New Yorker, The New York Times, Granta, McSweeney's Quarterly Concern,* and *Zyzzyva*. A former Stegner Fellow at Stanford University, she's also received support from the Headlands Center for the Arts, MacDowell, and Willapa Bay AiR. She lives in San Francisco.

katefolk.com
X: @katefolk
Instagram: @kate__folk